D1475400

PARTY OF THREE

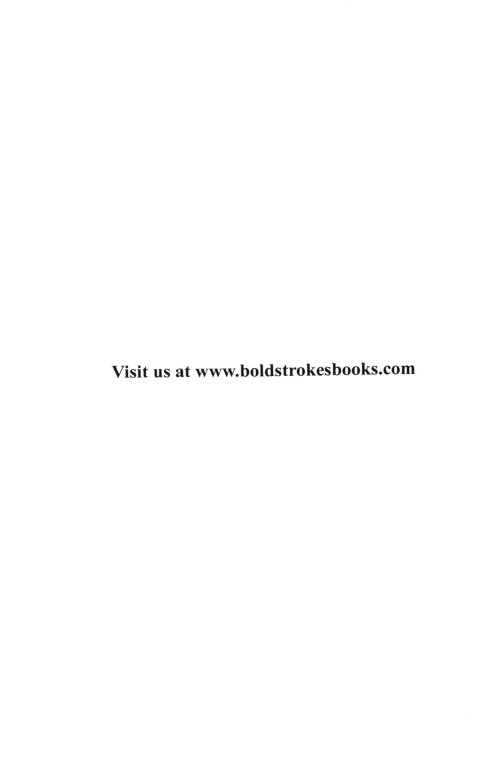

Visit us at www.boldstrokesbooks.com

PARTY OF THREE

by

Sandy Lowe

2019

PARTY OF THREE

ISBN 13: 978-1-63555-246-1

This Trade Paperback Original Is Published By
Bold Strokes Books, Inc.
P.O. Box 249
Valley Falls, NY 12185

First Edition: August 2019

Credits
Editor: Cindy Cresap
Production Design: Stacia Seaman
Cover Design by Tammy Seidick

Acknowledgments

No one knows better than me that it takes a village to publish a book. But when that book is mine? It takes a small city complete with round-the-clock emergency services and world-class psychiatric care. Thanks to the whole team at Bold Strokes, from the publisher to the proofreaders. You're the best in the business and you prove it every day.

Thanks to my ever-patient wisecracking editor, Cindy Cresap. I chose you as my editor because I didn't think you'd give a damn that I wrote a billion sex scenes. I'm so glad I was right. (How awkward would it be if I wasn't, though?) You made this book a better version of itself, and I can't think of a higher endorsement for superior editing than that.

Thanks to Eden Darry for reading the draft and cheering me on. I can't remember now if the enemy's fake threesome in the coat closet was your idea or mine, but whatever, it's brilliant and I'm taking the credit.

Thanks to Carsen Taite for the title and the sage advice that writing a novel in three parts was an insane idea. You were right, of course, but I did it anyway.

Lastly, thanks to Radclyffe. There aren't words big enough to express the gratitude I have for everything you've given me, not the least of which is guidance with this book. I promise to graduate from writing about whiny horny college kids soon, but in the meantime, thanks for the encouragement and mentorship.

To all the readers who buy romance novels for the "good parts."
This one is for you.

SARAH

CHAPTER ONE

Wait and See

Sarah Donovan was going to waste the most decadent weather of the year stuck inside, primping and preening for a party she'd resented since the moment the invitation had arrived. Winter released its icy grip on Manhattan, and Mother Nature had blessed the Upper East Side with a perfect seventy-degree day, so rare for the first week of April the sunshine on the back of her neck felt like a gift. Too bad she couldn't wrap it, or she'd have the perfect birthday present for Ms. I-Already-Have-Everything-I-Could-Ever-Want Eleanor.

"Do I have to go tonight?" She was doing it again, *whining*.

"Yes," Kaitlyn and Avery said in unison, neither bothering to glance in her direction. *The definition of insanity is asking the same question and expecting a different answer.* Sarah had to cut violently to the right as they dodged pedestrians wandering up Madison Avenue. New Yorkers kept their heads down and their feet moving. Strolling was for tourists, even on a day like this one.

"You should've just said no in the first place," Avery said, and not for the first time.

Sarah opened her mouth, then swallowed her retort. She loved her friends, but they didn't get it. Avery could tell Reginald McGregor no because *she* had a trust fund and a fashion mogul father who'd buy her a tropical island in the South Pacific if she so much as wanted a place to wear a bikini. Meanwhile, Sarah had Bob, and while she loved her three-legged tabby to death, he was more likely to eat the bacon than bring it home. He who holds the purse strings has the power, and McGregor was using his million-dollar investment in her fledgling gourmet bakery, Cakewalk, to ensure she attended his daughter's twenty-fifth birthday party.

Eleanor. She Who Must Not Be Underestimated. She probably didn't have any actual friends to invite.

They stopped outside tall, heavy glass doors with "Expressions Beauty and Spa" stamped in silver cursive at eye level. Kaitlyn slung an arm around her shoulders and squeezed. "Sometimes you just have to suck it up and get it done. Stop being such a baby."

Sarah smiled. "I love how you give heartless pragmatic advice that no one wants to hear in that adorable sweet-as-sugar tone. If I didn't listen closely, I'd think you were telling me I should go home and put my feet up. I don't really have to spend an evening with stuck-up snobby people who are so rich they should be embarrassed."

"Of course, I'm not going to tell you that. There's nothing embarrassing about being rich." Kaitlyn winked and pushed open the door.

Kaitlyn should know. Of the three of them, she was indeed the richest, thanks in no small part to her mother's tragic death. She was killed in a skiing accident when Kaitlyn was ten. While a ten-year-old mega-millionaire was mind-boggling, Sarah wouldn't have traded places. Her parents might be elementary school teachers, but they loved her and visited her minuscule studio in Brooklyn every third Sunday like clockwork.

Kaitlyn led the way to a long, thin counter that held up the longer and thinner woman standing behind it. She nodded to the receptionist. "We have an appointment under Forrester."

The woman smiled at Kaitlyn, no doubt noting her Chanel sunglasses and Tory Burch flats. Avery and Sarah didn't rate more than a cursory glance. Sarah's Gap V-neck and skinny jeans didn't cut it in a place like this. Which was exactly why she never went to places like this.

The receptionist ran a French-manicured finger down a list in front of her, and a small line struggled against the Botox between her brows. "Yes. I'm afraid Genevieve, Marcela, and Bridget are running late today. A wedding party ran over. *The bride.*" She waved a hand as if that said it all. "It'll be an hour."

They stared. "An hour?" Kaitlyn asked with the faintest edge of disbelief.

"There's a small cocktail bar two doors down if you'd like to wait there," the receptionist suggested with the air of a woman who really didn't give a fuck. That was New York for you, over eight million people and Sarah could count polite staff on one hand.

They waited, of course they waited. It took *months* to get an appointment at Expressions, let alone three at the same time, and, okay, maybe she was secretly glad they'd be a little late. It didn't make her a terrible person, did it? Every second she sat sipping a cosmo now was less time she had to spend talking to strangers and pretending to fawn over daddy's little girl.

Cocktail bar was a rather hopeful descriptor for the dark hole in the wall that comprised a scraggly looking bar and a few scattered tables so battered they appeared to have spent a previous life in a high school cafeteria. Even the walls looked exhausted, as if they might just give up the fight and the ceiling would come crashing in. If melancholy were a place, this would be the capital.

"Jesus." Avery sidestepped a mysterious sticky brown puddle on the floor and slid into a chair at one of the tables close to the bar. "How did this place not get swallowed by the gods of gentrification?"

"The owner believes a *real* bar should have a bit of character. Unfortunately, his definition is rather limited," said their bartender as she came sashaying over in tight black pants and a plain white long-sleeved Henley. A woman this gorgeous didn't need anything but rosy soft skin and deep chestnut eyes to be a knockout.

Avery gulped audibly. "Uh, hey."

Kaitlyn just sort of bobbed her head, words completely failing her.

"Hey right back. What can I get you?" Hot Bartender said

cheerfully, as if she hadn't noticed she'd reduced them all to prehistoric versions of themselves. Sarah gave her points. Pretty *and* nice was an unexpected bonus. She wouldn't have minded a handy cave to take her back to, maybe a wooden club to beat off the competition. Sarah had no idea how to use a wooden club, but for her, she'd be willing to give it a shot.

When the silence lasted a beat too long, Sarah jumped in to save her friends the trouble of thinking through their lust.

"Three cosmos, please." No one could say she wasn't doing her bit for the good of humanity and lesbians who happened to be breathing. "The salon up the street is running overtime and we have a bit of a wait."

Hot Bartender nodded. "That sucks. It's so annoying when people don't respect your time, isn't it?"

"Tell me about it. Have you been working here long?"

"I just started a couple of weeks ago. You know, living the cliché while I audition for commercials and hope to make it to Broadway."

She wouldn't be hot *and* nice for long, but it was fun while it lasted. "I hope you make it. You're certainly pretty enough."

"Thank you." Hot Bartender blushed a little, standing awkwardly and holding Sarah's gaze for a beat, before turning away to fill their order.

"So, last night's date was another disaster?" Avery was suddenly back in command of the English language now that they were alone again.

Sarah's dating woes were constant entertainment fodder and she played it up, embellishing details and stringing out the stories to the delight of her audience. It was all *so* amusing, and *so* outrageous, and she was *such* a good sport about it. The reality fell somewhere between her increasingly serious fantasy of going off grid and joining a commune so she'd never have to think about dating again, and sobbing into her wineglass at the thought of being single and sexless forever.

She smiled humorlessly. "You could say that. Her Tinder profile described her as a twenty-eight-year-old artist from Brooklyn, interested in classic literature and the Post-Impressionist movement. There's a photo of her at the New York symphony. On Tinder, she's my perfect dream girl. In reality, she's an unemployed art major who can't get her shit together. She does live in Brooklyn, in a walk-up with sixty-seven roommates, a feral cat, and a handful of cockroaches. I'm pretty sure they sleep on air mattresses and smoke pot all day."

"Seriously? She doesn't take prescription drugs at least?" Kaitlyn raised her eyebrows before smiling shyly as Hot Bartender placed drinks in front of them.

"Can't afford them." Sarah shrugged. "We're sitting there, drinking overpriced cocktails that I knew I'd be picking up the tab for, and she's telling me all this like she's *proud* to be a stoner. Like collecting unemployment and waffling on about Picasso is something we should all aspire to."

Avery punched her lightly on the arm. "You're being harsh. So she smells like moldy socks and is in a polyamorous relationship with sixty-seven people. Big deal. She's stood outside the symphony at least once. What's not to like?" Avery's bottle green eyes twinkled. She straddled the ancient chair with casual confidence and flicked her short dark hair out of her eyes, a little too preppy to be roguish, but sexy all the same. If they hadn't already been friends for a million years, Sarah suspected she might have had quite the thing for Avery Anders under the right circumstances.

Sarah closed her eyes for a second. She had a brief but fulfilling vision of throwing a temper tantrum worthy of a five-year-old denied a giant ice cream cone covered in chocolate sprinkles. Her life was funny, right up until it wasn't anymore.

"Hey." Avery rubbed the spot she'd just punched. "Forget about her. There are plenty of fish in the sea."

"There aren't, though. Let's face it. I haven't been on a good first date since Melinda."

"Don't tell me you're still hung up on her." Kaitlyn reached across to take her hand.

"I'm not." Or at least not exactly.

She was hung up on the comfort of a relationship, having

someone to come home to, to curl up on the couch with, to be her date at dinner parties. She didn't miss the terrible sex. The "hide your face and try to fake a convincing climax so it could be over" kind of bad, terrible, horrible sex. Melinda liked having sex about as much as Sarah liked hiking to the subway in the winter, as in, not at all. It was at best a duty and at worst an aggravating inconvenience. So they'd had less and less until, not knowing how to fix it, Sarah had called bullshit and they'd talked about it. She'd thought maybe Melinda was ace. Melinda didn't deny it. Not an orientation she was particularly thrilled by, given that Sarah absolutely, unequivocally, wasn't, but at least she'd had an answer. A reason. She could stop feeling as if she'd failed. Melinda was just wired differently. They'd work it out.

Except it wasn't asexuality. Not even close. The memory of what was really going on had her shoulders inching toward her ears and her insides going squirmy. She would *not* think about it. It was over. Done. In the past. She'd moved on. She was dating, getting out there, being a good, well-rounded, mentally healthy human. She wasn't lying awake at night thinking about Melinda. What Melinda had said. What she'd needed in order to get off. She wasn't thinking about it at all.

That went down six months ago, and she'd yet to find a woman who was even a remote contender for the role of sexy casual fling, let alone actual relationship material.

"I'm going to be thirty, watching Animal Planet in my pajamas, and eating sesame chicken straight out of the carton every Saturday night. I swear there are no attractive women with decent jobs in the city. She doesn't even have to be mentally stable. I'm willing to overlook a bit of crazy if she's hot and has a paycheck."

"Well, there are," Avery said, "but they're all in a pushy-shovey match for the two percent of eligible straight men."

"I should've been straight. I've heard a rumor that men aren't terribly complicated when it comes to sex," Sarah said.

"You shouldn't have to compromise at all." Kaitlyn gave her hand another squeeze. "Your one true love is out there."

Kaitlyn, ever the optimist. A rare woman who still believed in *The One.*

"You know what you need? Crazy hot, screw me up against the wall of the nearest bathroom, rebound sex," Avery said.

Sarah wrinkled her nose and made an obvious display of looking around. "Is the bathroom locale optional? And if not, does it have to be the nearest one?"

"Fine, let's make it the presidential suite at the Ritz Carlton then, Princess. The point is, you need to get laid without wading through all the dating hoopla."

Sarah considered it. Casual sex. No, not just casual. Avery was talking about sex with someone she didn't know. The irony had her biting back one of those hysterical laughs that always ended in tears. She'd have sex with a stranger the day hell froze over and angels did a jig on the iceberg.

She wanted sex. No, scratch that. She *needed* sex, like a plant needed water. All her girl parts were slowly withering in the unrelenting heat of her reluctant celibacy. Giving up the fight and curling in on themselves. But a stranger? Not a fucking chance. She couldn't make it work with a woman she'd loved, a woman who'd said she'd loved her back. What made Avery think doing it with a stranger would be easier? What made her think a stranger would even want Sarah, when her girlfriend hadn't? *Worse than hadn't.*

Avery tried again. "Tonight would be a great opportunity. You know the place will be filled with queers. Elle's on every diversity board there is."

Her friends didn't know what'd really happened with Melinda; her pride had forbidden it. Avery couldn't know how much the subject hurt. Sarah played for time. "I don't know. What am I supposed to do, walk up to someone and say, 'Um, hello, would you please fuck me?'"

Avery laughed. "Oh yes, please say that."

Kaitlyn shot her a look, and she shut up. "You order her a drink, chat for a bit, and then casually ask if she'd like to go somewhere more private."

Sarah stared at her. "How do *you* know that?" It was one thing for Avery to screw strangers, she was a total player, but Kaitlyn?

Kaitlyn suddenly became very interested in her phone. "Never you mind."

Were all her friends having amazing sex and she was the only one missing out? It didn't really surprise her, but she hated the way her stomach sank. Why was her life always the one that sucked by comparison?

Could she have rebound sex?

Tonight?

She ignored the way her heart thumped a few extra beats and her libido perked up. She wouldn't have sex with just anyone, and definitely not someone she didn't know really well. Taking another sip of her cosmo, she settled on *maybe*. If she found just the right not-a-stranger, then maybe. If it didn't happen, if no one at this fancy-pants social interrogation masquerading as a birthday party was interested in her, if she couldn't pull it off, well, then, she wouldn't have gotten her hopes up, would she?

CHAPTER TWO

The Problem with Paws

"Hey, there's Peter," Kaitlyn said.

Sarah turned toward the entrance and watched Peter Kingsley, Eleanor McGregor's longtime boyfriend, walk through the door, his arm around the shoulders of a blond woman so tiny she looked like an elf.

"What's he doing here?" Avery asked.

Peter sidled up to the bar and smiled charmingly at Hot Bartender. Hot Bartender didn't smile back; in fact, she looked downright pissed as she served them.

"Not exactly Peter's kind of place," Sarah said. Peter's silver spoon was so far up his ass he couldn't sit comfortably. His family money was so old that no one remembered quite where it had come from.

"Maybe it's his cousin or…" Kaitlyn winced when Peter tucked a strand of hair behind Blond Elf's ear and whispered something that made her giggle. "Or maybe not."

"His hand is way too low on her back." Avery studied them critically, her voice tense.

"Could be a college friend," Sarah suggested.

"Or maybe he's seducing the housekeeper. I heard they'd hired a girl younger than us," Kaitlyn said.

"Nah, the housekeeper's got to be there for Kingsley senior. It's just more civilized to keep that kind of thing behind closed doors and away from the wife's sewing circle of socialites," Sarah said.

"Can't say I like Peter, but he's rich and good-looking enough not to need to shit where he lies."

Kaitlyn groaned. "Really, Sarah? You have such a way with words."

"You know what I mean." Sarah threw her napkin at her.

"Whoever it is, he's seducing someone. Not that she looks as if she needs much persuading." Avery tipped back in her chair, scowling at them. "Elle deserves better."

Elle, Sarah mouthed to Kaitlyn and rolled her eyes. She was just about to start mocking the stupid nickname when the show at the far end of the bar started and they all fell silent to watch, as if the lights had just dimmed in a theater.

The girl was perched on a stool with Peter standing so close beside her it looked as if they were joined at the hip. He was rubbing her back in long, languid movements, catching his fingers on the hem of her tank top with every circuit, inching it up to reveal a tramp stamp, though Sarah couldn't quite tell what it was. A butterfly? A dragon? A flying space monkey? Peter wasn't even looking at her, still preoccupied trying to charm Hot Bartender, though he was up against a wall of ice there. Just what had he done to annoy pretty and nice? When his fingers dipped under the waistband of the blonde's denim miniskirt, they watched her lips part in a gasp, saw her tremble, as if no one, ever, in her whole life, had done anything as scandalous before, and would he please bend her over the bar and take her virginity before she burst?

Hot Bartender said something in a tone that resonated disgust and pointed to the restroom sign. Peter smiled, clearly not tuning in to her burn-in-hell vibe, paying in cash and leaving what looked to be an overly generous tip, before he grabbed the blonde by the hand and they headed toward the restroom.

"They're not going to…" Kaitlyn trailed off, clearly unwilling to finish the thought.

Avery drained the last third of her cosmo in one long pull. "I take back everything I said about crazy hot bathroom sex."

"Seriously. This ruins any kind of sex forever." Sarah heard the words come out of her mouth and knew they weren't true. What was about to happen looked to be ten kinds of fucked up, but she wasn't exactly what you'd call normal. Melinda had planted her flag squarely in the wild terrain of Sarah's psyche, so sex would never be the same again. The saddest part was that it hadn't been all that good to begin with.

Peter and the elf started kissing even before they got to the dim, stubby hallway with doors on either side.

"Oh, eew," Kaitlyn said.

That summed it up perfectly.

Peter was kissing the girl like she was a strip steak and he was trying to eat her face. He was all teeth, his jaw crunching. What he was hoping to achieve exactly, it was hard to tell. The elf moaned, and Peter hoisted her up with hands on her ass so she could wrap her legs around his waist. They fell against the wall of the hallway, not even bothering to go inside the restroom.

"You have got to be kidding me." Avery was halfway out of her chair, her face red, her eyes flashing like shards of broken glass.

Sarah grabbed her by the wrist and pulled her back down. "Don't even think about it. It's none of our business."

"Like hell it isn't."

"Avery, you can't go charging over there like Joan of fucking Arc. That's not the way to handle it," Sarah said.

"Seems like a good idea to me." Avery picked up Sarah's glass and drained her cosmo too. She hated that Avery cared. Did it really matter who Peter fucked? Of course it mattered, there was *Elle* to consider, wasn't there? Avery was going to be tied to that annoying bitch forever because of something she couldn't help feeling.

When Peter opened his zipper and shoved the denim mini up the girl's twig-like thighs, they all angled their chairs away from the hallway in silent agreement. A scattering of patrons were staring openly, but most either didn't notice or chose to ignore the scene. Hot Bartender had her back to them, cleaning glasses. Why didn't she do something? Give them a talking to, or kick them out, or call the police. *Anything.*

They sat quietly for a while, none of them quite sure what to do next. What on earth did you say to follow that?

"Well…" Kaitlyn finally managed, a blush creeping up her neck, "have you been to Bloomingdale's spring sale yet?"

❖

Sarah shot Kaitlyn a look that told her to get Avery outside as fast as possible, and she went to settle the tab. They had an unspoken agreement that Sarah paid when the bill was small. She couldn't treat her friends to Michelin star restaurants or front row seats at this season's must-see show on Broadway. Blowing a month's rent on *Hamilton* tickets wasn't an option. But paying for the things she could afford made her feel like she wasn't a total moocher.

She handed her credit card to Hot Bartender and tilted her head toward the restroom, not turning to see if they'd finished. She'd already caught enough to want to scrub the inside of her eyelids with bleach. "What's up with that?"

Hot Bartender shot a nasty look in the direction of the hallway. "Oh, Paws and his twelve-year-old companion have finally decided to copulate without need for an audience. Nice."

Sarah shot a glance over her shoulder. The hallway was empty, though the door to the women's room was still swinging. She turned back to Hot Bartender. "Paws?"

Hot Bartender shrugged. "No idea what his name is, but haven't you noticed his huge hands? I swear he tries to cop a feel anytime I walk past with an order. He comes in on Friday afternoons about this time and uses the place like it's his bedroom. Apparently, he and my boss have an *arrangement*, and I'm supposed to take his cash and keep my mouth shut."

Sarah couldn't believe it. Peter was using this seedy little bar, a rough in the diamonds of the Upper East Side, to screw a girl behind Eleanor's back. It was a regular thing. An arrangement. She felt a twinge of something she wasn't willing to admit was satisfaction. Being satisfied that Eleanor didn't have a perfect relationship, that she had bad hair days and cellulite and got duped by her boyfriend, would make her petty and mean. She wasn't. She wouldn't be satisfied. But she couldn't bring herself to be sorry either. "But why here? It's hardly an ideal location."

Hot Bartender shrugged. "He looks like money to me. He likes fucking her in public. It's always public. He's not likely to run into anyone he knows here, is he?"

"Geez." Sarah signed the credit card slip and slid it back across the bar. "That's unfortunate."

"It's like watching a gorilla hump a Teletubby." Hot Bartender glanced down at the slip of paper. "Sarah Donovan."

Sarah smiled. "That's me."

"Jennifer. Nice to meet you. I'm sorry you had to see that."

"So am I," Sarah said. "I don't think I'll be back on Friday afternoons."

"Will I see you around some other time? Maybe close to the end of my shift, say around seven?"

It took Sarah a second to catch on. *Oh.* "Um, sure. I can drop by after work."

Jennifer's smile brightened. "I'd really like that."

"Okay then." Wow, was she out of practice flirting. Way to go, Sarah. Charm her with your extensive vocabulary.

"Catch you next week then, maybe." Jennifer tossed her a wink before moving down the bar to help another customer.

"Catch you." It was a sad testament to her life that a perfectly G-rated conversation was the best thing to happen to her in a long time.

❖

Hair and makeup took till after four, and they used the salon's richly appointed changing room to slip into the cocktail dresses and heels that Kaitlyn had arranged to be messengered over from their respective apartments. Straight-legged black pants and a dove white tuxedo shirt for Avery. Ninety minutes of torture, by Sarah's estimate, to achieve a look that wasn't all that different from the tousled waves she saw in the bathroom mirror every morning. She'd have been better off staying home and taking a nap. She enjoyed wearing a nice dress as much as the next girl but didn't see the point of bringing in professional help. Why walk around as some glammed-up version of who you really were?

Kaitlyn's town car waited at the curb outside Expressions.

"It's still seventy-two. I can't believe we spent the whole afternoon inside," Sarah said.

"I've been looking forward to this all week. I love salon days." Kaitlyn settled back into the plush leather seat for the trip downtown to Cakewalk.

"Doesn't it bother you that you have to spend hours getting ready?" Sarah asked.

Kaitlyn shook her head. "Not everyone is blessed to be Barbie's second cousin."

"I always thought she could pass as Sienna Miller's kid sister." Avery pulled her iPhone out of her pocket and checked her text messages.

Sarah waved that away. "I could not. Anyway, that's not the point."

"What is the point, oh wise one?"

"The point," Sarah ignored Avery's sarcasm, "is that we only go to all this trouble because that's what everyone else does. We could save hours, and hundreds of dollars, just by being who we are."

Avery smirked. "Good luck taking on the beauty industry, Naomi Wolf."

"Some of us go to the trouble just to stand a chance of anyone noticing us next to you," Kaitlyn said.

"I…" Sarah started, but didn't know what to say. She knew she was pretty. It would be stupid to deny it. But so was Kaitlyn with her Irish legacy of lush auburn curls and alabaster skin. Not to mention the fact that she was completely loaded, a trait Sarah didn't have a snowball's chance in hell of competing with.

"You're beautiful. You know that." Except it was pretty clear Kaitlyn didn't.

Kaitlyn shrugged good-naturedly. "Uh-huh. That's why the gorgeous bartender couldn't take her eyes off me. Oh no, wait. I think that was you."

Sarah had to fight the urge to roll her eyes. It's not like she'd asked for it to happen. She only took charge because Kaitlyn was too busy blushing. "You just need to learn how to talk to girls. We should go out after work next week. I can be your wing-woman. Give you some pointers."

"God help you." Avery poked Kaitlyn in the side.

Kaitlyn's face softened. "Thanks. I should, I guess. I don't know."

"I'm a far better wing-woman," Avery said. "Sarah's track record is awful."

"This is true. But I can steer you away from all the losers and extricate you from an awkward situation in record time," Sarah said.

"Girl's gotta have some skills."

She shoved Avery's shoulder. "Shut up. You never know when you might need to make a hasty retreat."

"If you ever want to get laid again, Kaitlyn, don't listen to her," Avery said.

"What are you saying?" Sarah said.

"That you're so busy looking for Ms. Perfect Dream Girl you sabotage your chances of having a good time," Avery said without missing a beat.

Sarah could literally feel her hackles rising. She didn't know what hackles were exactly, or where they were located, but hers were standing on end. "So, I should settle?"

"No, you should relax. Go with it. Stop looking five years into the future, five minutes after meeting someone," Avery replied.

"I do *not*." Did she? God, Sarah didn't know anymore.

Kaitlyn laughed. "She's got you there."

It was *so* time to change the subject. "Do you think we should tell Eleanor about Peter and the girl at the bar?"

"I'm not sure that's a good idea."

Avery looked like Kaitlyn had just sucker punched her. "Why?"

"These things are delicate. It's possible she already knows."

"You're never going to convince me she doesn't care." Avery folded her arms. An immovable object.

"I'm not saying she cares or doesn't care." Kaitlyn sighed. "Come on. You weren't born yesterday. You know how this works. How people from certain families end up together."

Sarah frowned. "I don't get…" Then it hit her. "You're saying Peter and Eleanor are dating to keep their family money within their class. That marrying someone else would, what, dilute it? Dirty it?" God. Rich people pissed her off. Present company excluded, but still.

Kaitlyn threw a hand up as if defending herself. "Of course not. But relationships are sometimes…engineered. Or at the very least strongly encouraged between particular families."

"To keep money out of the hands of peasants?" Sarah asked.

"To strengthen social and business ties," Kaitlyn shot back. "I didn't invent the system, Sarah."

"How very eighteenth-century Britain."

"Not to disrupt the class wars or anything, but can we get back to Peter and the skank?" Avery asked.

"If she does care, it'll be a whole lot of drama, and you know how Eleanor loves to create drama. Whatever it is, she's happy to make it fifty times worse," Sarah said.

Avery frowned. "Are you ever going to let that go?"

"Let it go? She made my life a living hell for years," Sarah said.

"I'm sorry. *Really*. But it was seven years ago. It was high school. Can we be over it now?" Avery asked.

"You weren't the one on her shit list. She was *this close* to killing my chance of getting into culinary school. Did we just conveniently forget that little fact?"

Avery's shoulders slumped, the fight going out of her. "I know. It's totally my fault."

Sarah didn't say anything. It wasn't technically Avery's fault. She knew that. But fault and responsibility were two sides of the same coin. If Avery hadn't intervened at the eleventh hour, she might not have graduated valedictorian. She might not have had the grades to get into the best culinary school in the country. She might not have Cakewalk. The thought made her shudder. "I just don't want history to repeat itself. I'm staying out of the line of fire."

"The only way this will work is if we all tell her together," Kaitlyn said.

"I can—" Avery began, but Kaitlyn shook her head.

"No, you can't. You're the last person she'll want to hear this from."

"But—"

"She's right," Sarah agreed. "I think it would be better not to say anything at all. It's hardly our business anyway."

Kaitlyn shifted in her seat. "Well…"

"What?" Avery asked.

"I heard talk that Peter might use the occasion to propose."

Avery dropped her head back against the headrest and groaned. "You're kidding me."

"It's not confirmed."

"But likely."

"Yes, I think so," Kaitlyn said.

"Well, then, we have to tell her. I'm not letting her marry this scumbag. Sarah, *please.*" Avery sent her puppy dog eyes.

Sarah almost pointed out that Avery wasn't likely to have a lot of say in the matter if the couple was matched by their families, but kept her mouth shut. She wasn't thrilled to be doing a favor for the Queen of Snark, but Avery would just tell her anyway, and Kaitlyn was right. That wouldn't go over well. She didn't want to see Avery hurt. Sometimes, you just had to take one for the team. Even when it meant helping the mean girl who'd tried to ruin your life, one delicately placed lie at a time. "Fine. But let's all tell her. I'm not doing it alone. *Before* the proposal, if there is one," Sarah said.

"Agreed," Kaitlyn said.

Avery sent Sarah a sunny smile.

CHAPTER THREE

A Case of Mistaken McGrumpy

Two hours later, the driver pulled into the circular drive of the McGregors' Catskills estate and eased behind a sedate black Mercedes crawling along in a long line of equally glossy cars. The stately stone and brick colonial stood erect and imposing on the edge of a mountain, like a pompous elderly butler overlooking his master's domain. Enter if you dare. The fairy lights trailing over and around the ancient structure spoiled the lofty pretentiousness only slightly. The car finally stopped next to a pleasant-looking man in shirtsleeves and a thin black vest, and they all slid out. Avery handed Sarah the dessert they'd picked up at Cakewalk earlier. "I'll see you later, my darling," she whispered seductively, patting the bright pink cardboard before letting go with comical reluctance.

Sarah grinned. She loved that her cake was a crowd pleaser. They stood for a minute taking in the scene.

"We're underdressed," Avery said. "The house looks better than we do."

Kaitlyn led the way along manicured pathways to a front door so wide you could drive a semitrailer through with room to spare. There was no denying this shindig was expensive, and Sarah suspected the midnight black sheath dress that had looked so elegant on the rack at Macy's wasn't going to cut it with this crowd. She squeezed Avery's hand. "We're going to be fine. Promise." She might not be the richest or the classiest, even among her own friends, but she knew how to hold her head high. She'd been doing it all her life.

Believe it or not, there was an actual butler, though she was mid-fifties, female, and not the least bit stuffy. "Hello and welcome." Smiling warmly, she looked into their faces. "Kaitlyn Forrester, Sarah Donovan, and Avery Anders." She nodded as if checking them off a mental guest list. Wow. The woman must have studied photos, which was both weird and impressive. "Can I take that box for you, Ms. Donovan?"

Sarah hugged it to her chest like a teddy bear. "Um, no. If you don't mind, I'll take it to the kitchen myself."

"You're the baker. I understand you want to make sure everything is perfect for Miss Eleanor." The woman winked at her conspiratorially.

Uh-huh. That was totally my intention. More like she wanted some mission that would keep her from having to enter the fancy ballroom full of fancier people just a little longer. Delivering the cake wouldn't delay her much, but she would take what she could get. She nodded as if agreeing, and the woman smiled again. "You can all leave your purses and coats with me. If you head down the hallway, the kitchen is at the end." She turned to Kaitlyn and Avery. "Ladies, the ballroom is just to your right. Have a wonderful evening."

Kaitlyn and Avery gave Sarah a look that clearly said she was a chicken-hearted traitor. "We'll be at the bar when you're done procrastinating," Avery said as they turned in the opposite direction. Sarah lost them immediately to the swarm of people just inside the ballroom doors and was forced to move aside as yet more guests entered the house.

Time to stop loitering in the foyer.

She made her way down a wide hallway decorated with traditional landscapes and pushed open the door to the kitchen. Greeted with a blast of noise, heat, and controlled chaos, Sarah's unease fell from her shoulders like an itchy woolen coat. She was home. The kitchen had always been her safe place. She'd had a knack for cooking that she'd pursued despite the academic aptitude that got her through high school. She was good at school. But she was *phenomenal* at baking. It was her oxygen. Culinary school, a year interning with Chef DeMark, the best freaking baker in the history of the world, and then finally, with a little help from Mr. McGregor, Cakewalk. A tiny dot of a bakery a stone's throw from Times Square, squished indelicately between a McDonald's and an electronics store. It wasn't much, not nearly as prestigious as working beside the industry greats, and the truth was, she'd had more offers than she could count to do that. But she hadn't wanted to spend a decade working in someone else's kitchen before being deemed competent. She didn't want to pay the dues the older generation considered a rite of passage and refused to bend. She wanted a place of her own. Small and, for now, obscure maybe, but hers. And she was damn good at her job. She didn't plan on being a nobody for long. Some called her arrogant. She preferred to think of herself as ambitious.

Most of the noise came from a tall slim man issuing curt orders over the cacophony of chopping, sizzling, and mixing that surrounded her. God, how she hated asshole head chefs who ran their kitchens like drill sergeants. Was it really necessary to yell so loud and for so long? Cooking was supposed to be fun. At least it was for her.

She headed toward a heavyset woman weaving thin strips of pastry into exquisite if somewhat generic braids, and tapped her on the shoulder. "Hey, sorry to bother you. I'm Sarah. I have the German chocolate cake that was special ordered?" Special ordered in the crisply written email she'd received from McGregor, politely asking if she would bake a small cake for the party, claiming no other had ever compared to Sarah's specialty German chocolate with raspberry sauce. He'd added a smiley face to the request, and McGregor just didn't do smiley faces. She suspected it had more to do with circumventing the carb-conscious preferences of his society matron wife, but complied with the request nonetheless.

"Gem." The woman dusted her hands on an apron that was more flour than cotton and held one out for her to shake. "Non-refrigerated cakes, tarts, and dessert pastries go over there." She pointed to a thick wooden bench.

"Thanks. Bad day at the office?" Sarah tilted her chin toward

Chef Grumpy McGrumpy Pants who had stopped yelling and was now bending over an industrial oven. She blinked. His Grumpiness had a really nice ass. She could honestly say it was the first time in living memory she'd ever so much as glanced at a guy's ass, let alone allowed her eyes to linger on the curve of it, generously displayed for her as he leaned forward to lift a steaming dish from the middle rack. She'd only have to walk ten feet to sidle up behind him and—

Gem's laughter startled her back to the present, and she tore her eyes away. "Poor Ryan. The dessert chef was a no-show. It's been hell." Sarah could only nod, words not possible through the sirens blaring in her head. God. She was in worse shape than she thought if she was getting hot under the collar over some guy. She was gay, for Christ's sake. That settled it. She *had* to get laid tonight, if only to erase the twisting in her belly that had her lusting after some cranky dude. She thanked Gem and walked purposefully over to the dessert bench. It *was* looking a bit thin for a large party. Hell indeed. Depositing the cake, she took her time studying the offerings, giving each one her undivided attention like she was a tourist at the Louvre. Did she really have to go to the ballroom? She could just stand here all night, you know, keep the cakes company.

"Hey, you. Hey. Blond girl."

Sarah turned, surprised to find Lord Grumpton advancing, then looming over her. She hadn't thought it possible for anyone to actually *loom*, but it was the only apt descriptor for the way the man towered above her, all pissed off and reproachful. She backed up until her ass hit the edge of the bench and she had nowhere else to go. A fly caught in his net. Even with the couple of inches' extra distance, she had to tilt her chin up to meet his eyes. Rich, sweet toffee framed by dark chocolate lashes. Yummy. "Um, yes?"

"What are you doing here? This is a kitchen. You can't go walking around without protective clothing. We're not insured if you fall in those ridiculous contraptions."

It took her a second. "You're talking about my shoes."

He looked at her feet like her Dolce Vitas were covered in puke. "Is that what you call them?"

Okay. So weirdly attractive guy wasn't just grumpy, he was an asshole. Nice.

Sarah gestured vaguely toward the cake. She needed to leave. Push him back a step and get the hell out of the kitchen. Go to the bar where there were friends and alcohol. And people. So. Many. People. Eleanor type people. She stayed where she was.

The guy had such a striking face. Beautiful, really. His features were narrow and his skin looked smooth. Touchable and traceable and kissable. He had a sensuous pouty bottom lip she wanted to sink her teeth into. *What the hell is wrong with me?*

"Lady..." he started, but Sarah dragged her voice up from the back of her throat and cut him off. No one called her a lady in that, kid, I'm-losing-my-patience tone.

"I'm Sarah, friend of the birthday girl, well, the birthday girl's father. Actually, he's kind of my boss, well, we're partners. Anyway, that's not the point." *Which maybe I should get to sometime in the next five years.* "He asked me to make a cake, and I'm only delivering it. Here. To the kitchen. Nowhere near anything hot or dangerous." *Except the definition is standing right in front of me and I'm imagining him fucking me five ways to Sunday.*

He looked over her shoulder at the large pink box and finally relaxed. "Sorry. It's been a bad afternoon." He untied the soiled apron around his waist and whipped off his hairnet, running fingers through the short, inky black mess.

Sarah felt her knees wobble and grabbed for the bench. No need to actually fall on her ass and prove him right. Except this was no guy. Not a guy at all, but a woman. A tall, strong woman with broad shoulders and narrow hips, a great face, and a really exceptional ass. "Oh, thank God you're not a guy," she blurted, then snapped her mouth shut so fast her teeth clicked. *Fuck.*

Grumpy raised her eyebrows.

"I said that out loud, didn't I?"

"I'm afraid so. Now you have to tell me why."

"Any chance we can just forget it?"

"Not a one. The servers just left with the second round of canapés, and I have at least thirty seconds before all hell breaks loose again." She leaned around Sarah and grabbed a bottle of water from a cooler against the wall. Her breast grazed Sarah's arm, and Sarah bit her lip to prevent the embarrassing half-moan, half-sigh sound that wanted badly to escape.

Absolutely, positively, not a guy.

Grumpy McSexy Pants drank half the bottle in one long pull. "I've had a crap day. I could use a thirty-second break with a pretty girl. Entertain me."

Entertain her? Who the hell did this woman think she was?

"I'm not some…" Sarah searched wildly for inspiration, "*escort* here for your entertainment." She gave indignant outrage her best shot, though, honestly, the idea had more than a little appeal. Not that this *looming* woman needed to know that.

Grumpy grinned, and those eyes went from sweet toffee to molten caramel lava cake in an instant. She could all but feel the smolder. "An escort, huh? That could be interesting."

"I saw you from across the room and…"

Grumpy leaned closer. "And?"

The way her throat worked when she took another swallow from the bottle was making Sarah dizzy. If someone had tried to convince her that the simple act of a woman swallowing could be sexy as all fuck, she would have laughed them out of the room. But it really, really was. "I thought you were a man."

Grumpy just shrugged. "Easy to do. Why were you thanking God when you discovered I wasn't?"

"Because…" Grumpy was grinning at her, and Sarah realized she already knew the answer. Could this get any more embarrassing? She was losing her cool and off her game. She was also a little out of breath, her heart speeding up in a way that was biologically unnecessary. Her body needed to settle the hell down.

"What's your name?" Sarah asked.

The change in direction had her frowning. "Ryan."

Sarah pointed a finger into her chest. "That's a guy's name."

"It's Melody Ryan, but Melody doesn't suit me."

Sarah had to agree. This woman was no Melody. "Well, Ryan. I thought you had a nice ass, all bent over the oven as you were, and that took me off guard as I'm not accustomed to finding men attractive. I was thanking God I didn't have to go to another counselor to help me reevaluate my sexual identity. That kind of thing is expensive." Why had she told her about the stupid counselor? *Hello, sexiest woman I've ever seen, I'm kind of crazy, but it's super nice to meet you.*

Ryan's lips twitched, and she edged half an inch closer. "And what kind of person are you accustomed to finding attractive?"

Sarah's breath all but stopped. *Attractive is too tame a word for what you are.* "Smart, fun women. I usually go for the arty types, or the sporty types, you know, tennis players and softball players and such. Strong and toned, but soft where it counts. Usually." She was babbling. She had to stop babbling. Why was she babbling?

"Usually." Ryan made a small humming sound and caught a lock of Sarah's hair between her fingers, stroking the length before letting go. She grazed Sarah's cheek, and the touch made her shiver. "Perhaps you'd be in the mood for something other than your usual tonight. I only have a few hours—"

She was cut off by a yell from across the room. "Ryan, those tarts are gonna burn if you don't get them out of the oven in the next twenty seconds."

Ryan jolted as if she'd forgotten where she was and stepped back. "Sorry, Al." She strode across the kitchen like a military commander going into battle and whipped three trays of mini French apple tarts out of the oven, then slid them expertly onto a cooling rack.

Sarah instantly missed the closeness of their bodies almost-but-not-quite touching. Time to regroup. Assess the situation. Face facts. She was attracted to Ryan. Really attracted. Tear-my-panties-off-with-your-teeth attracted. But so what? It didn't have to mean anything, and she didn't have to act on it. Desire waged civil war against her better judgment and her previous experience. Experience won.

She wasn't going to have sex with Melody Ryan. No matter how much she wanted to.

Without her permission, her feet followed Ryan's path across the room. Sarah peered over her shoulder just as Ryan stepped back, and they collided.

"Whoa." Turning, Ryan grasped her shoulders to steady her. "Listen, you can't be here. When I get off shift I'll come and find you if you want me to. I need a few hours. I need to get these bloody desserts done."

This, she could do, especially if it meant spending less time in the ballroom. Sarah walked the three feet to a rack that held clean aprons and hairnets. With a short prayer for the death of her oh-so-long at the salon hairstyle, she flipped it on and faced Ryan. "Got a pair of enclosed shoes? I can help."

Ryan eyed her. "Aren't you here for a party?"

"Yeah. But my friends will understand. I can bake. McGregor and I own a bakery in the city. I can be your dessert chef." *Plus, if I'm cooking, I won't be thinking about sex. It's a win-win.*

Ryan's eyes widened. "Seriously? What are you, some gorgeous blond angel sent from the heavens?"

Sarah smiled, a light fluttering in her chest. "You think I'm gorgeous?"

"I think—"

"Ryan." Ryan caught the apple the sous chef threw at her before it hit her full in the face. "Get your head in the game. This ain't social hour."

"Don't get your panties in a twist, Al." She turned back to Sarah. "Can you make éclairs?"

"With my eyes closed."

Ryan tossed her a rolling pin. "You're a goddess."

"Just call me Aphrodite."

CHAPTER FOUR

When Love Means War

"So, uh, better late than never, right?"

"You'd better not be late again or you'll never keep this job."

The pimply-faced man-boy in black-and-white chef pants and a John Mayer T-shirt sighed as if the world rested on his scrawny shoulders. "I'm sorry, man. It was my gran, you know. She needed me to go to the store and—"

"Save it." Ryan scooped couscous from a dish on the warming stove onto twenty-five dinner plates lined up like soldiers preparing to march. Each spoonful precisely level, each flick of her wrist depositing the grain in exactly the same position on each plate. "Last week it was your great-aunt Mary who broke her wrist, and the week before some other long lost relative. I've had enough, Joe."

The man-boy stared at the ground and scowled. "Great-aunt Maisy."

"I don't get paid nearly enough to take up the role of your mother. Stop giving me reason to scold you. Now suit up and get busy. You get my share of cleanup." Ryan finished plating and made room for the guy behind her to slide salmon filets onto the china, adding garnish with a flick of fingers before the servers arrived to carry them out to guests.

Ryan strode to the same small cooler by the dessert bench and tossed Sarah a bottle of water. "We're off the clock, Aphrodite. Thanks for the help."

It wasn't as if she'd expected to be spending the night making a hundred éclairs, but now that her replacement had arrived, Sarah was reluctant to leave. It'd been fun. She wouldn't give up Cakewalk for all the frosting in heaven, but she missed working in a team. The banter, the casual insults, leaning into the rhythm of the group until you were all working with smooth efficiency. "You sure you don't still need me?"

"I never said that. I said we're off the clock."

"Both of us?" Sarah asked.

"That's right, if you want me to be. Joe here is a lazy ass, but he's not a half-bad chef when he bothers to show up."

Joe rolled his eyes at that and slid his arms into a pristine double-breasted white coat. "Yeah, yeah. I said I'd do the cleanup, man. Get out of here and stop ragging on me."

"You can just *leave*?" Sarah frowned. The last of the early dinner course was making its way into the ballroom on shiny silver trays held aloft by servers dressed in impenetrable black.

"My part of mission impossible is in the bag. All that's left is the dessert course in another hour or so. Then they'll all drink themselves into oblivion for the rest of the night. I can't leave the premises. I'm responsible for making sure all this stuff is cleared away. But now that Joe's here, I can take a break."

"Oh." A break sounded…intriguing, in a terrifying kind of way.

"Want to take a break with me?" Ryan asked.

The words were like warm cinnamon honey sliding down her skin. Smooth and sinful, with just a hint of spice. Did she want to? The wetness inside her panties had barely cooled in the hour they'd been working. And from the tone of her voice, Ryan seemed to feel the same way. Sarah flashed to Melinda's pained expression whenever she'd broached the idea of sex, her weighty silences, her oh-if-you-insist attempts at foreplay, as if touching Sarah had been a favor she was doing out of the goodness of her heart. Melinda said she'd loved her, said she'd wanted a life together. If Melinda couldn't stir up the energy to bother fucking, why should this woman, who didn't even know her last name, want to have sex with her? *What does it matter? You're not having sex with her anyway, remember? You decided.*

It hit her like a wave hitting rocks, smashing against her brain at full force, then sliding down her body in a rush. It was *because* Ryan didn't know Sarah that she wanted her. Of course, this crazy hot woman didn't want *her*. She couldn't possibly. Ryan didn't even know her. Melinda hadn't wanted her either. It's why she was scraping the bottom of the singles barrel. Sleeping with a stranger was the only option she had. She had to get it done, and get gone, before they got to know her. Her personality was that repulsive.

A boulder had lodged in her stomach, but she pushed around it. She'd dealt with bigger challenges than this. "I can't. I'm sorry."

Joe sniggered behind her, making Sarah realize she'd just turned down the boss in front of her entire staff. Fuck. She hadn't meant to do that. The last thing she wanted was to embarrass her. But Ryan didn't look embarrassed. She looked concerned.

"I owe you some food at least. You missed dinner."

"It doesn't matter. I—"

"Sarah." All too quickly, Ryan was in front of her, two fingers under her chin, tilting her head so their eyes met. "I was hoping to sit with you for a few minutes, enjoy a meal, maybe some conversation. That's all. Just a break from the work."

"Oh." It was wrong of her. She was the one who'd said no. She was the one who'd promised herself it wouldn't happen. But she was so freaking disappointed. Ryan just wanted to talk. She'd misinterpreted the whole thing. Whoop-de-do.

"Say yes." Ryan gave her a lopsided smile. "At least right here, right now, to save my dignity. If you want to bail, you can do it in a minute."

"Something tells me your ego would recover if I turned you down in front of your friends," Sarah said.

"Never. I'm a delicate flower." Ryan made a face that was half wounded, half pleading. "You wouldn't do that to me, would you?"

She didn't buy it for a second, but she did need to eat, especially since she planned on hanging by the bar and downing some liquid courage before being forced to mingle later. "Okay. Let's go."

Ryan nodded as if she'd expected nothing less. They shed their gear, Sarah changed her shoes, and they snagged a couple of plates of food left for the staff. "Follow me."

Ryan turned down a hall that ended in an exit that opened into the back gardens. Flowers were still weeks from blooming, but hopeful shoots of green foliage announced spring was coming. Seeming to know her way, Ryan led her to a solid picnic table tucked into an alcove.

While the house was only twenty feet away, the alcove was recessed in such a way no one looking out would see them.

Alone.

A thread of excitement sparked in her belly, then shot downward to simmer between her legs. *Stop it. She doesn't want you like that, Sarah. No one does.*

Ryan slid onto a long bench, set her plate down, and gestured for Sarah to sit beside her. "God, it's nice to be off my feet."

"How long have you been working?" Sarah picked up her fork to dig in.

"About six hours. Most of the actual work is over now that all the food's out."

Sarah knew the routine. She'd spent enough time at catering jobs, paying for her living expenses in college, to know even after all the food was prepared and served, the clean and pack up could take hours. "It's a sweet gig, though. You must be good."

"I am." Ryan's smile was slow and hot. "Very good."

Was this flirting? Or was Sarah just reading into it what she hoped to see? History told her the latter was more likely, so she pretended to ignore the way her pussy clenched in response to that sexy smile. "I believe it. McGregor's a stickler. How many interviews and test runs did he force you to endure?"

Ryan speared a cherry tomato from her side salad and popped it into her mouth, then swallowed before answering. "My dad's the groundskeeper here, so he had some pull."

"Your family isn't wealthy, then?" The words left her mouth

before they registered in her brain, and she realized the question had been rude. "Sorry, I didn't mean that the way it sounded. It's just, usually you need to be an insider to land a job like this."

"It's okay. You're right. I got really lucky. A few years back, I was fresh out of college and struggling to launch my business. I had trouble finding customers and was truly afraid the whole thing might sink before it had started. Mr. McGregor was planning a Fourth of July cookout, and Dad recommended me. Mr. McGregor gave me a chance. More, he went out of his way to recommend me to others afterward. It saved my business. It *is* my business."

"Wow. That was nice of him," Sarah said.

"He's a great guy, bets on the underdog."

Sarah scoffed.

"What?"

"Nothing."

"Come on, you said he's an investor in your bakery. You must know what I'm talking about. He helped you too," Ryan said.

She twirled pasta in a light cream sauce on her fork and considered her answer. "He loaned me money, with about a thousand conditions."

Ryan raised her eyebrows. "Such as?"

"He made me outline my plans for Cakewalk, the space, the tone, the inventory, the product. That's fine, I would've had to do that for a bank. But then he trashed seventy percent of what I'd outlined and told me if I wanted the money, I needed to focus on what actually mattered. Apparently, that wasn't baking, you know, that pesky little thing I'd spent four years learning how to do better than almost anyone else."

"What did he suggest was more important?" Ryan asked.

"Business school. He's got me taking night classes. He shredded my product list, limited my creative freedom, and every second week he's asking me to attend some annoying social function that's way out of my league. The man would rather see me in a party dress making small talk with strangers than in front of an oven."

Ryan looked at her in silence, her head tilted just slightly to one side, her brow creased as if trying to figure out a particularly tricky equation. "I don't really know you, and this is none of my business, but you're dead wrong."

"Excuse me?" Sarah put down her fork. "I think I know a little more about it than you do."

"Do you?" Ryan shifted and put a hand over the fist Sarah had made without even realizing it. Squeezed. It shouldn't have made her wet. "I've seen you work. You're fastidious, but you're also creative. You have flair. You're an artist. That's a rare combination."

"So?" This woman didn't know a damn thing. And why the hell was she so attractive? That wasn't remotely fair.

"So, Mr. McGregor's not stupid. Your talent is obvious. You can bake like nobody's business. But that doesn't mean you can run a successful business. A bakery is more than flour and butter. It's dollars and cents. It's cost projections and P&Ls. He's trying to help you."

"He's trying to control me." Sarah could feel the smoke coming out of her ears. "He loaned me the money, but he sure as hell let me know his fingerprints would be all over my dream."

Ryan pried open Sarah's fingers one by one, smoothing them out, stroking, soothing. God, if Ryan's touch felt this good on her hand, what would it feel like on her breasts? Her stomach? Those fingers pushing into her pussy? She pressed her thighs together and bit her lip to hold in a whimper. Perhaps it was time to reconsider her stance on sex with a stranger. Sex with Ryan.

"You'd never be successful without fabulous desserts and pastries. You spent four years mastering those pesky little things." Ryan smiled. "Mr. McGregor reined you in, yeah, okay, he trashed a bunch of your ideas, but you can't sit there and tell me the ones he kept, the ones he suggested himself, haven't panned out for you."

That…was a point.

How annoying.

"I'm guessing you didn't really want to come tonight," Ryan said.

Sarah stiffened. Was she that obvious? "What makes you say that?"

"You've spent an hour and a half avoiding the ballroom."

Damn her and her accurate observations. "It's not my kind of thing. Not my kind of people."

Ryan nodded. "I get that. Mr. McGregor gets that. That's why he asked you, why he keeps asking you."

"He asked me to a party because he knew I'd have a terrible time?"

Ryan laughed. "No, he asked you because he knew you'd meet new people, business people, money people, people with power who could help you."

"No, he—"

Ryan turned her hand over and made small circles in her palm. "Yes."

Yes. Those three simple letters confirmed a truth she hadn't seen. She'd believed McGregor enjoyed making her jump through hoops. That he saw her as just another obedient show pony he controlled with his deep pockets. But he'd been trying to *help* her. "Why? It doesn't make sense."

"What do you mean?" Ryan asked.

"Why would he help me like that? Why should he care? I'm nobody. Just the scrappy scholarship kid at his daughter's school," Sarah said.

"I don't know. Maybe you should ask him."

Sarah sat for a moment, trying to absorb this new perspective. "I've had it all wrong, haven't I? I'm usually not so quick to think the worst of people. I owe him a huge apology."

"Why did you?"

Ryan traced slow, tender circles in her palm, up over her wrist; the barely-there touch was so distracting she could hardly think. Luckily, it was an easy question. "His daughter is Satan incarnate."

"Eleanor?"

The shock in Ryan's voice made Sarah want to punch something. Why was it so hard for everyone to believe that beautiful perfect Eleanor had a heart of snake venom? "Yup. She hates me. She tried to ruin my chances of going to college."

"Shit, Sarah, are you serious? I'm so sorry."

Ryan's instant outrage, her unquestioning acceptance, warmed Sarah. "Yeah. It sucked."

"I can't believe it. I haven't been close to Eleanor in a long time, but we basically grew up together. I would've sworn she was a good person."

"She's a good actor."

Ryan shook her head. "What happened between you?"

Avery had happened.

Sarah sighed. "It's a long story."

Ryan glanced up at the setting sun. "I've got time. It's this, or go help wash dishes."

"Good to know talking to me is so alluring," Sarah said.

Ryan's hand stilled. "You're so fucking alluring, you have no idea."

All the blood rushed between Sarah's legs. *Oh.* "I am?"

"Yeah. But we'll get to that in a minute. Tell me why Eleanor hates you."

Right. In a minute. Melinda had always put her off too. *Later, maybe tomorrow. I just don't feel like it right now.* Or ever. Not with her. Ryan was just being casually flirty. God. Why did she always want more?

"I have two best friends. Kaitlyn and Avery. We went to school together. We're tight. We were all attracted to girls, so we bonded."

Ryan nodded.

"Kaitlyn ended up falling for this stoic butch type at about sixteen. They were together all through school, but Avery and I stayed single. Avery volunteered for one of those after-school looks-good-on-your-college-application extracurricular committees and got to know Eleanor. They became friends. Kaitlyn and I tried to include Eleanor in our group, we went out of our way to be nice, but she wasn't interested in hanging out with us. Only Avery. Like we weren't good enough for the hedge fund princess."

Ryan kept silent, giving Sarah her full attention even as she stroked up and down Sarah's arm in a maddening rhythm.

"But after about three months, Avery started hanging with

Eleanor less, downright avoiding her honestly, and she wouldn't tell us why. She got all moody. The woman can get a brood on better than Bronte's Rochester. There's no snapping her out of it. Then, one afternoon Avery asked me to let Eleanor know her hockey practice had switched to a different day and she couldn't make the committee that afternoon. I thought nothing of it. It wasn't a big deal."

"But it was to Eleanor." Ryan was already connecting the dots.

"Yup. I passed on the message, and she flipped out. She started crying, yelling at me, saying all kinds of ridiculous things that didn't make sense. Not then. I tried to hug her, figure out why Avery bailing on some school thing had her crying like her dog had just died."

"She was in love."

Sarah sighed. "Yeah. But she didn't tell me that. She just shoved me away and ran off. It was Avery who told me. Eleanor had been sending her signals. Clumsy, obvious ones, the way you do when you're seventeen and don't have any experience."

Ryan smiled.

"Avery's a good person. She didn't intentionally hurt her, but when you've never turned a girl down before, you fumble it. It's awkward, and embarrassing, and it didn't go smoothly."

"Where do you fit in?" Ryan asked.

Sarah shrugged. "I'm the one who passed on the message. The one who saw her break. Eleanor somehow got it into her head that Avery and I were dating and that's why Avery wasn't interested in her. I guess it made sense looking at it from the outside. We were close, single, and spent a lot of time together."

"Were you? Together, I mean."

"No. We've only ever been friends," Sarah said.

"So why didn't Avery just tell her that?"

And that's the sixty-four-thousand-dollar question. "She asked me to cover for her. She wanted someone else, someone she couldn't have, and she didn't want Eleanor to know," Sarah said.

Ryan frowned. "That's very *Days of Our Lives*, isn't it?"

"Totally. Her reasons made sense at the time. Seventeen-year-old logic is faulty logic."

"So, you let Eleanor believe you two were together," Ryan said.

"Yup. Honestly, it didn't seem like a sacrifice. I didn't like Eleanor much anyway. It didn't change anything for me. Not at first."

"But then she tried ruining your chances of college?"

"She *hated* me. She tried to get other girls to hate me too, but Kaitlyn, Avery, and some luck in the genetics department shielded me from most of that. Teenage girls are shallow," Sarah said.

"I don't think it's a teenage affliction. I felt pretty shallow when I turned around and saw you tonight. Looking like a runway model in those fuck me heels."

"My heels *do not* say fuck me."

"Baby, those heels say all kinds of things, the least of which is fuck me," Ryan said.

Sarah swallowed hard. *Baby*. The endearment settled on her skin, made her tingle. "Anyway, her great act of revenge was to go to the principal and claim I had cheated off her on our history final senior year. She got two other girls to back her up. Eleanor and I received exactly the same grade. It was her word against mine, and she was the daughter of the school's most generous donor. I was a nobody from Brooklyn there on scholarship."

"I'm so sorry," Ryan said.

"Thanks. The principal didn't want to piss off the golden girl. I was *this close* to receiving an F for that exam, at the very least. It would have dropped my GPA, and culinary school is competitive."

Ryan nodded. "What happened?"

"I went a round with Avery. I blamed her. It wasn't her fault, not really. But this little favor I'd done was about to ruin my life. I stormed off, had a sleepless night, and Avery used the time to convince Eleanor to come clean. I don't know how she did it, but two days later, Eleanor confesses, McGregor makes an extra-large donation, and the whole thing goes away."

Ryan whistled. "Wow."

"Yeah. I'm grateful that Avery backed me. If she hadn't, who knows what would've happened. But she's still friends with Eleanor. She thinks it's all a storm in a teacup. Girl drama," Sarah said.

"She's never felt powerless."

Sarah's whole body sagged, her righteous indignation slowly deflating. She hadn't realized how much her resentment had become a part of her until Ryan hit the nail on the head and she could let it go. Ryan got it. Got *her*.

"Yes. It wasn't so much what she did. We were kids. She had her heart broken, and she thought I was to blame. I let her think it. I'm not so cold I don't get how much that must have hurt. What pisses me off is that no one would have taken her as seriously if her family didn't have mountains of money. If she hadn't used that as leverage to get what she wanted, and used it again to clean up the mess she made. She never apologized for lying; she never had to pay. All because she was born rich, and I wasn't."

"And then Mr. McGregor approaches you to invest in your bakery," Ryan said.

Sarah laughed. "Yeah. He was so the last person I wanted to see. But banks don't loan large sums of money to twenty-somethings with no assets and no experience."

Ryan looked thoughtful.

"I'm sorry. I've been talking your ear off. You must think I'm nuts dragging up all this teenage angst," Sarah said.

"I don't think you're nuts. I think you're beautiful, smart, and determined." And with that, Ryan leaned into her personal space and kissed her. Not a friendly, thanks for the chat kiss. Not a sweet and soft first date kiss, but a full-on, knock your socks off, melt into a puddle on the floor, hot and sexy, I-want-you-naked-all-over-me kiss.

Even as Ryan's lips moved over hers, all Sarah could think was *more*.

CHAPTER FIVE

Cheer Up, Butter Cup

Ryan had the patience of an explorer in new terrain. Mapping every inch of Sarah's mouth with the glide of her lips and the sweep of her tongue, leaving no corner undiscovered. *Breathe.* It was like the touch of Ryan's lips to hers had flipped a switch, igniting her body. Her skin seemed to light up from the inside, every cell on high alert. Waiting. Wanting. Begging. *Just breathe.*

The kiss was demanding yet thorough. Purposeful but not hurried. When Ryan paused to suck Sarah's bottom lip into her mouth, darts of knee-weakening pleasure arrowed down her body, pooling in her clit, making her so, so wet. Someone made a sound, a small whimper filled with so much desire her cheeks burned. It wasn't until she heard it again that she realized she was the one making it. She wanted Ryan's body over hers. She wanted to arch up and rub herself against all the angles and planes of her skin, to beg for attention like a lonely kitten.

Sarah moaned. She couldn't stop herself. She wasn't sure how much more of this torturously patient, world-crashing-to-a-halt kissing she could take. When Ryan eased back a fraction of an inch and stared into her eyes, held the connection, Sarah literally forgot all about breathing. All she could do was stare back. The hungry look on Ryan's face stripped her bare. Whatever pretense of control she'd been deluding herself with shattered. No one had ever looked at her with so much want in their eyes.

Ryan cupped Sarah's cheeks in her palms and kissed her

tenderly, a kiss that had everything to do with attraction, yet felt like more. Sarah felt *cherished.* Fuck. She had no business feeling something like that. She'd given up on ridiculous romantic notions. When Melinda had walked out, she'd taken the espresso machine, an Andy Warhol print that had hung above their couch, and Sarah's faith in happily ever after. She didn't even know Ryan. Not really. Getting sentimental over some intense eye contact and kissing wasn't practical. Sarah pulled back. Tonight was supposed to be fun, a little release of sexual tension, not have her emotions churning and her body halfway to orgasm after just one kiss. And she wasn't supposed to be losing it over Ryan. Not a woman she'd only just met.

"Um, wow." Her vocabulary was *not* improving.

Ryan rested her forehead gently on Sarah's. "I'll say."

"You're pretty okay at that." Sarah desperately tried to inject some levity into the situation that had gotten all fog-the-windows steamy and intense way too fast. The persistent throbbing between her legs was getting difficult to ignore. It wasn't *natural* to be this turned on from a kiss, was it? Had Melinda's disinterest fucked with her so badly that one kiss, one moment of tenderness, had her ready to come? Was she really that needy? People kissed all the time. No big deal. She could pretend the kiss hadn't mattered. That she hadn't just had the hottest sexual experience of her whole life. No one needed to know just how desperate she was.

There was no denying she wanted Ryan to fuck her.

What the hell was she going to do about that?

Ryan narrowed her eyes. "*Pretty okay,* huh?"

Sarah struggled for nonchalance. "Somewhere or other in the top quartile of kisses. For two people who spend the majority of their time in the kitchen, we didn't do too bad."

There, see? She'd done it. No big deal.

Ryan didn't look amused. "There's something important you should know about me." She fingered a strand of Sarah's hair, twirling it and tugging just hard enough Sarah felt the pressure against her scalp. It was becoming a habit, as if Ryan just couldn't help touching her.

Ryan's face was so serious Sarah was almost afraid to ask. "What's that?"

"I'm very competitive. I can do so much better than pretty okay. I've been practicing since I was twelve."

"You—" Before Sarah could get another word out, Ryan's lips were back on hers, but this kiss was neither patient nor gentle. It was pure challenge. Ryan plundered her mouth, taking everything she had and demanding more. When her arms came around Sarah's waist, she would have luxuriated in the feel of those strong hands on her body if Ryan hadn't shifted Sarah into her lap as if she weighed no more than a bag of Doritos. Without thinking, Sarah moved with her, straddling her, her legs falling open on either side of Ryan's, her pussy flush against Ryan's thigh. Oh God. The material of her dress pulled taut, and when Ryan cupped her ass and brought their bodies together, she shuddered. It felt so good to be touched. Finally. Sarah gave in to temptation and rubbed herself against Ryan.

Her panties were so wet, slick fabric glided easily against her pussy as she rode Ryan's thigh. Her blood rushed and pleasure whipped through her, coiling low and tight in her belly, every nerve poised and ready to explode. Her breath came in quick, short pants as her pussy beat to the same rhythm.

The pressure against her clit was a thousand teasing fingers, pushing her to the edge and leaving her helpless. She needed more. Ryan's hand, her mouth. Ryan's everything, all over her everything, making the world spiral out of control until she was finally sated. But they hadn't even taken their clothes off, maybe they wouldn't. Maybe this was just a makeout session. They were in a semipublic place. She had to get a grip.

She'd always need more than she was going to get.

She was doing just exactly what she'd told herself she was strong enough to avoid.

Sarah backed it up before Ryan realized just how embarrassingly turned on she was. Why couldn't her body and brain get on the same page when it came to this woman? She came up for air, searched her sex-scrambled brain for something to say that wasn't *I think I could come just from your mouth on mine.*

Sliding off Ryan's lap and settling next to her again, trying not to look awkward about it, Sarah asked, "Twelve. You started early, didn't you?" There, that was a normal person question, right? They didn't have to talk about the kiss. It was a moment of weakness. No, less than that. It was a blip. Just a blip on the radar of her screwed up life.

Ryan took a moment to catch her breath, her fingers not quite steady when she brushed her hair out of her eyes. She glanced down at her empty lap and studied Sarah for a beat, as if deciding whether to answer the question or ask one of her own. "I spent a summer upstate in middle school, and Jessica Clements had a kissing booth at the county fair. My little lesbian heart just about beat itself out of my chest, she was so pretty. I used every dollar I had locking lips with my very own Mrs. Robinson until I was sure I had it just right and the tri-county beauty queen would be mine forever."

Sarah laughed. "How old was she?"

"About seventeen. But when you're a scrawny twelve-year-old tomboy, seventeen is an insurmountable level of sophistication. Almost as scarily adult as Frappuccinos or staying up past midnight."

"I take it she didn't feel quite the same way about you?"

"Not so much. She had a boyfriend on the football team. There's something ironic about working a kissing booth to raise money for your boyfriend's sports team, don't you think?"

"Sounds kind of sexy to me."

Ryan's eyes lit with appreciation. "Oh, I never thought of it like that. Maybe she liked kissing half the town, showing off for him."

"Maybe he liked having a girlfriend everyone wanted to kiss."

"You know, I bet you're right. I like the way your mind works, Aphrodite."

Sarah smiled. She liked the way her mind worked too. She'd just never known anyone who could meet her halfway. "Oh, my mind is packed full of wicked thoughts."

"You're very sexy."

Sarah scoffed and looked away. She wasn't sexy.

Their bottles of water were sweating on the picnic table. She should really go find a coaster or there would be water rings on the wood in the morning.

"What just happened?"

"Sorry?"

"I told you that you were sexy and the conversation stopped dead."

"Oh. That."

"Yeah. *That*."

McGregor would surely flip out if his three-thousand-dollar made-to-look-rustic Frontgate picnic table was ruined. Should she tell him? Probably. Now would be a good time. She'd go do that.

"Sarah."

Sarah sighed. "I'm not sexy."

"Well, that's ridiculous."

"It's true. My last girlfriend told me so. In unfortunate graphic detail."

"She sounds like a colossal bitch."

"Maybe." Sarah picked up the water and set it on a folded napkin.

Ryan put an arm around her shoulders. The gesture was so warm and comforting Sarah couldn't help but lean into the heat of her body.

"I'm having a real hard time believing anyone could make a case for you not being sexy. Does this woman have eyes? Ears? Functioning brain cells?"

"All of the above. We were together about a year, so she had plenty of time to use them all to draw her conclusion." Then, almost as an afterthought. "I loved her."

Ryan's hand moved to her back, traced the curve of Sarah's spine in silent encouragement. "I'm sorry you were hurt."

"The sex was never very good, I can see that now, but at the time I only saw how much I wanted Melinda. How attractive she was. How turned on I got just from looking at her. I was totally crazy for her. But just because you *want* the sex to be good doesn't mean it is." She stopped suddenly. "Sorry, I shouldn't be talking about this to someone I just made out with." *Correction. Someone I almost came with.*

"I don't mind. Jealousy is overrated."

Jealousy was overrated. She liked that. "I fell hard, and for me, a big part of that was sexual attraction. But over time the sex became less frequent. She was never in the mood. Always too busy. Too distracted. Whenever we had sex, it felt like some monumental effort for her." Sarah stopped. After all this time, it still hurt.

"No one should feel as if they're an obligation."

She nodded. That was it exactly. "Eventually, we stopped. I wanted her to want *me*, not to have sex out of some sense of duty. I thought maybe I'd done something wrong. Turned her off in some way. I tried to bring it up, but didn't push very hard. I was afraid I was right, and who wants to face the fact their girlfriend thinks they're unattractive? Sticking my head in the sand isn't my style, but I wanted it to work between us, so I tried it. What they don't tell you about that tactic is that after a while, it's impossible to breathe. You just suffocate in the loneliness."

"Sarah." That one simple word, two short syllables, her word, her name, held an endless supply of compassion and support.

"The week before we broke up, I'd gone out into the city with Avery. Kaitlyn had a cold and couldn't make it, and after one too many cocktails, we'd ended up at an upscale strip joint in Times Square. One of the dancers took a special interest in me, and Avery bought me a lap dance." She realized how sleazy it must sound and didn't want Ryan to think she was a wanton hussy. "It was a joke. A bit of fun. I don't do that kind of thing all the time. I wasn't really into it, just caught up in the idea."

"I'll buy that it's not something you do regularly, but no woman with a pulse isn't into a lap dance. I think it's really sexy that you were there and very cool of your friend to do that for you."

Surprise had her mouth opening slightly and her tears drying up. "You do?"

"Oh yeah. I'd love to have watched."

Sarah's pussy clenched. *Oh.* A woman who thought jealousy was overrated and wanted to watch another woman turn her on? She needed to learn how to say "yes please" in at least ten languages. STAT. One just wasn't enough.

"Did you like the other patrons in the club watching?" Ryan's voice was velvety rough.

"I would've liked it better if you were watching."

Ryan groaned. "Did you come?"

Sarah shook her head, the question vanquishing the fantasy of Ryan in a dimly lit club, watching her get hotter and hotter as a sexy stripper worked her magic. "I didn't let it get that far. It felt disloyal. I was with Melinda after all."

Ryan nodded.

"When I got home that night, I was really keyed up. I begged Melinda, told her how much I needed her, and she begrudgingly agreed to make love. She started stroking me and I was happy I hadn't come in the club. But she fell back asleep in less than a minute, literally with her fingers on my clit."

Ryan winced. "God. I'm so sorry."

"Yeah. It wasn't my finest moment. Turned on and drunk isn't a great combination. The next morning, we talked. I apologized for coming on too strong too fast, but I wanted to get to the bottom of what was going on with us. A paid stripper had more interest in me than my own girlfriend." That fact had eaten away at her, leaving her tossing and turning, confusion and desire an unsettling mix in her belly.

"What happened?"

"She told me I was making a big deal out of nothing; she'd just been tired. That was such bullshit. We were on totally different planets when it came to sex. It was about more than one night. So I asked if she was asexual."

Ryan whistled softly. "Wow."

"Yeah. It would've explained a lot. She didn't confirm or deny, and I took her non-answer as a yes. I thought she was embarrassed to admit it. In retrospect I can see that I *wanted* to believe she was asexual. It was easier than thinking she wasn't into me. She was just wired differently. That wasn't personal."

"Makes sense." Ryan's hand moved down to the small of her

back, rubbing circles only an inch above her ass. Sarah shivered. She wanted to grab Ryan's hand and slide it lower, then higher up under her dress. She'd been imagining the feel of those hands on her bare skin all night, and the heat of Ryan's palm though her dress was making her crave the real deal.

But she *needed* to finish this story. She'd never told anyone all of it before, and for some reason she couldn't explain, she wanted Ryan to know the truth. Even if that meant Ryan walked away.

The sky had begun to darken in earnest, a faint smattering of starlight dotting the sky. Warm yellow garden lights flickered to life along the edge of the flowerbeds and pathways, lighting the grounds in a faint glow. The shadows they cast made it hard to see Ryan's face beside hers.

"I felt better. I mentally committed to doing everything I could to be there for her. I had no idea what box I would shove my overwhelming attraction into, but that seemed unimportant when she was coming to terms with an identity that could change her life. I hoped it would make her happier. I so badly wanted to make her happy.

"On Sunday afternoon, they'd closed half of Times Square for a parade and I shut up the shop early. I decided to surprise Melinda with a romantic dinner. Candlelight, a movie, cuddling on the couch. She was constantly complaining I worked too hard and was never home, so this was my chance to show her how important she was to me."

"And?"

"When I got there, she wasn't in the main part of our apartment so I went looking for her. The bedroom door was cracked a couple of inches and I glanced in. Melinda was in bed with another woman."

Ryan sucked in a breath. "So, she wasn't asexual then."

"Nope. Not by a long shot. I couldn't believe it. It made no sense."

"Did you confront them?"

Sarah shook her head. "Most people would have, I guess. I was too confused to consider barging in there. I just left the apartment, took a walk."

"But you confronted Melinda later?"

"When I was sure the other woman had left. It didn't go well."

"Why did she have sex with this other woman?" Ryan asked, getting straight to the point.

Sarah sighed and rubbed a hand over the back of her neck. "Long story short? Melinda got off on having sex with strangers. Apparently, actually getting to know someone killed her sex drive."

"That's...wow."

"Yeah. It gets worse."

"Is that possible?" Ryan's touch on her back was tense, her body still and tight, as if she was steeling herself for Sarah's pain.

"I made the mistake of trying to understand. I'm not like most people. If Melinda had been honest with me, told me she liked sex with strangers, I would have found a way to accommodate that desire. I wasn't totally against the idea of seeing her with someone else. Watching them, maybe. But when I suggested that, when I fucking offered to give her exactly what she wanted after she'd been cheating on me for God knows how long, she looked incredibly awkward. Like I'd just pooped all over her cupcake and she wasn't sure how to tell me she didn't want it anymore. She said it was really sweet of me, but that that wouldn't work for her. She didn't want me there."

"Are you serious? But why?" Ryan asked.

"When she's done with someone she's done. She loved me according to her. She wanted the picture-perfect relationship, but she had no interest in me sexually anymore. I was used goods. She'd been there and done me. Having me there would have been distracting, diverting her attention from what she really wanted. She oh-so-generously told me I could sleep with other people, too, if I wanted."

Ryan all but growled. "I want to kill her. Chop her bones into little pieces."

"Thanks, I guess. Anyway, I wish I could say I flayed her with the fury of a thousand swords, but all I did was sit on the floor and cry. Right there in front of her. Talk about pathetic."

Ryan didn't say anything, just scooped Sarah back onto her lap and wrapped her arms tight around her as Sarah's tears fell and the last of her grief soaked into the front of Ryan's shirt.

"Tell me the rest," Ryan murmured against her hair.

"That's when she told me I wasn't sexy. I don't think she meant to insult me, but she crouched down, all concerned girlfriend, and told me in a so-reasonable-and-mature tone that it wasn't unusual for two people in a relationship to find different things sexy. That she didn't find me sexy anymore, but that didn't mean we couldn't have a great life together. Like picking out furniture and sharing the same Netflix account somehow made up for not wanting to touch me."

Ryan shook her head. "I don't have words for how fucked up that is. You deserve someone who wants you with every breath they take and shows you just how much every day."

Sarah knew all too well that life was about dealing with what you got, not dreaming about what you deserved. She'd stopped deluding herself that day, and she wasn't about to start again now.

"I can't have sex with you."

CHAPTER SIX

Stripped Bare

Ryan put her hands on Sarah's shoulders and nudged her back to look into her eyes. "Huh?"

"I can't have sex with you."

"Sarah, with everything you've been through, everything you told me tonight, I can certainly understand why sex with me would be the last thing on your mind. But those kisses were amazing, even on my awesome kissing booth scale, so maybe you could explain your logic?"

"I don't know you."

Ryan frowned.

"I don't want to have sex with someone I don't know. That's what she did, what she wanted more than she wanted me. I don't want to want it, too."

"Oh, baby."

There it was again. *Baby.* Why did it have to feel so good?

"Melinda was a crazy person. Maybe it's not that unusual to have a kink for sex with strangers, I don't know, but it sure as hell isn't right that she preferred it to sex with you. That she deliberately and cruelly denied you any chance to be with her. What she did to you was awful, but I'm not sorry you're not with her anymore. She didn't deserve you."

Sarah rested her head against Ryan's shoulder and blew out a slow breath. Logically, she knew that wanting to have sex with Ryan wasn't the same thing as Melinda not wanting to have sex with her, but if felt too close for comfort. "I'm sorry."

"Don't apologize. If you don't want to kiss me again, if you're not interested in seeing where this leads tonight, tomorrow, a week from now, that's okay. We can get up and go inside. But hear me when I say that what's happening between us isn't the same as Melinda wanting to screw strangers. I *like* you, Sarah."

"I like you too."

"See? It's not the same. Do you think Melinda liked that girl? Do you think she even knew her name? That she ever really saw her?"

I like you.

I know you.

I see you.

Sarah felt each simple admission as if it were a suture in her wounded heart. She was being an idiot. Ryan wasn't a stranger. Hell, she'd spilled more about her life in the last thirty minutes than even her best friends knew. You couldn't get more personal. So what if they'd only just met? Sometimes it happened that way. An instant connection.

"What are your feelings on rebound sex?"

Ryan's eyes went deep and swirly. "I'm a big fan. It's right up there with first-thing-in-the-morning sex; frustrated, we're-in-the-middle-of-an-argument sex; and my personal favorite, we're-gonna-be-late-because-you're-so-fucking-gorgeous sex."

"Late to where?"

"Wherever it is I'm taking you on our first date."

She chewed on her bottom lip. "I'm not sure I'm ready for—"

The briefest touch of Ryan's lips to hers cut her off. "I know. I've got time, and I've got patience. Whenever you're ready, I'll be waiting, and in the meantime I'd love nothing more than to show you just how sexy you are and make you come all over this picnic table." She considered for a moment. "Twice. Possibly three times."

"Confident, are we?"

"Just sure of how much I want you."

"That feels really good to hear."

"I promise it will feel even better when I show you. Say yes."

Sarah knew what she'd say before she threaded her fingers in Ryan's hair, before she pressed against Ryan's chest, before her lips hovered over Ryan's mouth, but she did all those things for the simple pleasure of being able to, of being sure they'd be welcomed.

Finally, with this woman, she would be able to breathe.

"Yes."

❖

They were tucked into a secluded corner of the gardens, stretched out next to each other on a checkered picnic blanket that Ryan had rustled up from the caretaker's shed. The moment was sweetly awkward, like teenagers on a third date, inching ever closer and secretly hoping the other would make a move.

"Tell me about the stripper."

Sarah halted mid-inch. "Huh?"

"The stripper at the club in Times Square. Tell me about her."

"You can't be serious."

"Come on, you can't drop that bombshell into a conversation and withhold details." Ryan tugged at her hair again. Sarah was starting to love when she did that.

"It was part of the story. My *tragic* story, remember? I didn't tell you so you could get off."

Ryan's breath was warm against her cheek. "I bet it would make you hot and wet to watch me get off on the details."

Fuck. It so would.

"I seem to recall telling you I wasn't here to be your escort." She tried for prim and proper and made it roughly halfway there.

"That's true. Good thing I prefer you as the do-ee rather than the do-er."

"The *do-ee*? How old are you?" She made a face.

"Old enough to want the details. Spill."

"You're not going to let this go, huh?"

"Not a chance."

"Well, if you're going to drag it out of me against my will, then

I have no choice but to tell you that she was incredibly beautiful. Tall, dark, and willowy."

Ryan exhaled a measured breath slowly. Stroked a hand down Sarah's hair, slid it to the nape of her neck. "Keep going."

"I noticed her the second we sat down. She was working the pole to the left of the one in front of us. She had amazing legs. She was at least five eight, probably taller. She had flawless skin and all of it on display, save for her fire engine red panties."

"Red's my new favorite color." Ryan traced the curve of Sarah's neck down the column of her throat. She closed the gap between them, kissed the spot, then sucked until Sarah gasped. "Don't stop now, Aphrodite."

Where was she again?

"Avery noticed her too and commented on how hot she was. When you find someone genuinely attractive in a strip club, she stands out. We ordered drinks and after a while, I saw her glancing my way. Not all the time, but enough that Avery started teasing me."

Ryan kissed down her collarbone. "Did you like that the stripper had noticed you? Singled you out?"

Sarah groaned. Both in frustration at the sensual open-mouthed kisses that weren't nearly enough and the damning accuracy of the question. "Maybe."

"Be honest."

"Okay, yes. I liked that she'd noticed me. It felt good to know someone found me attractive."

Ryan looked up and smiled wickedly. "You're a very dirty girl."

Sarah couldn't help the laugh that burst out. "*Excuse me?*" No one had ever called her a dirty girl before. It ought to be porn flick cringey. But when Ryan said it, it sounded honest and sexy.

"You heard me. Your girlfriend refuses to put out, but you have needs that aren't being met. It makes you a little crazy, willing to take risks. You're half-drunk in a strip joint, and you really shouldn't be there, but a sexy dancer is into you. It makes you hot and it doesn't take much to get you wet, you're so ready for it, you've been deprived for so long. Don't tell me you didn't sit there, in your heels and night out on the town clothes, sipping your girly pink drink, your friend chatting away next to you, and all the time imagining her mouth on your pussy."

On the word *pussy*, Ryan's hand moved to her breast, circling her nipple though the fabric of her dress, pinching lightly.

"Oh God." Sarah closed her eyes, the picture Ryan had painted flashing across her eyelids. It did sound dirty the way she told it, and now she wasn't sure if that was what had actually happened or if Ryan was making her believe it. She arched her back and pushed her breast into Ryan's hand. "More, please."

"You'll get more when you give me more. Were you imagining her mouth on your pussy, baby?"

"Yes." Sarah felt Ryan's other hand move to her breast. "I was thinking about how good it would feel if she licked my clit."

Ryan made a sound that could have been a moan or could have been a growl, and her hand tightened on Sarah's breast. "Straight to the action." She reached around and slowly, with the care of a woman unwrapping a treasured heirloom, lowered the zipper on Sarah's dress.

"I was lonely."

Ryan caressed the bare skin of her back and every circuit Sarah had sizzled. *Oh God yes.*

"Don't give me that. People don't go to strip clubs because they're lonely. They go because they're horny. Because they want to come. Did you need to come, Aphrodite?"

Ryan slipped the dress from her shoulders.

"I didn't—"

"If you're not honest with me we'll go back inside, and you can walk around all night with the ache that you primed in my lap earlier. Is that what you want?"

Sarah opened her eyes. Ryan's mouth was level with her breasts, still covered by her black satin bra. The way Ryan touched her was so careful, torturously slow, allowing her to absorb every sensation, somehow knowing that a woman starved would need to savor the texture of every fingertip against her skin. This was the Ryan who'd wrapped her in her arms and told her she was sexy, the one who knew she deserved more than she'd been given.

But the longer she stared into those caramel eyes, the clearer she saw the edge just under the surface. That hint of steel. Ryan would be gentle. But that didn't mean she'd play nice.

"I don't want to go back inside," Sarah said.

"What do you want?"

"I want you to keep touching me. Please."

Ryan shook her head. "You're going to have to do better than that."

"I don't know what to say."

"It was a simple question."

Sarah wanted to wring her neck and kiss her at the same time. Yeah, it was a simple question, but that didn't mean the answer was easy. She hadn't had sex, all the way to orgasm, in more months than she cared to think about. She'd pushed the need down, diverted it and rerouted it until she'd convinced herself it wasn't there. Admitting it now was…embarrassing. Bringing it into the light made it real. Ryan wasn't going to let her hide her desire. She wanted it out in the open. She wanted Sarah to face it.

"Tell me that admitting you wanted the stripper to lick your clit didn't make you wetter just now," Ryan said.

Heat rose up her neck. "I can't."

Ryan nodded. "It makes you hot to tell me how much she turned you on, doesn't it?"

She hesitated and Ryan squeezed her hand, one corner of her mouth tilting in a half-smile. *I've got you.* "Yes."

"Now tell me if you went to that strip club because you were horny and wanted to come."

Embarrassment wanted to submerge her, but she fought against it. "Yes. I didn't consciously think about it like that because I was there with Avery, but I wanted another woman's hands on me. Touching myself wasn't enough anymore. If Avery hadn't bought me the lap dance, I would've paid for it myself."

Ryan's eyes shuttered closed, as if the words were too much for her to take. When she opened them again, the edge was even sharper. "Good girl. For that, you deserve a reward." She pushed the strap of Sarah's bra down her shoulder and cupped Sarah's breast in her palm. Lowering her head, she sucked on the exposed nipple.

Sarah shuddered, her pussy clenching as if Ryan had sucked on her clit. She was so wet it was obscene, soaking her panties and inner thighs. "More, I need...please." The garbled half sentence was all she could manage as heat shot from her nipple to every erogenous zone ever discovered. Her hips rose and a small, desperate sound escaped her parted lips.

"What happened next?" Ryan unclasped the front hook on her bra and her breasts spilled out into the moonlight. Ryan just stared for a second, her breath catching. "God. You're so beautiful."

The words were spontaneous, not part of the game they'd constructed. They bolstered her nerve. Tonight, spread out for Ryan like cream cheese on crackers, she was beautiful. "We sat for a couple of songs. I wasn't listening to anything Avery was saying. All I could think about was her long dark hair threaded through my fingers, her tongue circling my clit. I was so wet I was afraid to move, scared that someone would notice. I was sure I must have soaked through my jeans."

Ryan groaned against her breast, scraping her teeth along the hard ridge of her nipple. "You're making me so hot, Aphrodite."

She was so focused on how Ryan was making her feel, on the lewd story Ryan had demanded she tell, she hadn't considered it might be turning her on as well. "Are you wet?"

She'd meant the question to come out low and seductive, a little payback. But it was too high-pitched. Too real.

Ryan released her breast and shifted so they were face-to-face. "You never have to doubt how much I want you."

Sarah bit her lip. She wanted to believe her, but they were just words. Pretty words, sure. But she'd been lied to with pretty words plenty. The body never lied. "Yeah. But are you wet?"

"Stroke my clit."

The command was so unexpected Sarah blinked. "Huh?"

"Find out for yourself whether you made me wet."

Oh.

With fingers that weren't as steady as she'd have liked, Sarah reached for the waistband of Ryan's white chef pants. She tugged the zipper down. Her heart started to race, her vision narrowed, her fingers on Ryan's pants, sliding in, sliding under. She eased past the barrier of Ryan's underwear and shuddered out a moan.

Ryan wasn't just wet. Wasn't just turned on. She was *soaked.*

Sarah's throat clogged, a lump settling itself where her breath should have been. Tears stung her eyes. She felt her way down to the folds of Ryan's pussy, bypassing her clit. Dipping into Ryan's cashmere soft center, she spun her fingers in a slow circle, scooping up the evidence of her desire, wet and hot and slick. "You want me."

"So much."

She buried her face in Ryan's neck and took a second to process. To breathe through the swell of emotion. The fluid painting her fingers irrefutable evidence that Ryan was attracted to her. She slid a finger to Ryan's opening and pressed, felt the flutter of muscles in response.

"Careful." Ryan's voice was sandpaper.

She smiled. No doubt in her mind now. "Why? You like it."

"Ladies come first." Ryan's eyes were screwed shut, the look on her face almost painful.

"And what are you, an alien from another planet?" But she eased back an inch and played with the folds guarding Ryan's entrance. *So wet.*

"You know what I mean."

"I'm not sure I agree with that rule. Maybe I can convince you to change your mind." Before she had a chance to argue, Sarah slid a finger on either side of Ryan's clit and tugged.

Ryan's head snapped back and her breath sawed out in a harsh pant. "Jesus, fuck, woman."

Sarah grinned. "I don't think Jesus is going to help you." She tugged again, circled, felt Ryan's clit grow hard beneath her touch. Was there anything sexier than a woman's clit hardening under your hand?

Ryan gripped her wrist and pulled her hand away and out of

her pants, not releasing her until Sarah felt the night air chill her wet fingertips. "Enough. You've had your fun."

She pouted. A full, puffy bottom lip pout. "What a tease. I wasn't done."

"You're the tease. For someone who's been on the sidelines, you sure know what you're doing."

She liked that Ryan thought she had skills. Sarah brought her fingers to her mouth and sucked Ryan's come off them as if they were a lollipop. "Mmm. You taste good. I bet you'd taste even better if I licked it off your clit. Maybe I should lick all that come from your pussy, and if that made you wet again, well, I'd just have to start over."

Ryan grabbed her hand to stop her from swirling her tongue around her fingers a second time. "You like to play with fire, don't you, dirty girl?"

She'd never thought of herself that way before, but the heat in Ryan's eyes made it impossible not to fan the flames. She glanced down at herself, her dress pushed down to her waist and her bra still hanging half off her shoulders. She met Ryan's eyes. *Look how shameless you make me.*

"You'd better make me come soon, or I'm going down on you, whether you like it or not."

CHAPTER SEVEN

So. Fucking. Sexy.

"Baby, you couldn't take me, even if you wanted to. You're about as tough as a kitten in a herd of elephants."

Sarah narrowed her eyes, glided a hand down Ryan's belly, cupped her pussy through her pants, and squeezed. "Tough isn't what's required here."

"God." Ryan squirmed. Her eyelids fluttered and she thrust once, hard, into Sarah's palm. Before Sarah could amp up the pressure, Ryan flipped her, rolling on top and pinning her to the picnic blanket. "I'm going to make you come so hard."

Sarah's brain fogged like a windshield in a summer storm. "That's the best idea you've had all night."

Ryan traced the curve of Sarah's earlobe with her tongue. Nipped. "Anyone ever tell you you have a smart mouth?"

"Occasionally."

"I'm going to make you pay for it, and for that grab-and-squeeze you just pulled."

"But I was provoked."

"Too bad. Tell me what happens next."

Sarah struggled to remember. The stripper. The club. She'd needed to come. *God, how she needed to come.* "When the music changed, the dancers switched and the stripper came down onto the floor. She circled a couple of tables, collecting bills from appreciative patrons, but I knew she was heading for me. I had to bite the inside of my cheek to stop from making a sound. I couldn't have moved if a tsunami flattened the building."

Ryan eased down her body, pulling Sarah's dress along with her, down her hips and off. "Do you think she knew that she'd been making you crazy?"

"I think that was her plan when I walked in. She sauntered over to our table, asked if we liked the show. Her voice was the most beautiful thing I'd ever heard. Like the purr of a Jaguar at eighty miles an hour."

Ryan lifted her ankle and kissed her toes. "Were you wearing these fuck-me heels?"

"Not this pair."

"You have others?"

"I may have a slight weakness. I'm in recovery. It's under control."

Ryan snorted. "You like the way they make your ass perky and your legs endless, even though you're short."

Sarah didn't like being called short, but she couldn't deny it. No woman would walk around in five-inch heels unless they made her feel good about herself. Ryan ran her hands slowly up the insides of Sarah's thighs, and everything inside her clenched like a fist. Pulsed. When Ryan brushed her fingers against the silky material of Sarah's panties, the fist melted and her muscles pooled to sticky honey. She fell back against the blanket, her thighs falling open. She was completely helpless against the tide of need. "Please, Ryan."

"You're not finished yet. When you're finished, you get to come."

Sarah whimpered. The scent of her arousal perfuming the air. "I said something stupid, like, for sure, or something like that. I couldn't think. I looked at Avery for help. What I saw in her eyes made it worse."

Ryan pressed a finger to her clit through her panties, and the sound Sarah made was pitifully needy. She shuddered. "Please hurry."

"What did you see on Avery's face?"

"That she liked it. She knew I was turned on and enjoyed

watching me try to keep it together. We're friends and nothing like that had ever happened before. I was surprised."

"And aroused." Ryan hooked a thumb around the ribbons holding her panties up and tugged, dragging them down her legs.

"Yes." She blushed. So wrong in the very best way to find Avery watching her. She had a poker face Sarah could only dream of mastering, but her eyes were bottomless. Avery was turned on by watching her get turned on, and that only made her wetter. The need to come, for this sexy stranger, for her best friend, ticked mercilessly close to detonation. "The stripper asked if I wanted a lap dance. My mind just about exploded. No way would I survive a lap dance. I just stared at her."

Ryan stroked a finger from her clit all the way down her pussy.

"Oh yes. That. Just that."

Ryan's hand stilled. "Tell me the rest."

"When I couldn't speak, Avery asked me if I wanted the dance. She was really asking if I wanted the stripper to make me come, right there at the table, while she watched. My face was on fire, but I was so hot I didn't care. I told her yes."

Ryan groaned, circled her clit. "So. Fucking. Sexy."

Sarah canted her hips forward, wanting more, wanting Ryan inside. "I have to come."

"As much as you had to come with the stripper in your lap and Avery watching?"

"So much more. Please. I can't wait." Ryan's mouth covered her pussy. She thrust her tongue inside Sarah and her body bowed, her pussy gushing her desire directly on Ryan's tongue. "Oh, fuck yes." Color exploded behind her eyelids as Sarah shoved her fingers into Ryan's hair and rode her face. "Don't stop. Please, don't stop." *So close.*

"Finish it."

The words were barely audible as Ryan licked her pussy in fast strokes, ratcheting up the sensation until she was sure she'd shatter from the tension twisting every muscle in her body. "They exchanged cash and the stripper sat on my lap. Not all the way, that just barely touching thing they do. Her breasts were in my face and she was too tall so her ass stuck up in the air every time she moved. It was filthy. It felt so good. I heard Avery's quiet gasp, and knowing that she was watching, that she was probably wet, made me crazy, brought me right to the brink."

Past talking now, Ryan sucked Sarah's clit, her breath coming out in pants and washing over Sarah's thighs.

I'm going to come any second. The knowledge came right on the heels of *I haven't finished the story*, and she hurried to tell the rest, her words tumbling over themselves as her mind began to shut its doors, all her circuits in crisis mode, alert and focused on the rhythm of Ryan's tongue and the impending destruction of her sanity. "Then the stripper broke the rules, she sat fully in my lap, her pussy pressed right against my crotch, and whispered, 'Are you going to come, sweetheart?' I wanted to, I wanted to, but..." Her heart started to pound, the memory of the anxiety she'd felt at being disloyal to Melinda pushing its way into the present. "Ryan, I..."

Ryan lifted her mouth for barely a second. "Tell me what you wish happened, Sarah." She parted Sarah's folds and buried her fingers deep inside her pussy, curling them a fraction and thrusting. Not a patient, gentle lover now. Not a woman intent on making her admit her secrets. This was instinctual. Carnal in the most basic way.

"'Yes,' I whispered back, every roll of her hips driving me higher. I looked over her shoulder and came hard, my hips jerking up into her body and my knuckles white from gripping the chair. I came looking into the bottomless depths of Avery's eyes."

Then she forgot about Avery, about the stripper, about the story, and let her own eyes close, her mind click off. She sank into pleasure, reveling in the joining of their bodies. Her hips rose to meet Ryan's demand. She surrendered. She cried out when she came, she knew she had, but it seemed far away, like a voice at the end of a long tunnel. Only pleasure existed, hitting her like the sharp snap of a rubber band and then fanning out in molten ripples until she was limp and worthless for anything but gasping in air.

Ryan pulled her into her arms and held her, rocked her, whispering things she couldn't quite decipher over the roaring in her head. *Well, one thing is for sure. That was worth the wait.*

She rested her forehead against Ryan's and murmured, "You're pretty okay at that."

Ryan groaned. "You're hell on my ego, Aphrodite."

"You know better. Thank you. Really. That was…just exactly what I needed."

"Anytime." Ryan's lips brushed her forehead. "It's getting cold. We should head inside."

Sarah froze. A twinge of unease twined itself around her post-sex haze. "You're done?"

"No. I mean, I want to see you again. But the party is half-over, and you haven't even entered the ballroom."

Ryan had dropped a bucket of ice water on her head, only the chills were on the inside. "I see. That's it then. I'm the do-ee and you're, what? Just going to take care of that little problem in your pants later? Find some other girl to get you off? Plenty of willing bodies just inside the ballroom, I suspect." Sarah pushed away. As close as she'd felt to Ryan, as open as she'd just been, she now wanted to be as far away as possible. Ethiopia wasn't far enough.

"No. I didn't mean it like that." Ryan grabbed Sarah's wrist before she could escape. Run away. Freaking fly a UFO out of there if she had to.

Sarah didn't trust herself to speak, all her mental energy focused on not crying. She'd cried for Melinda. She wasn't going to cry again.

Ryan picked at a loose thread on the blanket. "I don't want to assume reciprocation. You've been through so much tonight."

"And that impedes my ability to bring you to a screaming climax?" Sarah asked.

Ryan had the decency to look sheepish. "I almost lost it when you did. Without being touched."

Sarah softened a little. "So why are you sending me away?"

"I wasn't. Okay, I was. But I didn't mean it like that. I just wanted to give you a night you'd always remember. A night just for you."

Sarah thought for a moment. "We could pretend I'm some narcissistic fairy-tale princess who desires to be pleasured and isn't fussed with getting my hands, or mouth, dirty by returning the favor. Or you can be honest and admit you're scared to be vulnerable in front of me."

Ryan's head whipped up. "What?"

"You're telling me that you can't trust me, too. You'll shoulder the responsibility of my fucked-up past, of my need to feel good about sex again. You're quite the hero coming to my rescue. But when it comes down to the wire, you can't admit you want to lie back and let me rock your world. Do I have that about right?"

Ryan groaned. "It's not like that."

Sarah wanted to smack her. Instead of giving in to it, possibly proving the kitten versus elephant theory correct, she pushed against Ryan's shoulder. Hard. The fact that Ryan didn't so much as flinch made her even madder. "Lie down."

"Listen, I—"

"Shut up. You've said more than enough already. Just lie the fuck down."

Ryan did as she was told.

Sarah straddled her, buck naked, and more annoyed than she could ever remember being. If Ryan hadn't pushed her to face what Melinda had done to her, if she hadn't made her feel safe enough to get past it, she might never have been able to have sex again. Not the kind of sex where you come so hard you can't hear your own voice. Ryan had done that for her. There was no way Sarah was going to let her go back to work with a terminal case of blue balls. She *wanted* her, dammit.

"Tell me that you want me to make you come." Sarah kissed her. A kiss fueled by frustration as much as need. She shoved inside Ryan's mouth, took what she wanted with lips and tongue, and barreled through any defenses Ryan might construct. They came up gasping.

"I like feisty. You'll have to take what you want. Let's see if you can break me," Ryan said, her tone teasing.

Making Ryan come wouldn't break her; it would bind them together. That's what made it scary. That it was hard for Ryan to let go only made Sarah more determined to make her beg. To be the one who showed her how exhilarating falling could be when you had a net.

Sarah ripped open Ryan's shirt. She pulled her sports bra up and off before Ryan caught up and tried to stop her. She palmed Ryan's breasts, rolling small pink nipples between her fingers. She was rough, but Ryan didn't need gentle. She needed Sarah, and Sarah she was going to get. "Tell me you want me to make you come."

Ryan's head tipped back, her eyes fluttered closed. "God. That feels so good."

"So good you're going to come. Tell me you want it."

"I do."

"Not good enough. I want to hear you say it."

Ryan's chest flushed, her breath wheezing as Sarah handled her breasts, tweaking and rolling and pinching her nipples until Ryan started to rock under her. God, she was stubborn. An elephant was right. Sarah shifted down and tore open Ryan's pants, shoving them to her knees. Ryan's underwear was the next victim in Sarah's battle to show her how powerful surrender could be. When she was completely naked, Sarah cupped a hand over her pussy. Her palm slicked instantly. No matter how much Ryan tried to fight it, her body wanted release.

"Tell me you want me to make you come."

"Please."

"You're going to say it. You're going to trust me to be the one who makes the world shatter when you come. You're going to trust me not to let that break you."

Ryan's eyes bored into hers, and in them Sarah saw insecurity battle desire in a war only one would win.

Her heart was beating so fast she was afraid she'd have a heart attack. She thrust inside, burying her fingers in Ryan's pussy as far as they'd go. Ryan cursed, her body bowstring taut, but Sarah didn't stop. She thrust again and again. Sarah fucked her. There was just no other word for it. She drove her fingers into the most vulnerable and needy part of Ryan, her palm slapping against Ryan's folds. "Tell me you want me to make you come."

Sarah used her other hand to stroke Ryan's clit. Gripping with fingers on either side, she jerked her off, working furiously. Everything, *everything*, rested on this moment. On Ryan's ability to trust her.

"Sarah." The word was a plea.

She had no patience for it.

She never stopped working Ryan's clit, fucking her pussy shamelessly, but she freed a hand and levered herself over Ryan so they were nose to nose. "Say. It. Now."

"I want you to make me come. Please. Please, oh fuck. I need you." Ryan's body seemed to liquefy and knot at the same time, her admission the key to her surrender.

"Don't worry, I've got you." Sarah's heart filled with emotion she wasn't interested in examining right at the moment. She was going to make this strong, sexy woman come like the fate of the world depended on it. She was beginning to think the fate of her world did.

She focused on the tilt of Ryan's hips into her palm, the pulse around her fingers. She concentrated on Ryan's clit, using finesse now instead of fury.

Ryan moaned, the sound filling their garden sanctuary.

"That's it. Moan for me. Show me how badly you want me to keep fucking you. How sexy you are when you come." With one last precise stroke, Sarah sent Ryan over the edge, her moans the hottest damn thing Sarah had ever heard in her life. She held on as Ryan's whole body quaked, her pussy banding tight around the fingers still buried inside her. Sarah breathed again. *Thank God.*

As destroyed as if she'd come herself, Sarah collapsed on top of her, as Ryan rode out the last of her orgasm.

So. Fucking. Sexy.

"I can't believe I did that," Ryan said. "Actually, I can't believe *you* did that."

Sarah brushed Ryan's hair out of her eyes and grinned. "Believe it. This kitten whupped your ass."

Ryan laughed and the sound was starlight in the night sky. "You absolutely did. Wow. Way to rock my world, Aphrodite." Brushing Sarah's lips with hers, she murmured, "Thank you."

"I'd say we're even." Sarah mustered the energy to flop off of her and stare up at the sky. This party didn't suck so much after all. In fact, it might be the best night she'd ever had.

Ryan staggered to her feet like a drunk and pulled her pants back on as if in slow motion. A mountain of effort, and no grace whatsoever. So, Sarah wasn't the only one whose bones had melted to putty. Nice.

Ryan tugged her shirt in place and offered Sarah her hand. "Come on, Aphrodite, now that you've had your wicked way with me, want to head inside and find your friends?"

Sarah smiled, more content than she'd ever thought possible. "I'll introduce you to Avery. You two have a lot in common."

AVERY

CHAPTER EIGHT

No Princess Charming

The McGregors' grand ballroom sparkled like a Tiffany jewel. Superbly tasteful, sleekly elegant, and absolutely dignified, it epitomized class in that understated way of really old money. As beautiful as it was, the space better suited the fifty- and sixty-somethings that comprised the majority of the party's guest list. Avery Anders found it just a bit too refined, a bit too stuffy to be Elle's taste. Elle might be heiress to a kingdom of riches, but Avery didn't envy her for the compromises she'd had to make for the sake of the family image.

Huge crystal chandeliers spun their soft light into every corner, casting the partygoers in an eerie glow that magicked away a decade of flaws like a superhuman eraser. The photos in tomorrow's society pages would be flawless. Avery was far from a society wife, but she was convinced all those long lunches were a front for super-secret perfect light bulb insider trading. They just had to be.

She perched on a stool at the bar, a ripple of richly grained wood and glass that slunk along one wall of the room like a sulky snake. She'd been nursing a glass of pinot noir for an hour and was already wishing she could call it a night. Sarah hated parties and was hiding in the kitchen. Kaitlyn loved them and had ditched Avery the moment their drinks had arrived. Avery found parties boring and sat people watching. In the world she'd been born into, parties were obligatory. She didn't usually resent the call of duty, but this was the last place in the world she wanted to be tonight. Especially tonight.

"You get more delectable every time I see you." Daniella Rosenberger, daughter of this week's Wall Street kingpin, bestowed a smile so dazzling it could have melted stone. Had probably melted hearts just as hard.

Avery rose to hug her. "Flattery will get you everywhere."

"Will it?" Daniella grinned, letting the silence hang just long enough to call Avery's bluff.

Avery looked away. She flagged the bartender and ordered a Manhattan for Dani. She wasn't going to go there. In fact, she spent a good portion of her time with Dani steering them away from exactly right there. The right there that was now, unfortunately, right here, right now.

Dani was the kind of beautiful people described as striking. Her mouth just slightly too wide in her narrow face, her eyes an unremarkable nut brown, framed by thick dark lashes. Her hair not quite the right shade of salon blond, but perfectly cut. Yet somehow, when you put it all together, she was striking.

Avery stifled a sigh. She shouldn't be thinking Dani was striking. "What fundraiser are you neck deep in? Finding a cure for the liver disease all these cocktails will give you? Research for the next great scientific breakthrough? Saving cute, cuddly dolphins?"

Dani smirked as if cute dolphins were far too small a fish for her. "A dinner. St Peter's is looking to add a new wing to the children's hospital in the Bronx, with auxiliary apartments for families. We could go together." She accepted her drink from the bartender, sipped, and waited for Avery's reply. Dani enjoyed the witty repartee, edged with the keen blade of challenge that they always seemed to fall into. That Dani always seemed to maneuver them into. That Avery had to navigate around with the caution of an explosives technician.

It didn't matter how many times she'd told Dani no, it never seemed to stick, and being put in the position of constantly rejecting her advances was exhausting. It wasn't like women hit on her all the time, but she felt like shit when she told any of them no. She always wanted to add "It's not you, it's me. Please don't feel bad about yourself." But she'd learned long ago that it didn't help. It was the cliché of clichés and it didn't matter that it was true. The problem was that the it's-me-not-you excuse lacked credibility. Avery dated other people. Other not-like-Dani-at-all people. She escorted women to benefits, parties, restaurants. She kissed them; she even slept with a few, when it'd been so long her body craved the feel of skin against skin.

"Think of the children," Dani went on, "so sweet, so fragile. If that doesn't convince you, think of me in the little black Valentino I bought yesterday. I have lingerie to match. I guarantee you'll never be able to resist me again." Flawlessly adept in social situations, Dani smoothed away any awkwardness by waggling her perfectly arched eyebrows. A gesture that wouldn't have been out of place on Avery's eighty-seven-year-old grandpa and looked downright ridiculous on Dani.

She couldn't help but laugh. "How could I possibly resist after that?"

"I have no idea." Dani's deadpan delivery almost concealed the seriousness of her response.

"Count me in for two seats. I'd love to gift them to my mother and Richard."

Dani pouted, clearly annoyed Avery hadn't taken the bait. "Come on, it's just one night. I know you're not dating anyone right now. Why not have some fun?"

Things with Dani were the kind of complicated that settled comfortably into moral gray space, sneaking in between the black of what you knew was very wrong and the shining white of being a good and decent person. Avery always aimed for good, and always came up short. Dating Dani would be wrong, but turning her down, breaking her heart one crack at a time. Was that the right thing?

Not used to taking no for an answer in anything in life, Dani took Avery's refusal as a personal mission to persuade her otherwise. Avery wasn't bothered by the innate arrogance that made Dani think no one would possibly refuse her. She'd grown up on the Upper East Side, after all. Arrogance was as common as snow in January. No, what bothered her was the way Dani just never let it go, her insistence on knowing if Avery's decision wasn't about Dani specifically, then *why* didn't Avery want to date her? And just like the one who'd asked before her, Avery couldn't bring herself to tell the truth. Only Sarah and Kaitlyn knew the whole story.

Dani put her glass on the bar and her shoulders fell a little. "I toured the hospital last week, spoke to the chairman. Those poor kids. Some of them have been in the hospital half their lives and their parents visit on weekends because they can't afford to live in the city, can't afford not to work. Can you imagine?"

Oh, the irony. If Avery'd liked Dani less, she'd have been happy to take her out. She'd have made Dani one of the girls on her arm at a party, one of the faceless bodies she used to assuage the loneliness that sometimes crept up on her like an intruder in the night. But Avery actually liked her. Maybe not in the this-could-be-our-engagement-party-one-day way that Dani hoped, but still. Dani was as comfortable in this silver spoon world as Avery was in a pair of old socks, and she used her time and influence for good. She could've spent her days shopping at Barney's and getting pedicures, but instead she was touring a children's hospital and looking to help. Avery respected that.

So, yeah. Complicated. Avery didn't know how to tell her that what she wanted was for Dani not to be Dani. She didn't want nice and kind and charitable. If Dani wasn't everything Avery knew she *should* want in a woman, then she could take her out because it was more convenient than going alone, kiss her because it was expected, sleep with her because her body needed to come even if her mind had shut down. She wanted a woman who didn't really want her, so she wouldn't have to feel bad about feeling nothing.

Avery wasn't ever going to be able to give Dani what she deserved. Her heart was a stubborn, unreasonable bastard.

Dani tapped her lightly on the nose. "Did I lose you?"

Avery blinked. "We're so lucky to be so fortunate, I try to never forget to be grateful." She set her glass on the bar. It was still half full. Her alcoholic mother had taught her the don't get falling down drunk life rule the hard way. How long had she been sitting here? Almost an hour? Avery bargained with her inner sense of duty. She'd stay one more hour, make sure she caught up with

Elle, and then get the hell out of here. Maybe, if she was lucky, she wouldn't see the rest of Elle's family. After dreading this night all week, she might actually escape unscathed. It was a plan. It could work, right?

And, as if by magic, Elle appeared at Dani's side. "Are you two having fun?"

Avery smiled. "Happy birthday. Good God. You look amazing."

And she did. Her hair was piled on top of her head in a complicated-looking updo, and the strapless emerald dress left her tan shoulders bare. The dress was more of a gown really, the skirt billowing out from the fitted bodice in shimmering layers of material that Avery guessed might be silk, but what the hell did she know about dresses? When you put it all together it was a bit too Disney princess for Avery's taste, but it was so completely Elle.

Elle blushed prettily. "Thanks. I had it designed. It's a Frederik original."

Dani saluted her with her glass. "Nice. It's a beautiful dress for a beautiful woman."

"Oh please. Look at you, you get skinnier every time I see you. That's so annoying. Skinny friends are just bad for my ego." Elle stopped a passing waiter to sample brie arranged atop a bone thin cracker.

"I've lost ten pounds on the South Beach diet." Dani looked at Elle's cracker the way an organic-only, gluten-free vegan looks at a cheeseburger. With lust in her eyes.

"Mmm," Elle responded, deliberately licking her lips. "This is amazing."

"Bitch." Dani took another sip of her wine. "You used to be nice."

"You used to be a size six." Elle grinned and they both dissolved into giggles.

Somewhere between Elle picking up the cracker and Dani calling her a bitch Avery had missed the joke. Girls like Elle and Dani communicated in a language that sounded like English but made absolutely no sense to her. If Dani had called *her* beautiful, Avery would've taken it as an expression of interest. But when she said it to Elle it was so obviously a friendly compliment, Elle hadn't even blinked. How did you tell the difference?

"So, what were you talking about before I rudely interrupted?" Elle asked.

Dani gave an exaggerated sigh. "I was trying to convince Avery to go to the St. Peter's charity dinner with me next month. But you know how she is. Stubborn as an ox and determined to thwart me."

Elle made a tut-tut sound in the back of her throat and turned on her. "Don't you dare take one of your brainless skanks to that dinner. Why not go with Dani? You could do a lot worse. You *do* do a lot worse."

Avery felt her shoulders start to bunch up around her ears and ordered herself not to lose her temper. *Brainless skank* was a favorite term of Elle's, and that she'd once used it on Sarah made it particularly distasteful. "I'm very happy with my choice of partners, thanks. I wasn't planning on attending. I was just telling Dani I'd purchase tickets for Mom."

Elle rolled her eyes.

As if sensing the rising tension, Dani rose. "You're a good person, Avery. So good you're going to dance with me. I love this song, and I'm going to let loose and have some fun. Now take me out there and show me off. Let's make every woman in the room wish they were you and line up to take your place."

Avery didn't respond for a few seconds, racking her brain for a sensible reason to decline. When she didn't immediately come up with one, she offered her hand. She couldn't refuse Dani the opportunity to find someone else on whom to bestow her attention. "Okay then. Let's dance." She could feel Elle's eyes burning a hole in her back all the way to the dance floor.

They swayed to a piece Avery remembered vaguely from *Swan Lake*, their feet moving to the rise and fall of the music as if they'd been born dancing together. In reality, they'd both been forced to take years of dance lessons in preparation for moments exactly like these. For Manhattan's elite, socializing was a sport one trained for from birth.

Avery closed her eyes and let her mind drift. Dani's hands had moved all the way to her hips before Avery registered a difference. The music changed, the classical melting into the soft crooning of Sinatra. The beat grew sensual, thrumming around them as couples paired up to slow dance. The lights dimmed just a little and Dani breathed into her ear, "Don't go."

"Dani, I—"

Dani slid closer, closing the respectable distance between them, bringing their bodies together, threading her arms around Avery's neck. "Please. It feels good to dance. Doesn't it feel good?"

Did it? Avery couldn't tell anymore, but leaving Dani alone in the middle of the dance floor in the middle of a song wasn't an option. Neither was hurting her feelings. "Of course, just one more dance." She closed her eyes again, but the feel of Dani's body against hers, Dani's breasts pressed lightly against her shirt started to feel good, little tingles of heat shooting out from the places where they touched. Avery opened her eyes and tried to shake it off.

She caught a flash of gold over Dani's shoulder and the whole world stopped. Even before she took her next breath, before she'd fully focused on the woman who was watching them intently, her body had tensed. Before her brain remembered and her senses sharpened, her heart just knew. Would always know.

Spencer.

CHAPTER NINE

All Roads Lead to Threesomes

Time ground to a halt and hung there, heavy and expectant, reality suspended for the heart-stopping second when eyes the color of faded denim met hers.

Spencer.

Then as quickly as it had receded, the world came rushing back. Stronger, sharper, clearer. Sounds louder, colors brighter, her senses attuned to every nuance around her. She felt the moment in a way she didn't even know she'd been missing until it came crashing back.

Spencer.

Avery would be able to find her face in a crowd of millions. Tens of millions. Her heart had beat to the rhythm of this woman for longer than she would admit. And despite herself, despite the years of frustration she smiled.

It was always Spencer.

When Spencer didn't return her smile, Avery felt hers fall. Spencer looked upset. No, she looked annoyed. More than annoyed, she looked pissed. The music eased to a finish and Avery stepped back, not giving Dani a chance to protest. "Thank you. I see Claire Presley headed our way. I think your plan worked."

Dani didn't look thrilled to be passed to the closest possible alternative, but all Avery could think about was Spencer. She was back. She was here. Of course, Avery had known she would be, but right now she couldn't remember why seeing Spencer again could possibly be a bad thing. All she wanted was to be close to her, to touch her, to… God, she wanted. Wanting Spencer had been the epicenter of her life for seven years.

She should probably circle the room so as not to make her beeline to Spencer so obvious, but she didn't have it in her. It had been too long. She'd missed her desperately and wanted to drink her in, savor her like vintage wine.

"Hi." Avery stepped up beside Spencer, badly wanting to take her hand. She didn't. She'd wait for Spencer to initiate contact.

"Hello, Avery. Nice to see you again."

To her absolute horror, Avery felt herself grow wet at the sound of Spencer's voice. A hint of chimes on a summer breeze. Light and sweet and innocent. And so sinfully erotic a pulse began to beat between her thighs. She'd thought about that voice and imagined all the sweet and sexy things fantasy-Spencer would say to her when they saw each other again. Twelve long months of torment. And now Spencer was so close Avery's fingers trembled with desire. Hell. This could not be happening.

Act normal. You can do it. Just say something that isn't "You make me so wet."

"That's a bit formal, isn't it?" Avery said. "What happened to the teenager who used to throw her arms around me in a bear hug at every possible opportunity?" She poked Spencer playfully in the ribs. She was always playful. Careful to keep just the right amount of teasing in her voice, terrified Spencer would discover how she truly felt.

Spencer just rolled her eyes, but she slid her arms around Avery and hugged her. "I'm not a teenager anymore."

The flames that had simmered during her dance with Dani leapt to life when Spencer drew close. Avery wanted the moment to last forever so much that she forced herself to step back.

Spencer had always been beautiful, but a year away had chiseled her softer edges into strong lines. The woman standing in front of Avery was simply stunning in a deceptively plain burgundy gown that poured like honey over every curve and highlighted her long, straight corn silk hair. Her eyes were outlined in dramatic eyeliner, making the blue of her irises even more startling. Even the way she held herself was different; the year abroad had given her a confidence she'd struggled to form under the overbearing influence of her family. She'd grown into herself and it looked good on her.

When Spencer held her gaze, Avery couldn't have looked away if dancing warthogs cartwheeled into the ballroom. "Do you like what you see?" The corner of Spencer's mouth tipped up.

Avery gulped. Jesus. Was she being totally obvious? She was usually a better actor. Not able to tell Spencer the truth but unwilling to brush off the question, Avery replied, "You've changed. It's so good to see you again. How was Norway?"

There. A safe topic. Avery took a slow breath, ordered her heart to stop pounding and her body to relax. She'd had plenty of experience hiding her feelings for Spencer. This was no different; she just had to get used to it again.

"Amazing and scary at the same time. Do you know what I mean? God. We're so isolated in the city. We have no idea what's out there in the world, other cultures, ways of life, smaller bank balances." Spencer smiled, and as much as Avery had missed her, she was happy Spencer had taken a gap year after college to experience the world.

"What's next on the agenda? Do you think you'll go back?"

Spencer shook her head and took a sip from her wineglass, pausing to consider her answer. "I'm applying for a position in a graduate psychology program at NYU. Actually, I really hope I get it. It's the only specialty specific program in the country."

"What specialty?" Avery asked, distracted by the way the sip of wine had wet Spencer's bottom lip so it glistened.

"Sex therapy," Spencer answered mildly.

Avery stopped breathing. Whatever miracle kept her standing, it wasn't oxygen. "What?"

Spencer's nose crinkled. "It's therapy designed to assist couples and singles with sexual issues that may impede their desire or sexual functioning."

Avery coughed. She swallowed hard, wishing she hadn't left her drink on the bar. "I know what sex therapy is. Is that really what you want to do?"

"Is there something wrong with it?" Spencer frowned.

"No, of course not. I'm just surprised."

And intrigued.

And aroused.

"You're really going to grad school to study sex?" Avery tried to picture it and went weak at the knees. Spencer would be thinking about sex all day. The why and how and where of sex. She'd probably study erogenous zones, and sex toys, and porn. Did sex therapists study porn? Avery had no idea, but suddenly it seemed vital to find out.

Spencer laughed. "Don't try to convince me you're all prim and proper these days. Not when you were just dirty dancing with Daniella Rosenberger for the whole world to see."

Huh? It took Avery a few seconds to drag her mind away from the mental image of Spencer sprawled across her bed, erotic images scrolling on the screen opposite, an unopened textbook on the nightstand. Spencer's blond hair would look amazing against her navy sheets, her soft skin the perfect contrast. Would it flush pink when she was aroused?

Spencer waved a hand in front of her face.

Avery shook her head. "I was not."

Spencer gave her a don't-bullshit-me look, completely unaware of where her mind had just been. "Her hands were practically on your ass and you were so close syrup wouldn't have slid between you."

"Syrup?"

"What's wrong with syrup? It's slidey."

"It is," Avery agreed, unsure how to respond. Had she been dirty dancing? She didn't think so, but she couldn't deny the slight thrill being so close to Dani had given her. Realizing Spencer had noticed made her a little sick. Avery rubbed a hand over her face, suddenly more tired than she could remember being in years. "I guess I might have been. I didn't intend to. Dani is persuasive."

Spencer snorted. "That's one word for it."

"There's another?"

"I'd say it was more like she got her claws in you and planned to eat you for supper."

"Dani's just being Dani." Avery shrugged it off.

That expression of annoyance flickered over Spencer's face again. "Have I mentioned lately you're a dumbass sometimes?"

Was there a right way to respond to a question like that? "Uh, not recently."

"She wants to sleep with you. You know this." Spencer's tone was flat.

Avery nodded. No point denying the obvious.

"And you're not willing to accommodate her for reasons of your own. I know, or you would have slept with her already, and Ellie would have told me."

Elle talked about her to Spencer? They talked about her sex life? Holy hell. What did Elle say? What did Spencer say back? "That's true."

"But you let Daniella drag you out there and rub herself all over you even though you didn't really want it."

"Well…" Avery *so* didn't want to admit dancing with Dani had turned her on. Especially not to Spencer.

As if reading her mind, Spencer continued. "You got into it at the end, but you had to close your eyes to do it, and you dropped her cold the second the music stopped."

Avery balked. "No, I didn't. She had another offer."

Spencer made a sound in the back of her throat like a puppy staking its claim. "Avery, don't you get it?"

"No, not really," Avery said honestly.

"You don't *owe* Daniella anything just because you turned her down. You don't have to dance with her like that's some fucked up consolation prize for not sleeping with her."

Avery stared at Spencer. "I wasn't."

"So, the dance was your idea?"

"No."

"But you were happy she asked you."

"Well, no."

"But you were the one who changed the tone from perfectly innocent to let's get it on."

"Not exactly."

"Then why did you dance with her when you didn't want to?"

Because…well, because she'd felt bad about turning down Dani's invitation to attend the charity dinner together. Because she had to carefully navigate Dani's feelings, and all because Avery didn't want to sleep with her.

Spencer was right. How had she put all of that together so fast? Avery had no doubt she'd make an excellent therapist. "It just seemed like the right thing to do."

Spencer shrugged. "Yeah. I get that. I often find myself in a bump and grind with someone I'm not attracted to. It's just good manners, you know what I mean?"

Avery gave her shoulder a gentle push. "Sarcasm doesn't suit you."

"Denial doesn't suit you either."

Avery inclined her head. "Fair enough."

Spencer took another sip of her wine, studying Avery. "My sister did a number on you, didn't she?"

"Elle? Of course not. She's one of my closest friends. You know that."

Spencer shook her head. "That's where it comes from. You think you let Ellie down because you didn't love her back."

Avery grabbed Spencer's wineglass, their fingers brushing, sending delicious tingles down Avery's arm. She took a generous sip before handing it back. "I can't believe she told you about that."

"We're sisters," Spencer replied as if that said it all.

"Can we forgo the psychoanalysis, at least until I can get my own drink?" Avery glanced around rather desperately for a passing waiter, but of course when you wanted one there were none to be found.

"Sure. But don't you think it's time you stopped trying to please everyone and gave yourself a chance to fall in love?"

I'm already in love. Not saying the words out loud didn't make them any less true.

❖

Drinks in hand, Avery found Spencer again on the balcony, her back to the railing, checking her phone. She set down the two wineglasses and small plate of appetizers she'd snagged just before wait staff whisked them away to be replaced by the main course. She offered the plate. "Canapé?"

Spencer took one and popped it in her mouth. "These are good."

"They are." The sun was just beginning to set over the garden below, and the impossible swirl of orange and purple was the perfect backdrop, emphasizing the highlights in Spencer's hair, the slender curve of her neck. "Am I monopolizing you? Do you have to mingle or network or whatever?"

Spencer shook her head. "We both know this party is more for Mom and Dad. I'm a free agent as long as I don't get in trouble or do something embarrassing."

"What could you possibly do that would be embarrassing?"

"Well, let's see. I could get ridiculously drunk and set up that karaoke machine we have in the basement. I have an unfortunate tendency to think I'm Beyoncé when I've had too much to drink."

Avery couldn't think of anything cuter than a tipsy Spencer singing karaoke but kept that to herself. "Hmm. That would be embarrassing. Okay, I'm cutting you off. One glass of wine is your limit."

Spencer made a grab for the second wineglass. "No way. I'm here with you. You'll save me from myself."

I'm here with you. Avery fought against the ache in her chest. "But what if I also get ridiculously drunk? I could be k.d. lang."

Spencer looked blank. "Who?"

"k.d. lang. Singer-songwriter from the eighties."

Spencer rolled her eyes. "Yeah, okay, Grandma, you can be k.d. whatever."

Avery's mouth fell open. "Grandma? k.d.lang is a lesbian *icon*. She put lesbians in music on the map. She—"

"Is an historic artifact. Maybe I can read about her in a museum one day." Spencer grinned.

"You have no taste."

"Why is it that old people think any music written after nineteen ninety is terrible? Like the freaking Beatles are the lynchpin of the music industry. Give me a break."

Spencer had said some things. Complete sentences worth of things that were probably important, but Avery only heard two words. "You think I'm *old*?"

"I…" Spencer frowned. "No."

"But you just said I was old people."

"I didn't mean you were old. Just older. Older than me."

Avery narrowed her eyes. "I'm *two years* older. You're going to have to do better than that, kid."

"Hey!" Spencer stepped closer, stuck a finger in her chest. "Just because you're older doesn't mean I'm a kid."

"Doesn't it?" *Didn't it?* Wasn't that what had kept them apart for so long?

Spencer shook her head emphatically. "Uh-uh. We're both adults. You're older."

Avery groaned.

"By a little bit. A smidgen. A smidgen of a smidgen."

"Great. Remind me to call about long-term care insurance."

The silence fell naturally and neither of them tried to break it, just stared out across the garden that in early April looked more like a horticultural wasteland. The plant hospice of November turned into the plant graveyard of January. But Avery knew in a couple of weeks it would spring back to life, because, well, it would be spring. She didn't envy people who lived in warmer climates. Sure, it might be fun to live by the beach and wear flip-flops year-round, but there was something comforting about the change from one season to the next. How dramatic it was. Each spring was its own mini-miracle. Avery wouldn't give that up for the world.

Her miracle season had been summer at the McGregor house.

Endless, lazy weeks of bumming around the city, swimming in the pool, eating her weight in Ben & Jerry's. Never ending, heart pounding, torturous, ecstatic weeks of looking-but-not-looking at Spencer. Her breath catching and then twisting in her throat whenever Spencer entered a room. Country songs and romance novels described love as an emotion, as if it were something you generated and gave away. As if it could be controlled. That was total bullshit. Love was a stampede. You were either swept up and carried away, or crushed by sheer force.

Spencer twisted and untwisted a stand of hair that had fallen in front of her shoulder. "Avery..."

The way Spencer had said her name made it sound like there was more. Avery waited. She would wait forever if that's what it took.

"I've been wanting to ask you something."

Spencer wasn't looking at her, but Avery's heart started to hammer in her chest. This sounded serious. Not their usual banter. Was Spencer going to bring up what had happened the last time they'd been alone together? Also known as that time Spencer's sunshine yellow bikini had made Avery lose her mind, and she'd kissed her. Was *she* ready to talk about it? She wasn't sure. "What is it?"

Spencer set her glass down and gripped the railing, fingers tight. Her blue eyes gleamed dark and mysterious in the growing dusk. She looked entirely too sexy. "Have you ever had a threesome?"

CHAPTER TEN

A Flight of Fantasy

Avery needed to see an ENT doctor. She couldn't possibly have heard that correctly. She was off her game, so distracted, so…okay, why not just admit it, so helplessly, hopelessly aroused just being in the same space as Spencer, her ears had deceived her. They had to have. Spencer had *not* just asked her if she'd had a threesome. She didn't. Nope. No way. Could the floor please swallow her now? She could die. That'd be fine.

"I'm sorry, what?"

"Have you ever had a threesome?"

Avery stared. What else could she do? Really, no one could expect more at a time like this. She tried not to have a panic attack. "Well, uh, um…"

The corner of Spencer's mouth twitched. "Is that a yes?"

Why didn't women come with an instruction manual? Why wasn't there a book, a magazine, a Wikipedia page that outlined what in holy hell she was supposed to do when the girl she loved asked about her sex life? And threesomes, for fuck's sake. *Threesomes.*

The problem wasn't actually the threesomes, not really, even if threesomes were better in books than in real life. No, the problem was the kaleidoscope of dirty-as-fuck images that flashed through her mind and lingered like smoke. The deadly kind of smoke that killed you inch by inch, so you didn't even know you were dying until it was too late. Spencer bent over a desk while a nameless, faceless, woman fucked her from behind, another woman in front on her knees, sucking Spencer's clit. Or even better, Spencer curled into the curve of a woman's chest while she played with Spencer's breasts, someone else straddling her lap. Avery couldn't think straight, every cell leaving its post and migrating to the one part of her body she needed desperately to ignore. She wanted to kiss her so badly she could already feel Spencer's mouth on hers. The soft glide, the surprising dominance, the hungry rush. She knew what that kiss felt like, and knowing only made her crave it more. She couldn't do this. There was no way she could chat to Spencer about threesomes and not spontaneously combust.

Unfortunately, what came out of her mouth was, "Yes." Damn her brain and its lust induced logic. She could feel heat rise up her neck and willed it down. No reason to be embarrassed. She was an adult; adults had sex. Sometimes with more than one person. So there, she'd answered the bizarre question that had come from nowhere like a lightning strike to her sanity. Now they could move to safer topics. Like the weather, their families, or… She'd go to the basement for the karaoke machine if that's what it took. She just didn't want the conversation to end. Soon the party would be over, and she'd have no reason to see Spencer. She wanted to hold on to the moment, and if that meant admitting to some not-as-sexy-as-she'd-hoped escapades, well, it was a small price to pay.

"What was it like?" Spencer's face was serious. She didn't look awkward or shy. She could've been asking Avery what it was like to hike the Appalachian Trail for all it showed.

Avery hoped the sound that had pushed its way up from the back of her throat passed as surprise. She was strung so tight she could feel herself vibrating. "Why exactly are you asking?"

"Did you know that people who talk honestly about sex actually have better and more frequent sex? They also score higher on overall happiness and well-being."

"Good for them. I still don't understand why you're asking me about threesomes."

"I'm putting together my application for NYU, and I have to write an essay." Spencer shrugged and gulped the rest of her wine.

"On the impact that psychological readiness and interpersonal dynamics have on sexual arousal during intercourse."

Avery swallowed. She wished hearing Spencer say "sexual arousal" didn't make her want to drop to her knees and give a practical demonstration. "In English that means?"

"How the way we think and feel about sex, and those people we're having sex with, impacts the level of arousal we feel. Like, how it's not just biological or physical, but mental and changes and adapts depending on the circumstances."

Right. That. Easy-peasy.

"I'm sure there is a textbook or a journal article that you could..." Avery said.

"No. You don't get it." Spencer waved a hand in the air in frustration. "This is more embarrassing than I thought it would be, and I'm not explaining myself well, so I'll just say it." She took a steadying breath. "I'm a virgin."

Spencer was a virgin.

Well, of course she was. Obviously, she was. She had to be. No one had the right to touch her. No one was worthy. If anyone tried, Avery would've killed them, she'd maim them, she'd cut off their fingers. She'd... Avery smothered the irrational fury. Tried to focus. Tried not to be ridiculously, outrageously pleased that Spencer was a virgin. *Thank God.*

"So, what you're telling me is that you have to write an essay on sex, but you've never had sex."

"Yes." The relief on Spencer's face was palpable.

"Okay. But I'm still blurry on what that has to do with asking me about threesomes."

"Come on. You've got a degree. You know there's more to an essay than research and statistics. You need detail, insight, analysis. I'm asking because you have experience and I don't. I want to interview you."

For what felt like the umpteenth time in the last hour, Avery was floored. "You want to interview me. About sex. About why I was aroused."

"And also what you were thinking, and who you were with, and why." Spencer nodded.

"No."

"Avery—"

"No. No, no, no." *This was not happening.*

Spencer's face fell. "Why?"

Because I love you. Because I don't want to talk about other women, or all the sex I've had that was meaningless because it wasn't with you. "It's personal."

Spencer nodded again. "Okay, sure. I get it. I didn't mean to make you uncomfortable." She turned to head back into the ballroom, and Avery grabbed her hand like she was a diabetic and Spencer was the last candy bar on earth. Avery's heart was galloping; she was confused and cranky, and so unbelievably wet. But Spencer didn't know that. Would never know that. She had to get her shit together. Spencer leaving wasn't an option.

"Just give me a second, okay? Just a second."

Spencer's hand was warm in hers, and Avery didn't have the metal fortitude to do the right thing and drop it. Spencer's fingers were long and slender, each topped by a perfectly manicured nail. It felt right to be holding her hand. The more right it felt, the worse it hurt. "Why are you asking me? Why not Elle? You two talk about everything, and she's not a virgin."

"Ellie's never had sex with a woman. I wouldn't say she's straight exactly, well, you know that better than anyone I guess, but she's only ever had sex with men. I did talk to her and she gave me lots of great information, but I want the perspective of someone who's been with women."

Avery traced the curve of Spencer's wrist, played her fingers along the pulse that beat there. Steady and strong. That was Spencer. She knew the answer but asked anyway. "Why?"

"Because I think I could empathize more. Be able to offer more genuine insight. I'm attracted to women. If, no, *when*, I have sex, it will be with a woman."

"And you want to know what it's like," Avery paused a beat, "for research."

Spencer took their joined hands in hers and squeezed. "Yes."

Avery nodded and came to her decision. It should've been difficult, but somehow the words just came. "Don't settle. Don't sleep with the first woman who asks you, or the first one you're interested in. Take your time. Make sure it's what you really want and that she's special enough for the honor."

Avery couldn't look at her now, not without betraying her feelings. "Try not to be self-conscious. It's not a performance. Focus on your body, on how you feel, on how you want the woman you're with to feel. Have fun. Laugh."

"Okay," Spencer said softly. "Is that how sex is for you? With someone special who makes you feel good and who makes you laugh?"

Avery closed her eyes. She was the biggest damn hypocrite she knew. But maybe she could save Spencer from her own fate. "Sure."

"You're lying."

"You don't know that."

"Then tell me I'm wrong."

Avery groaned and met her gaze. "Don't be like me, Spencer. Be better than me."

"What's wrong with you?"

If only she knew.

When the silence lasted too long, Spencer said, "Okay, we can come back to that. Tell me about the threesome instead."

"You're relentless, you know that?"

"I've heard the rumor. Now tell me."

"There were two. Which one?"

Spencer coughed.

"Ah, I surprised the unflappable sex-therapist-to-be. You'll have to work on that poker face." Avery grinned.

Spencer immediately schooled her expression into an unreadable mask. "Tell me about both and how they were different."

Sex was never that easy. It had only been easy once. One simple kiss that changed, and then confirmed, every damn thing she already knew about herself. So easy that the kiss had shattered her.

"The first time," Avery said. "I was a freshman in college. I was seeing a woman who was bisexual and she convinced me it would be fun to have a threesome with a man, just to see if I liked it. It wasn't and I didn't. Arousal wasn't much of an issue, seeing as there wasn't any."

Spencer winkled her nose. "That sounds like it sucked."

"It was uncomfortable, and eventually I just left. But it was a good lesson. If you're pretty sure you're not going to like something sexually, you're probably right."

Spencer nodded. "And the other one?"

"About two years ago, I got to know a couple who lived in my building. They were friendly, and I fed their cats when they went on vacation. They invited me over for dinner one night, and it was clear they were flirting with me, both of them. It just kind of happened."

"Happened because it seemed like the right thing to do, or happened because you really wanted it?"

"I wanted it. I wanted them. I was fascinated. I'd always had this fantasy…" The words jammed in her throat. She just couldn't reveal her deepest, darkest fantasy so Spencer could use it in a psychology paper. Her masochism had its limits.

"What kind of fantasy?"

"Spencer." Avery wasn't sure if she'd said Spencer's name as a plea for mercy or a dire warning.

"Don't be a wuss. Fantasies are normal. Ninety-seven percent of men and eighty-nine percent of women admit to having sexual fantasies. Let's be embarrassed that you indulge in an activity that almost every single adult on the planet earth does. What a weirdo. We should lock you up to run tests."

Avery couldn't help but laugh. "Eighty-nine percent of women, huh? I feel sorry for the other eleven percent."

"Right? I wonder what they do when they masturbate? Like are their minds just totally blank?"

"They probably don't masturbate."

Spencer's mouth fell open. "Well, they should. Everyone should."

Avery grinned. "Hey, preaching to the choir here."

"So, you masturbate then? Do you think about the fantasy you're too modest to tell me about?"

Avery's mouth was desert dry, and the steady thrum between her legs kicked from a pleasant hum to all-I-can-think-about-is-fucking-you level distracting. Spencer's words ran over her like open palms, silky and sensual. There was no way she was going to survive. "Sometimes." *Mostly I think about you.*

Spencer's shoulders slumped and she sighed dramatically. "Damn. A fantasy hot enough to get the famous Stone Anders to orgasm, and I'm never going to hear it. It sucks to be me."

"The famous *what*?"

Spencer looked amused. "Didn't you know that's what people call you? Avery Anders, a lover hot enough to coax multiple orgasms out of countless women, but so controlled she never comes herself."

Avery would have been less surprised if Spencer had just gone ahead and punched her in the nose. "Seriously?"

"It's not true then?"

"Of course it's not true. Jesus. That would make me..."

"Kind of a jackass?" Spencer supplied helpfully.

"Well, yeah. I mean, sure, there have been times I haven't come for one reason or another, but it's not a regular thing. I'm certainly not stone. That's not even what stone means anyway, which is an actual not-a-jackass thing."

"Good." Spencer appeared to be satisfied by this. "You can tell me what it really means later, but I wonder why Ellie told me you were."

Avery thought she knew why and would be giving Elle a piece of her mind in short order. Of course, that meant admitting she'd been talking about sex with Spencer, but she'd cross that bridge later. "I guess she got her wires crossed. Sex isn't something I discuss with your sister." *Your annoying as hell sister.*

Spencer tapped her fingers on the railing. "I bet it was wishful thinking. She can't delude herself that you don't have sex at all, so she pretends you don't enjoy it. I love Ellie deeply, but when she's unhappy, she tends to make stuff up."

Avery was baffled by the injustice of it all. Having her emotions and her sexuality misrepresented by someone she cared about, *to* someone she more than just cared for. She'd put up with Elle's passive-aggressive bullshit for years, and no matter what she did it never seemed to get better. But the way Spencer said it, like it was truth, like it was something that just was, and wasn't hers to fix, felt like a revelation. What if she could just accept that Elle had feelings for her that she'd never return? That it wasn't her responsibility to make them go away? What if she could understand that Elle lied to protect herself, and not let that bother her?

Well, hell. Talk about a freaking aha moment.

Spencer had just unraveled in a couple of sentences what Avery had been struggling to get her head around for years. Spencer was insightful and empathic, and she wanted to use those skills to fix people's sex lives. Maybe to enhance them. To make the world a better place by helping people understand how to fuck each other. How could Avery not be madly in love with a woman like that?

"Do you really want to know the fantasy?" Avery asked.

Spencer's eyes sparkled. "I really do."

This was a terrible idea. But what the hell, it's not like she had a lot to lose, except, you know, her dignity.

"I have a fantasy about the woman I'm with having sex with someone else, while I watch them. Sometimes they know I'm there, sometimes they don't. I love the idea of charting her pleasure from an outsider's point of view, taking in every angle of her body, every gasp and sigh. I watch her desire ebb and flow. I pay close attention to the way her hands caress and her mouth kisses. So much the same yet, in many ways, different from how she is with me. The distance between us makes her more mysterious and alluring. Watching makes me want to ravish her. When I can't stand it any longer I slide my hand down over my belly, between my thighs, and stroke my clit. She's always on the brink of orgasm when I do, so close. Caught up in passion, she's wild. An untamed and unedited version of herself, set free by a need she can't control. When she comes, she looks straight at me and we explode together." Avery shrugged.

"I've never had the chance to live out the fantasy. So, the threesome, being able to watch, it really turned me on."

Spencer's gasp was so faint Avery would've missed it if she hadn't been so aware of Spencer beside her. Daylight was fading fast, and amber security lights began to flicker on in the garden below them. She could just make out the slight pink to Spencer's cheeks. Had she embarrassed her? Surely there were more embarrassing fantasies. Toe-sucking fantasies or stepmother fantasies, or something. Hers was embarrassing to her because, well, it was hers, and it did it for her in amazing ways she didn't really care to understand. But it wasn't, like, pervert level embarrassing. Right?

"Are you okay? I didn't mean to freak you out."

Spencer dropped her hand from Avery's and rubbed it over her face. "I'm fine."

Spencer's chest rose and fell just a bit faster than normal and she wouldn't look at her. She clearly wasn't fine. Avery slid an arm around her shoulders. "Hey, what's wrong? You have my self-esteem hanging by a thread here."

"I'm sorry." Spencer shrugged away from her touch. "This was a bad idea. I should go inside, find my parents, my sister, the biggest glass of wine in the universe."

Oh, no way was Spencer ducking out of this now. She grabbed Spencer by the shoulders and twisted her around, then cupped her cheeks so she was looking right into her eyes. "Not a chance. You don't get to ask me to bare my soul and then freak out and walk away. Now what's wrong? Is my fantasy that bad?" *Good idea, bully the girl. That'll do the trick.*

Spencer blushed scarlet. "Your fantasy isn't bad. I, God, this is so humiliating, as you were talking I got this mental image of you and…" Spencer averted her gaze. "I'm sorry, I couldn't help it."

It finally clicked into place. "You pictured me in the fantasy getting off."

Spencer nodded. Avery could feel the heat radiating from her cheeks. It was so goddammed sexy she just lost her mind. Her common sense fled the building, every restraint, every boundary, every wall she'd so carefully erected, came crashing down as she stared into Spencer's eyes and saw a mirror of her own need.

"You're blushing."

Spencer groaned. "Shut up."

Avery shook her head. Embarrassed Spencer was unbelievably hot. "Don't you know that seventy-two percent of women admit to blushing when picturing people naked in lurid sex acts. No need to be embarrassed. It's normal."

"I hate you. And you just made that up."

"So, do I look good in the buff, Dr. Sex Brain?"

"No. Picturing you naked does nothing for me." Spencer's eyes were boundless, her breath choppy. "And assuming that it would makes you a conceited jerk."

Avery was sure Spencer meant the words as an insult, but they came out on the edge of a whimper with an undercurrent of *I want you all over me.*

"You're lying," Avery said.

"You don't know that."

"Then tell me I'm wrong."

"I can't."

"Tell me no, Spencer. Tell me to back off."

"I can't."

"Tell me you don't want me to kiss you right now." Spencer was so close Avery could see the flecks of brown in her blue eyes.

"I can't."

"God." Avery all but breathed the word into her hair.

Spencer kissed her.

The shock of Spencer's mouth on hers paralyzed her for a moment. She planned to reach out and push Spencer away, tell her that they couldn't, they mustn't, but found herself pulling Spencer closer instead, wrapping an arm around her waist and threading fingers through her hair, angling her mouth, deepening the kiss. Avery slid her tongue into Spencer's mouth and Spencer whimpered, a full-bodied throaty sound that had all the blood rushing between Avery's legs. The subtle rose scent of Spencer's perfume, the way Spencer's body molded to hers had her common sense waving a white flag. She was done pretending she didn't want to rip Spencer's clothes off. Done pretending she didn't want to be the first woman to touch her. To make her come. To make Spencer hers.

Avery kissed her like she was dying and Spencer was oxygen. Kissed her like she'd never have the opportunity to kiss again, like kissing Spencer was all there was in the whole world and they were going to self-destruct at any second.

"God." Her vocabulary seemed to be limited to just that single word, but Avery couldn't breathe, couldn't think. Could barely stand. She gasped in the cold night air knowing that only Spencer could cool the heat raging inside.

"I've always wondered what it would be like if we kissed again," Spencer said.

"You have?"

"Yeah." Spencer smiled shyly.

"And did it meet your expectations?"

Spencer tilted her head to the side. "Met and exceeded. I thought you'd be all sweet and gentle, though, and I would be the one to dial things up, to make you want me enough that you lost control. I was wrong about that."

Avery groaned. Spencer had kissed her and she'd completely forgotten how inexperienced she was. *Jesus.* "I can do sweet and gentle." Avery stroked her cheek.

Spencer scoffed. "If you think I want sweet and gentle after I got a taste of *that* kiss, you're so wrong."

"No, love, sweet and gentle can be just as sexy. It can drive you crazy."

"You're already driving me crazy."

Avery kissed her again. Sweetly and gently, exploring the curve of her lips and the sweep of her tongue. She took her time, cataloguing each new part of Spencer's mouth like it was a precious artifact in a grand collection. She stroked Spencer's hair, traced the line of her spine, curled a palm around her hip. Avery cherished her in a way she'd never let herself imagine was possible. Sure, she'd thought about sex with Spencer, she could even admit to herself that she loved Spencer. But to know herself capable of *treasuring*

Spencer, even while part, a really big part, of her wanted to fuck Spencer senseless, was a revelation. She felt alive again. She felt *good*. Happy. Avery couldn't remember the last time she'd felt happy before tonight.

And just as she said she would, Spencer dialed up the kiss, planting hands on the back of Avery's head and angling her thigh so it slid between Avery's legs. *Ohjesusfuck.* She made a noise that sounded desperate and needy even to her own ears. If she wasn't careful, she was going to come in her pants like a band geek making out with a cheerleader at junior prom.

"What the fuck do you think you're doing?" The voice wasn't merely a bucket of cold water over Avery's head. No, exactly that voice, at exactly that moment, it was more like an Arctic apocalypse. Harsh halogen light flooded the balcony, exposing their tangled embrace. She must have flipped the outdoor lights. Avery broke away from the kiss as gently as she could, careful to steady Spencer, and put a couple of inches between them. Then she looked over Spencer's shoulder to the open balcony doors and met the fate she'd spent her entire adult life trying to avoid.

"Hello, Elle."

CHAPTER ELEVEN

I'll Cry If I Want To

Spencer's eyes went wide; she whipped around, wiping her mouth with the back of her hand. "Ellie. What are you doing here?"

"What am I doing here?" Elle's voice was so cold Avery could imagine a wall of ice forming. "It's my birthday party, Spence. I'm twenty-five today and my *kid* sister is nowhere to be found. My *best* friend has disappeared, and when I search for them, because clearly neither of them care enough to spend my birthday with me, I find them humping like rabbits."

Avery rubbed a hand over her face in a fuck-my-life gesture. "That's enough."

"Don't tell me what's enough. You were kissing my sister. You were practically eating her face."

"Ellie—" Spencer began, but Avery cut her off with a hand on her shoulder.

"This is between Elle and me. We have some things to sort out that we should've talked about years ago. That's my fault. I didn't handle it well."

"*It.*" Elle was practically vibrating with indignation. "*Me*, you mean. You didn't handle me. My feelings were an atom bomb and you had to run for your life." Tears ran down Elle's face and Avery's heart ached. Ached for the teenagers they were and for the way they'd let all this define their friendship for almost a decade.

"You're right."

That stopped Elle short. "What?"

"I said you're right. You had feelings for me that I didn't return, and instead of understanding, instead of being a friend, I completely freaked and screwed up everything. I ignored your feelings like you meant nothing to me. I broke your heart, then rather than be honest, I asked Sarah to lie for me so I'd have an easy way out. I let her take the fall. And the worst part of all is that I never said I was sorry. I just wanted it all to go away and for us to be friends again. I know it's too late, but I'll say it now. I'm sorry for the way I treated you in high school. I'd just turned seventeen and didn't know what the fuck I was doing. I'm not excusing myself, but I hope you can understand I acted that way because of *me,* because *I* couldn't deal. I'm so sorry."

Elle's spine stiffened and she lifted her chin. "What does all that have to do with you forcing yourself on my sister?"

"What the hell—" Spencer took a step forward.

Elle scowled at her. "Stay out of this, Spencer. Or better yet, go inside and find Mom and Dad. Clearly, you need a babysitter."

"You've got to be kidding me."

Outrage seemed to make Spencer taller, and she looked ready to defend their honor with all her might. Despite the horrific awkwardness of the situation, Avery wanted to smile.

"It's time we put the past in the past," Avery said. "You're happy with Peter now, and I'll apologize for being a jerk as many times as it takes, but what happens between Spencer and me is none of your business. We're adults."

"She's twenty-two," Elle said in a tone that made twenty-two sound like twelve.

"Like I said, Spencer is an adult who can make her own decisions."

All the icy rage seemed to melt at that, leaving Elle in a miserable puddle. "How could you?"

Avery took a deep breath. This was not how she wanted to tell Spencer the truth, but Elle deserved it as much as Spencer did, and she needed to hear it now. Avery took Spencer's hand and squeezed tightly. "I had a crush on Spencer back then. That's why I reacted so badly when you told me you loved me." Avery felt the old shame well up inside her and fought it down. "I had a crush on your little sister, and I didn't know how to tell you without making things worse."

Elle had gone deathly pale, and Spencer was squeezing her hand so hard Avery couldn't feel her fingers. She could barely look at either of them. "She was only fifteen, and when you're teenagers two years seems like a lifetime. She was way too young for the kind of relationship I wanted, so I avoided her, tried to convince myself my feelings were just friendly. But they weren't, and I was ashamed. Then you told me you loved me, and I had no idea what to do. If it'd been anything, anyone, else I think I could have been honest with you, I might've been a better friend, but I couldn't tell you I loved your sister instead."

Spencer's eyes were wide as saucers. When she spoke her voice was barely more than a whisper. "You loved me?"

"Yes," Avery said simply. She didn't know if Elle would ever get past it, or if Spencer would ever return her feelings the way she hoped, but finally, *finally*, having the truth out in the open would help them all to heal.

"I had no idea." Spencer ran a hand through her hair. "You loved me all those years ago?"

Loved you then. Love you now. "Yes," Avery said again. She had to stop herself from saying more. She didn't want to be having this conversation in front of Elle. They all deserved better than that.

Elle just stood there like a forgotten scarecrow abandoned in a snowy field, untended and useless. Avery couldn't stand the wounded look in her eyes. "I'm sorry. I should have had the guts to tell you then."

Elle tried to speak, then cleared her throat like she was forcing the words up from some hollow place deep inside. "No. You were right not to tell me. I wish you hadn't ever told me." She looked ready to crumple. "Of all the girls you had to fall for."

"I know." Avery walked to her, then touched her shoulder. "I'm sorry, Elle. I'm so sorry I couldn't be what you needed."

Elle threw her arms around Avery and clung to her, tears seeping into Avery's shirt. "You asshole. I thought you were disgusted by me. You told me you were with *Sarah*."

Avery winced. "Yeah. That was a dumb move."

Elle lifted her face from Avery's shoulder and glared. "I went crazy and almost had her thrown out of school."

"Oh, I know. You do have a bit of a green-eyed monster lurking in there."

Elle pressed a hand to her mouth. "You were never actually sleeping with her?"

Avery shook her head. "I asked her to lie. You were so hurt, and I didn't want you to think it was *you*. It wasn't you. It was me and how I felt about Spencer. But because I couldn't tell you, I had to come up with another reason."

"Guess I owe her an apology."

"You've owed her one long before tonight. Even if I'd been dating Sarah, lying to make sure she failed an exam was harsh."

"I know." Elle sighed. "I hated her. I kind of still hate her. Did you know Dad fronted the money for her little cake shop? *Millions* of dollars."

"It's a gourmet bakery."

Elle scowled and waved a hand in the air in exactly the same way Spencer did when she was frustrated. "Whatever."

"He'd give you millions of dollars if you asked him, no flour or sugar required."

"And that's the point. He gives me whatever I want. But he *invested* in Sarah. He believes in her stupid mini cupcakes. He's never paid that kind of attention to me."

Avery slid a finger under Elle's chin and tilted her face until their eyes met. "He invested in Sarah because he knew his daughter had done wrong by her. And also, because she's brilliant. Sorry, but she is. Those mini cupcakes are to die for."

Elle groaned. "I know. I'm secretly addicted. I think they're laced with cocaine."

"Just because she's brilliant doesn't mean you're not. You're just as smart. You wouldn't have been able to pull off that crazy stunt at school if you hadn't been neck-and-neck for grades. Make your dad proud, but on your own terms. Do it your way."

"Yeah. Okay." She glanced toward Spencer who was still standing by the railing, turned away, and doing her best to give them privacy. "You still kissed my sister. My kid sister. On my birthday. At my own party."

"Forgive me?"

Elle didn't reply; she just stared at Spencer sadly.

"I do love you, you know. But like a sister." Avery held her breath.

"You love me like a sister and you love my sister like, well, if that kiss was anything to go by, like you're dying of thirst and she's the damn ocean."

Avery shifted uncomfortably. "We don't have to go there." *Especially before I have a chance to tell Spencer myself.*

Elle sighed. "We're already there. I want to take this memory from my brain and run it through the sanitize cycle on an industrial washer."

Avery winced again. "Sorry. It's got to be weird seeing your sister all hot and—"

"Shut up, shut up, shut up!" Elle covered her ears like that would prevent her from hearing.

"Shutting up now."

When Elle dropped her hands, Avery smiled.

Slowly, tentatively, Elle smiled back. "If you lay so much as a finger on her before she's ready, I'll cut it off with a rusty knife and force it down your throat. When I'm done, I'll disembowel you and feed your insides to a shark, no, wait, a mountain lion. They have smaller teeth and it will take longer for you to die."

Avery bit her bottom lip. "A mountain lion, huh? That sounds painful."

"It will be."

"I'm not going to hurt her, and we'll be taking things just as slowly as she needs, if we take them anywhere at all."

Elle looked back at Spencer and sighed. "She wants to be a sex therapist, you know."

"She told me."

"She's, like, twelve. Twelve to me anyway, and she wants to study *sex*."

Avery tried to think of a response that wouldn't make Elle tell her to shut up again. "She's going to be a great therapist. She's already really talented." Elle's face turned murderous and Avery added hastily, "At listening and understanding people." Then she laughed. "Geez. I don't work *that* fast."

"Did she ask you about sex? Oh my God."

"She—"

"No. I don't want to know." Elle put a hand up between them as if she could physically stop the conversation from happening. "I should go back inside, give you guys some privacy to…Jesus, Avery, just do me a favor and don't put your hands on her out here for the whole world to see. If Dad catches you, he'll feed you to a mouse and it will take you *years* to die."

"Noted. I'll put my hands on her in private only."

"*Shut up*," Elle said, but she was laughing.

❖

Elle was just about to head back inside when Kaitlyn, Sarah, and a dark-haired, good-looking stranger appeared in the doorway. "There you are." Kaitlyn pointed a finger at Elle. "We've been looking for the two of you everywhere. Oh, hi, Spencer."

"Hi." Spencer walked up to stand beside Avery, took her hand, and snuggled close. "Great party."

Avery tried really hard not to grin like an idiot and beat her chest like the chief gorilla in the rainforest. She really, really tried but had a feeling she was failing miserably.

"Awesome," Kaitlyn agreed, eyeing their joined hands. "Better for some than others I suspect."

Elle shifted and cleared her throat. That topic was no longer up for discussion.

"Hi," Avery said to the stranger. "Avery Anders."

"Ryan." They shook hands.

Sarah and Kaitlyn both looked at Avery, and for the first time since she'd gotten to the party, she remembered the scene in the little dive bar on Madison. Crap. The last thing Elle needed was a double gut punch. But if Peter really was going to propose…

"Eleanor, we need to tell you something. It's not going to be easy." Kaitlyn's voice was soft but resolute.

A wrinkle planted itself between Elle's brows. "Not easy appears to be the order of the night. All of you do remember it's my birthday, right? It's fairly traditional to have fun on your birthday, expected even. Next birthday, I'm definitely requesting more fun."

Kaitlyn's gaze slid back to Avery's and Spencer's joined hands.

Sarah shifted uncomfortably, and Ryan wrapped an arm around her shoulders. She leaned into the touch and her nervous energy disappeared. Interesting. Looked like Sarah found what she'd needed tonight. Avery wasn't surprised; she had no idea how stunning she was. Sarah, her whole body trembling with need and a dancer in her lap, flashed through Avery's mind. Yeah, it was still pretty hot, she had a pulse after all, but it didn't do it for her the way kissing Spencer did. Kissing Spencer was about a bazillion times hotter. Now Spencer at that club…

"What is it?" Elle's voice had an edge now, sounding like she was done with their chickenshit stalling.

Kaitlyn looked at Sarah, who looked at Avery, who sighed deeply. This was turning into the longest night of her life. She'd already broken Elle's heart, then given it another good wallop when Elle had caught her with Spencer. How on earth did she say what came next?

"We were at a bar on Madison this afternoon, waiting for salon appointments, and Peter walked in. He was with a woman, and they had sex in the bathroom." God, she felt like the world's biggest ass, and this time she hadn't been the one in the wrong. Being the messenger was almost as bad. "I'm so sorry."

Spencer gave a small yelp and rushed to Elle's side. "Oh my God. What a fucking dirtbag. Are you okay? I'm going to kill the fucker. Kill him dead."

The sisters had a serious mean streak.

Elle's spine stiffened as if she were a marionette and someone had just pulled her strings. Her eyes weren't in focus, like reality was all too much and she'd checked out. But the longer the silence hung, the stiffer she got, and Avery wondered if she'd ever speak again. Or if everything that made Elle Elle would just snap in two from all the lies that had been revealed tonight.

Surprisingly, it was Sarah who spoke next. "You already knew, didn't you?"

That brought Elle back with a jerk. "Of course I—"

Sarah shook her head. "Don't do that. Denying it only makes it harder. Trust me on that."

Elle shot her a look that radiated, don't-you-tell-me-what-to-do. "I didn't know for sure, but I had a pretty good idea. Believe it or not, there are some things that just aren't any of your business. Why are you here anyway? I didn't invite you."

"Reginald invited me."

Elle rolled her eyes. "Of course he did."

Sarah shrugged. "If it makes you feel better, I spent most of the night in the kitchen so I wouldn't have to talk to you."

"You should've stayed there."

Sarah glanced at Ryan and her eyes went soft. "That's the smartest thing you've ever said to me, Eleanor."

Elle scowled at that. "Why don't you just—"

"Whoa." Spencer cut them off. "Let's save that fight for later. Ellie, I don't know what's going on, but you can't date a guy who's cheating on you."

"I'm going to marry him." Elle said it the way someone else might've said, "I'm going to the store for milk."

"No, you're not," Spencer and Sarah said in unison.

Avery's head spun. Hadn't Sarah been all prepared to let Elle say yes only a few hours ago? "We didn't think you knew about his engagement plans," Avery said. "We couldn't let you say yes without telling you."

"We're not letting you say yes at all." Spencer gave her a none too gentle shove the way only siblings could get away with. "What the hell is wrong with you? Do you even love him?"

"Yes." But the word was so insubstantial Avery didn't believe her.

Avery didn't know what to do. If Elle knew, then maybe she and Peter had an open relationship? It wasn't very common and it didn't sound like Elle at all, but what did she know. Spencer looked ready to charge into the ballroom guns blazing and confront him, and Avery was right behind her on that, but Elle was so freaking detached right now, that didn't seem like the right approach. Girls were so confusing.

Kaitlyn looked just as torn. "Okay, well, we should go back inside, let you deal." But she didn't move.

Sarah made a long-suffering sound and frowned at Elle. "I don't like you."

"Sarah," Avery warned her.

"But," Sarah said, raising her voice a little over Avery's protest, "you don't deserve some fucker screwing a tramp in a hole-in-the-wall bar. She wasn't even pretty."

The corner of Elle's mouth twitched. "No?"

Sarah chewed her bottom lip thoughtfully. "She looked like Alvin the Chipmunk and Smurfette's illicit love child."

How could this possibly be helping? But it seemed like it was. The twitch turned into the tiniest of smiles. Avery had no idea why the hell it even mattered if the girl was pretty or not. Cheating was cheating.

"That's gross," Elle said.

"Like you wouldn't believe," Sarah agreed.

"They really had sex in the bathroom?"

"Yup."

Elle's shoulders slumped. "Perfect."

"A year ago, I went on vacation to Miami with my ex. She screwed some stranger, who was probably just as ugly, at the top of a lifeguard stand. You know the ones that are just a ladder and a chair? They climbed all the way to the top at three in the morning to have sex while I was asleep in the hotel room."

"What the fuck?" The words were out of her mouth before Avery could stop them. How had Sarah not told her? She knew

Sarah and Melinda had problems, sex kind of problems, but... And seriously, a lifeguard stand?

Elle raised her eyebrows. "Who would cheat on you?" She waved a hand at Sarah. "You're perfect. You're like Barbie, but with an actual brain. You're Smart Baker Barbie."

Sarah smirked. "Gee, Eleanor, I had no idea you had such a thing for me."

The wave turned into a poke. "Shut up. You know what I mean. You're hot."

Sarah's eyes twinkled. "Please, by all means, keep going."

Elle scowled. "You're also annoying. I don't like you either."

"But you think I'm hot."

"I didn't mean—"

"Children, please settle down," Kaitlyn said, rolling her eyes.

"Look, all I'm saying is that it happened to me too. I didn't have any idea it was going on, but it absolutely completely sucked. It took me a long time to get over, until tonight actually. I thought she'd cheated because I wasn't sexy enough and she had to go looking elsewhere. But screw that. I'm awesome sexy and it's her loss. It's Peter's loss too." Sarah gave Elle an appraising head-to-toe. "You look like you can do sexy just fine."

"I can," Elle said with another of those tiny smiles.

If someone had told her that it was Sarah who'd get all life-coach empowering and make Elle see the truth, Avery would have sworn on her life it'd never happen. Tonight was turning out stranger than a double episode of *Fringe*.

"But why are you still with him?" Spencer asked Elle.

"I don't know. It's easier, I guess. We've been together so long our families would be devastated if we split."

Spencer looked at her like Elle had just told her she'd decided to become a nudist and was going to give her entire wardrobe to charity. "You're with him because our family likes him? Are you crazy?"

Avery tucked Spencer's hand back in hers and squeezed. Apparently, her knack for empathy and insight was lost when it came to her big sister's love life.

"I thought maybe once we'd married, gotten a little bit older, things would change." Elle shrugged. "That's probably wishful thinking."

"You think?" Spencer said.

Avery wanted to cover her mouth.

"He was going to ask you tonight, only hours after sleeping with that girl," Kaitlyn said quietly. "He was going to stand up in front of your friends and family and talk about how you were the only girl in the world for him. He'd have lied his face off."

"What am I supposed to do? Everyone expects us to get married. You know who my father is, it's not that easy to just break things off."

"Do you really want to marry him?" Sarah stared holes through Elle like a perky blond drill sergeant.

"Not anymore, but I don't know how…"

"Don't worry." Sarah patted Elle's shoulder. "I have a plan."

Elle narrowed her eyes. "Why are you helping me?"

Sarah smiled. "Because you didn't flay Avery alive for cuddling up to your little sister. That was classy."

"I still might." Elle shuddered. "I caught them kissing."

Sarah burst out laughing. "Oh, to have been a fly on the wall. Okay, now I'm definitely going to help you. I bet you wanted to puke."

"These are eight-hundred-dollar shoes," Elle said, deadpan. "No way."

"Let's all move inside, shall we?" The last thing Avery needed was Sarah and Elle talking about the kiss. She wanted nothing more than for them to all go the hell away so she could go back to doing just that with Spencer. Preferably alone, in a room with a bed.

As they stepped back into the ballroom, Avery slung an arm around Spencer's shoulders. "Is this okay?"

"More than okay." Spencer twined her fingers with the ones Avery had rested on her shoulder. "But don't think for a second I'm letting you get away with not telling me *every single detail* of your crush on me."

Avery let out a windy sigh. "Do I have to?"

Spencer laughed, reminding Avery again of chimes in the breeze. "You had it bad, huh?"

"So bad," Avery whispered, pulling Spencer even tighter against her side. "If we can manage to make a clean escape tonight, I'll be happy to show you all the many and varied things I fantasize about, Dr. Sex Brain."

Spencer appeared to be considering this. "Well, I do want to write a really good essay. What do you say we skip the cake?"

Avery's heart started to pound so hard she was sure her ribs would be sore in the morning. "Are you sure? We don't have to do anything. I know you're probably not ready, and…" *And your sister threatened to feed me to a mountain lion. Let's not forget that small detail.*

"Oh, we are definitely going to do something. You're not the only one with a crush, you know."

Avery's grin was so wide her cheeks hurt. Tonight, Spencer would be hers. *Finally.*

Chapter Twelve

Never Forget Your First

Avery and Spencer sped down a deserted hallway in the McGregor mansion like they were executing a prison break and freedom was an unlocked bedroom away.

"Quick, in here." Spencer pushed open an antique wooden door and motioned for Avery to hurry up. Safely inside, she fell against it, kicking off her heels and groaning as her bare feet sank into the inch of oatmeal colored carpet. "Those heels are not made for sneaking around."

"They're made to drive me to distraction."

"Worth every penny then." Spencer wiggled her toes in the carpet.

"I'm shocked we ever made it out of there. When your mother cornered us, I thought we were goners for sure," Avery said.

Spencer shook her head. "Please. That was easy. I have eons of experience handling Pamela McGregor."

Seeing Spencer's goddess-of-the-social-circuit mother blocking the ballroom doorway and looking none too happy about them heading in that direction had set off alarms in Avery's brain so screechily persistent she hadn't taken in any of the conversation that followed. It wasn't exactly a heroic trait, to say the least. She was embarrassingly terrible in a crisis.

"What did you say to her?"

"I told her you were taking me upstairs to ravish me, and grandbabies would shortly follow."

Avery gaped. "What?"

"Yeah, in hindsight it would have been a lot more convincing if you'd have had a penis. Oh well."

Avery shoved a hand through her hair. "Spencer, please tell me you didn't…"

Spencer grinned and slid into Avery's arms. "I told her I'd had too much wine and you were being gallant and escorting me upstairs. Mom hates it when people get drunk at her parties."

Relief flooded Avery like water over a levee. "Well, thank God for that."

"The grandbabies thing might have worked though. She wants them more than life itself. Do you know the guilt trips I've had to endure over not finding a partner yet? It's like I'm fifty-two instead of twenty-two."

Avery had sympathy, but couldn't help but wonder the same thing. "Why don't you have a girlfriend yet?"

"Because I was waiting for this gorgeous as sin, slightly left of androgynous, lesbian fantasy come true to notice I existed and kiss me senseless. Again."

Spencer had been waiting for her? Butterflies launched into flight inside her belly. "Huh. And how's that working out?"

"So far? Pretty nicely. She can be a bit of a blockhead though, so I had to get creative and ask her inappropriately personal questions about sexual arousal. It made her hot."

Avery laughed. "Did it? You must be very sexy then."

Spencer's smile turned shy. "I hope she thinks so, at least."

Avery cupped Spencer's cheek. "She thinks you're the sexiest woman alive. Sexier even than Angelina Jolie in *Gia*."

"She was way hotter in *Mr. and Mrs. Smith*."

Avery shook her head sadly. "You really have no taste."

"Who made you the judge?" Spencer shoved her.

"I'm older and therefore wiser."

"Sure you are." Spencer rolled her eyes. "Are you going to put all that wisdom to better use? Perhaps by showing me your best kissing technique?"

"Well, if it will help you to write a better paper, I think I'm obligated. It's for research, after all."

Spencer rose up on her toes in her bare feet and whispered against Avery's lips, "Less talking, more touching. I want your hands on my skin."

For the first time, Avery felt nerves sliding into the cracks around the giant ball of lust that was her brain. She'd never had sex with a virgin before, not that she knew of anyway. That she was now, that it was Spencer, that she'd thought about exactly this every single night since she was seventeen—it was all starting to freak her out just a bit. Sure, she could promise herself she'd just be making out with Spencer, they could take things slowly, but slow didn't seem to be a viable option when they touched. God, all she'd done was kiss Spencer and she'd been ready to tear her clothes off in an almost-public place. She wasn't sure she'd be able to do the right thing and stop before things got out of hand, wasn't sure she'd want to.

If by some miracle, Spencer was ready to have sex tonight, what if Avery screwed it up? What if it wasn't everything Spencer wanted? What if she couldn't make Spencer come, or she accidentally elbowed her in the face? Rogue elbows were a safety hazard. It might be best if they just aborted this whole thing before someone ended up in the hospital. How would she ever explain *that* to Mrs. McGregor?

And anyway, what the hell was she thinking sneaking around with Spencer at her sister's party, under the nose of all her family? People might start looking for them, and Spencer deserved better than an upscale version of the do-it-at-the-kegger college-style lay. They should be downstairs having a good time and making plans to go out on a date. That's what normal people did, right? They didn't drag the girl of their dreams upstairs to fuck without so much as buying her a drink first.

Avery wanted a do-over of the whole evening. Except the kiss. That part she'd keep.

Spencer dropped back on her heels. "Something wrong?"

"No," Avery said. Then she sighed. "Yes. I think we might be making a mistake here."

"Oh?" Spencer began tugging at Avery's shirttails. "How so?"

"You deserve better than this. You deserve a woman who'll take you out on a date."

"And are you planning to lose my phone number in the morning?" Spencer slid soft, warm hands up the inside of Avery's shirt and over her stomach, making her gasp.

"Of course not." Was that the answer? She couldn't focus, couldn't think.

"So, then you'll take me out on a date."

Spencer raked her nails gently across Avery's stomach, and every muscle in her body tensed and readied.

Avery's hormones were in a fight to the death battle with her brain. She wanted to throw Spencer on the bed and make her come in deliciously creative ways, but she wanted Spencer to be satisfied with her first time even more than that, and not all satisfaction was sexual. "It's traditional to date first. I don't want you to think I expect sex tonight. I want to…" Avery searched for the right word and eventually came up with, "Court you. Make you feel special."

Spencer burst out laughing, then bit her lip when she realized Avery was dead serious. Her bottom lip trembled. "You want to *court* me? Did we enter a time machine and go back to nineteen thirty-nine?"

Avery pulled Spencer's hands out from under her shirt. She couldn't think when Spencer touched her, and this was important. "I want to do this right. You deserve someone who makes you feel as special as you are. I want to take you out and—"

"Treat me like a princess," Spencer supplied.

"Yes, exactly."

Spencer took a step back and folded her arms. Avery had never seen a woman look so annoyed at the idea of a date. "Avery, do you want to have sex with me?"

"Of course I do. I just want to be sure you're ready."

Spencer shook her head. "I'm here. I'm doing the best I can to throw myself at you. I'm ready. It's you who's not ready."

Well, that was absurd. "I'm ready."

"Then unless you're calling me a liar who doesn't know her own mind, we don't have a problem here."

Avery shoved a hand through her hair. Spencer didn't get it. Though, honestly, she was pretty sure she wasn't making any sense. "I'm sorry. I just think we should wait."

"Okay. We'll wait as long as you want. I'm sorry if I made you uncomfortable by coming on too strong." Spencer's tone was so polite, Avery felt every word like an arrow to her heart. Spencer grabbed her shoes and turned the doorknob.

"Wait." Spencer was leaving. Avery had said no, she knew she had, but she hadn't really meant *no* no, had she?

Spencer turned back to her and some of the stiffness in her posture eased. "I care about you, and I really want to be with you tonight and have that date you mentioned as well. But you're sending mixed signals. You need to decide what you really want." *And stop jerking me around.* She didn't say the words, but they hung in the air.

Avery had spent her entire life trying to do the right thing, say the right thing, put her own needs second, and now she had no idea what the right thing was. Spencer thought she wasn't ready to have sex with her, which was so far from the truth this situation would be comedic if it was happening to someone else.

"Forget about me and that I'm a virgin and that we haven't done more than kiss. Forget we're at my sister's party or standing in my childhood bedroom or that there's a whopping two years age difference. What do *you* want?" Spencer asked her.

That answer was easy. "I want you."

"Maybe you're not sure you want to sleep with me," Spencer said, folding her arms across her chest like they'd protect her. "Fifteen-year-old fantasy me may be a whole lot better than awkward virgin trying to get laid me. Maybe the reality will ruin the fantasy and now you're not sure you want to follow through."

"No." Avery took Spencer's shoes and deposited them on the floor, then she pulled Spencer back into her arms and wrapped her in a tight hug. "Don't think that. I promise you that's not true."

"Then what *is* true?"

God, why was being honest so hard? Though of course, it wasn't honestly. It was vulnerability. Spencer thought they were talking about sex, but the problem had nothing to do with sex. No, the problem was love and always had been. If she told Spencer how she really felt and Spencer still left? Avery wasn't sure she'd ever recover. But if she never took the chance, she'd be letting the one woman she could never forget walk away thinking she didn't want her. In Avery's mom's AA meetings, they said that people change when the pain in their lives becomes greater than their fear of change. For the first time, Avery understood that. Tonight, everything was going to change one way or the other, but if there was even a tiny chance Spencer could love her back, she'd take the risk.

"When I first started hanging at Elle's house, you were fifteen. You were so bright and happy and sure of everything you wanted, even back then. I didn't just have a crush on you, Spencer. I fell in love with you. The two years between us wasn't just a number. You want to know what my deepest, most secret, most fulfilling fantasy was at seventeen? It was marrying you one day. It was watching you walk down the aisle in a white dress and knowing that I'd wake up next to you every morning for the rest of my life. I loved you and I'm pretty sure you loved Justin Timberlake." Avery smiled weakly. "You weren't ready for what I wanted. No one is at fifteen. It didn't seem fair to burden you with my feelings."

"I'm not fifteen anymore," Spencer said, taking Avery's hands and squeezing them.

"I know that. But I still feel like I'm way ahead of you. Spencer, I still love you. I never stopped loving you, and no other woman has ever come close. My life without you in it is empty. I don't just want tonight. I want forever. And if saying no tonight, if taking things slower and making sure you're ready for the same things I'm ready for means we have a better chance at forever, then I want to wait."

Spencer stared at her for a long moment. "Forever is a long time." She brought her hand up to Avery's face and traced the curve of her lips with a fingertip. "Kind of similar to the span of time between when you kissed me at fifteen and when you kissed me tonight."

Avery closed her eyes. "I'm sorry. I never should have kissed you then. You were so young, and that was unforgivable."

Spencer tilted her head to the side as if considering this statement seriously. "Unforgivable is the wrong word. Surprising, maybe. Unexpected, for sure. But the word that really comes to mind is arousing."

Avery groaned. "That couldn't possibly be true. You never saw me as anything but your big sister's friend."

Spencer walked around Avery to sit on the bed as if she needed a little distance to have a conversation about how close they'd been. How close they'd come. "You're right. I meanm I never considered that we'd get together before that kiss. I didn't even know I was gay. Actually, it was you who planted that seed."

"The kiss made you think you might be gay?"

Spencer shrugged. "Yeah. A girl kisses you and you get all squirmy in all the right places, it makes you wonder if you might be gay."

Avery felt as if the floor was spinning and she was rooted to the spot. "But you freaked out."

Spencer shook her head. "No. You freaked out. I was innocently going about my business looking for the spare sun umbrella in the pool house and there you were, all dark and broody, cranky at me for no reason I could see."

"I wasn't cranky at you."

"You were. You wouldn't even look at me, let alone talk to me. I assumed you thought I was the dork kid sister and couldn't be bothered."

Avery shoved a hand through her hair for what had to be the twentieth time that night. She was sure it must be sticking on end by now and the Einstein look was doing wonders for her sex appeal. "Spence. For God's sake. You were practically naked bent over looking for that stupid umbrella."

Spencer frowned. "What?"

"Do you even remember what you were wearing? Or rather, not wearing?"

Spencer looked blank, and Avery sighed. "A yellow bikini. A shade darker than your hair. The kind that tied together at the hips with flimsy strings. One good tug and the whole thing would've fallen off you. I spent the whole day trying and failing not to notice your endless legs or your flawless skin or the sweet little breasts you were so embarrassed to have then. I spent the whole day trying and failing not to imagine tugging at those ties with my teeth. That bikini drove me crazy, and I go to the pool house looking for a bottle of water and five minutes alone and there you are, with your sunshine yellow ass in the air."

Spencer's cheeks went red. "It was *not* in the air."

"It was, trust me on that. The memory has never left me. I was so fucking turned on I didn't know what to do. And, God, you were so *innocent*, chatting away oblivious. I felt like a complete ass."

A smile tugged at Spencer's lips. "How turned on exactly?"

"Turned on enough that I couldn't help kissing you. I knew it was wrong, that you were too young and you'd never shown a lick of interest in me. But I couldn't help myself." Avery sat next to Spencer on the bed. "I want you to know that's not an excuse. A bikini doesn't mean you invite that kind of reaction or that you were asking for it. I was the asshole who took advantage of you."

Spencer took her hand. "In an alternate universe where everyone is politically correct and no one has a reaction they can't help, that might be true. But that isn't the real world. Kissing someone you're attracted to isn't wrong. Not unless they push you away and tell you no, and that definitely didn't happen."

"You didn't know what you wanted."

Spencer rolled her eyes. "You say the memory never left you, but you seem to be forgetting a crucial point. When you kissed me, I kissed you back."

"Spence—"

"No, listen." Spencer cut her off gently. "You're beating yourself up for nothing. Was it one hundred percent appropriate to kiss me at fifteen? Maybe. Maybe not. But you were a teenager too.

I have complete confidence that if I had pushed you away you would have respected that, am I right?"

"Of course." Avery said it so fervently it was almost a shout.

"But I didn't. I kissed you back. It felt amazing. It made me feel sexy and special."

"Thank God. I thought I'd pressured you."

"Oh, I know. You completely freaked out and apologized your ass off without letting me say a word, then ran out of there like I was on fire."

Avery poked her in the side. "Hey now, I was a teenager too, remember? I hadn't learned to be cool yet."

Spencer snorted. "Got cool covered now, do you?"

"I've learned to shut the hell up so a girl can talk after you kiss her. Usually because I'm hoping to hear, 'No one's ever kissed me like that. Take me to bed immediately.'"

"And just how many women have you seduced and bedded, Avery Anders?"

Avery leaned in and brushed her mouth over Spencer's in a kiss as sweet as a candy apple. "None that were you. None that I loved."

Spencer pouted. "You're just saying that."

"I'm not." Avery slid closer so their thighs pressed together. "You're the only one I've ever loved."

"All this time?"

Avery nodded, emotion clogging her throat. Words a distant island off the mainland of possibility.

"Wow. Thank you, I guess. Is thank you right? It seems like there should be bigger words than that for this."

The lump in her throat swelled a little more, and the unfamiliar sting of tears built behind her eyes. Oh hell no. She would *not* cry. Crying wasn't an option, even if Spencer had said "thank you" instead of "I love you too." That's why they were talking instead of touching, because even though Spencer was attracted to her, she wasn't in love with her. *Yet,* Avery reminded herself, blinking hard. Spencer wasn't in love with her *yet.* Avery had wanted and waited for her for seven years, and she'd wait seventy more if there was even a chance future Spencer might love her one day. She had to try.

"Thank you is perfect." Avery brushed her lips over Spencer's again. Her mouth was so soft, full lips and gloss that tasted faintly of berries. She couldn't help but remember their first kiss. Spencer's skin warm from the sun and oh so bare. The faint smell of sunscreen and chlorine. The way Spencer had gasped in surprise and melted, the perfect way she fit against Avery like they were two pieces of the same puzzle. And the kiss. God. She'd only had a little more idea than Spencer what she was doing, and finesse seemed insignificant up against the desire she'd been repressing for months. It hadn't been a movie star kiss, not the kind girls like Spencer dreamed their first kiss to be. It hadn't even been sweet and gentle the way Avery'd imagined kissing her after their first date one day. Hell no. The kiss had been all fumbling passion and overwhelming desire. She'd wanted Spencer. Wanted her naked. Still did.

Just as she was about to pull back and suggest they head back downstairs, Spencer threaded her fingers in her hair and held her close. "I love it when you kiss me."

Simple happiness chased away the last of the lump in her throat. "Then I promise to kiss you any time, any way, for as long as you like." Avery kissed her lips again, the tip of her nose, the space between her brows. All the kisses.

"That's good because kissing you is making me crazy hot."

"Hot, huh?"

Spencer smiled but looked away, pulled at a ruffle on the quilt they were sitting on. "I have to apologize too, for back then. I let you walk away. I let you think I didn't like that kiss just as much as you did. I'm sorry. You kind of rocked my world, and it took me a while to be okay with being attracted to girls. Like really attracted."

"That's totally normal. You have nothing to be sorry for. Sexual development at seventeen is a whole lot different than fifteen, even if we were only two years apart."

The corner of Spencer's mouth tipped up. "Not so different really. I have a confession to make."

"What do you possibly have to confess?"

"That night, after you'd left and I was in bed I couldn't stop thinking about you. Of course, I replayed the kiss a hundred times, but I also thought about you in the pool, wet and dripping, and stretched out on the sun lounger with your eyes closed. I thought about you asking me if I'd rub sunscreen into your shoulders. How you'd lie there on your belly while I ran my hands all over you, and you wouldn't have stopped me."

All the blood in Avery's body shot down between her legs. "God."

"Yeah," Spencer said a little uncertainly. "I touched myself, thinking about you and what would've happened if you hadn't stopped kissing me."

"You…" Avery couldn't get the words out. It was like all her insides had just packed up and gone on holiday. Holy Jesus. Spencer had masturbated thinking about her back then. "Did you come?" Okay, so probably not the subtlest question but definitely the most vital one.

"Oh, you're all about the payoff, are you? Just want to get right to the finale? Nice. That's real romantic of you." A grin broke out over Spencer's face.

Avery chewed her bottom lip. Yeah. Not subtle. "In this circumstance, I feel the question is warranted, though I definitely want every single detail of the in-between."

Spencer laughed. "Yes, I came. My first, actually."

"Your first orgasm?" Wow. Just, wow.

"Yup. That kiss was pretty inspirational."

"So, what you're saying is that while I was picturing us having picnics on the beach and growing old together, you were picturing pornographic sex acts and getting what I'm sure is a very pretty pussy all wet. You started young, Dr. Sex Brain."

Spencer groaned. "Shut up. It wasn't pornographic. Kissing and being vigilant about your skincare and sun protection was plenty to get the job done."

Avery tipped Spencer's face up with a finger under her chin. "But you don't deny it made your pussy wet, do you?"

Spencer's mouth twitched. "Can I plead the Fifth?"

"You'll have to pay for it." Avery narrowed her eyes jokingly. "What do you want?"

The question was simple, four little words. So insignificant on their own but enough to have her own pussy growing damp when Spencer put them together in that tone. The one that said she'd be happy to pay whatever the price.

Avery thought for a second. She didn't want to go back downstairs and share Spencer with everyone at the party just yet. It was also pretty interesting that Spencer's fantasy had been touching her and not the other way around. To her mind, most girls at that age would've pictured lying back and being tended to. But not Spencer. She'd wanted to explore, and she'd waited just as long as Avery had. "I think I'm going to require a little reenactment, Miss McGregor."

Spencer's brow creased. "Huh?"

Avery spread a palm over the quilt. "This isn't a sun lounger, but it'll do fine. I believe you said your fantasy was that I lay on my stomach and you rubbed my shoulders? I wouldn't have stopped you then, and I'm not going to now."

Avery could practically hear Spencer gulp, but she wet her lips and took a long breath. Oh yeah, she liked this idea. Avery liked it too. Maybe too much.

Her body craved it.

But her heart was ringing alarm bells.

The trick was not letting things go too far too fast.

CHAPTER THIRTEEN

Lessons in Losing It

"Take off my shirt." Avery stood in front of Spencer, looking at her expectantly.

Spencer froze. "I...You want me to...You want to be naked?"

Avery wasn't sure if Spencer was going to start ripping her clothes off or start running for the door. From her expression, it could go either way. For all her bravado about getting laid tonight, she was still a virgin about to take a woman's shirt off for the first time. Avery reminded herself to go slow, be patient, not act like an ass again.

"No, love, I want you to take my shirt off. I wasn't exactly expecting to re-create your poolside fantasy tonight, but I think my sports bra is as close as we'll get to a swim top."

"Oh!" Spencer laughed awkwardly. "Sorry. I suck at this already, don't I?"

"Absolutely not." Avery tugged her up so they were nose to nose. "We don't have to do anything you're not ready for. You know that."

"You're just afraid my sister will feed you to a mountain lion."

Avery winced. "Definitely a factor. She's scary when she's mad."

"You don't have to worry. I'm ready. I've been ready since I made myself come for the first time thinking about it."

Avery groaned. She didn't think she'd ever get used to hearing that Spencer had touched herself thinking about her, thinking about touching her, wanting her so much it had made her come. "Take off my shirt."

Spencer's slender piano player fingers got to work on her buttons, tugging the starched cotton off her shoulders until her shirt fell like a fat snowflake to the floor. Her tongue peeked out to wet her lips as she gave Avery the slow once-over. It was stupid to feel insecure. Avery'd been a lot more naked than this plenty of times in her life, and modesty wasn't a virtue she possessed. But Spencer's gaze on her bare skin had goose bumps breaking out along her arms. It might be juvenile and not a little shallow to wish she had a bodybuilder's physique, but right this second, she'd have traded every cent in her bank account for a few muscles worthy of *American Ninja Warrior*. "Maybe fantasy Avery doesn't compare to the real version either," she said, trying to disperse the sudden weight in the air.

Spencer met her eyes. "It doesn't compare at all. I could never have imagined real Avery to be this sexy."

Avery's breath whooshed out of her. That was a pretty good answer, as answers went. "Thanks, love. I could use some more time in the weight room."

Spencer trailed her fingertips along Avery's bicep, "You look strong to me. But in a Pilates enthusiast, daily swimmer kind of way."

Avery winced. "Pilates?" Was there anything girlier? Just the idea of those skintight workout pants made her want to cross her legs in defense.

Spencer grinned. "No? Well, just born toned then. I could learn to hate you."

I'd rather you loved me. Avery caught Spencer's wandering fingers in hers and kissed them. "Now that you have me at your mercy, Dr. Sex Brain, what are we going to do?"

Spencer smiled. "I believe this is the part where you lie down and pretend to be sunbathing."

Spencer was right, but somehow it didn't seem fair that she just lie there while Spencer did all the work. She wanted to touch her too. "Maybe we should engage in a little revisionist history."

An abridged version where she had Spencer naked and panting within the next twenty seconds. The CliffsNotes guide to getting it on.

Spencer shook her head. "Uh-uh. On your belly. Before I lose patience."

"You sure? I could make you feel really good you know."

Spencer made a little sound that under any other circumstances Avery would've interpreted as pain. When she spoke her voice was strained. "I want this. I want to run my hands all over you and have you not stop me."

God. Yes. Okay. Sure. That'd be fine.

Avery settled on the bed with her face in Spencer's pillow. It smelled like her, the subtlest hint of rosewater wrapped in sandalwood. She could feel Spencer kneeling on the bed beside her, looking down at her bare back save for the straps of her bra.

"It's getting hot," Spencer said. "You don't want to burn."

Too late for that. "Um. Too lazy to move." She stretched languidly, making sure to wiggle her ass just a little. "Do you have any sunscreen? Maybe you could keep me from burning." *Or be the flame that scorches me.* She could hear Spencer's breathing change above her, a slight uptick that had her own pulse racing.

"Sure. Some right here." Spencer paused. "Keep still. I don't want to miss a spot."

Her fingers were trembling when she brushed small circles along the nape of Avery's neck. Her touch was tentative at first, like she was half afraid she was doing something wrong, but as a minute ticked by, and then another, she grew bold, confident. Spencer threaded fingers into her hair and tugged just hard enough to make her scalp tingle and her hips jerk. *Fuck.*

"You like that?" Spencer's tone more incredulous surprise than tempting seductress.

"Oh yeah," Avery murmured, wishing she'd do it again. "It feels really good."

"I read about it in a book once," Spencer said, "but I wasn't really sure it could be a sexual turn-on. Hair seems so..." She thought for a second, "banal, like your elbow or your big toe."

"Everything's a turn-on for somebody," Avery said. "You just wait till it's your turn, you're going to find out all kinds of things about yourself you never knew."

Spencer's fingers tightened in her hair again, and she leaned down to whisper in Avery's ear, "I can't wait." Her hands slid along Avery's shoulder blades, mapping the contours of her body. "You're going to get tan lines."

"Take it off then." Avery made sure to keep her voice just this side of sleepy. The fantasy had all the trappings of innocence, and she didn't want to spook her. Spencer might be the virgin, but she was in control of the pace tonight.

"O-okay." Spencer stumbled a little on the word, like she'd tripped but caught herself before a full-blown stutter. She released the clasp on Avery's bra and pushed the straps down her arms. Avery levered up on her elbows and pulled free, tossing the garment to the side. She settled back down, but not before giving Spencer a good long glimpse of her breasts.

"Thanks," Avery said, "that feels better."

"You're welcome." The gravel in Spencer's voice made "you're welcome" sound a hell of a lot like "turn over and fuck me," but Avery kept still, more than a little pleased their impromptu role-play was turning Spencer on as well.

When Spencer touched her again, running her palms along Avery's waist and up across the expanse of her back, she had to stifle a moan. God. She'd thought a cute little fantasy sunscreen would be light and easy, a step toward intimacy that would be fun for them both. But this wasn't fun; this should be in the urban dictionary under *The Scenic Route to Torment City*. Spencer's hands on her back made Avery want them on her front, on her everywhere, especially, most particularly, between her legs. She pressed her pelvis into the quilt trying and failing to relieve some of the pressure without being too obvious. The very last thing she wanted was to freak Spencer out by getting too hot too fast. Again.

Spencer's fingers dipped down her sides, grazing the side of her breasts, and Avery couldn't help the shudder that ran through her. When Spencer did it again, then again, she knew she must have noticed and was teasing her on purpose. Whose dumb idea was this to reenact a fantasy where she had to lie passively while Spencer drove her out of her mind?

Oh yeah. That's right. Hers. Dumbass.

When Spencer ran her palms down Avery's waist and curled her fingers around her hips just above the waistband of her pants, Avery groaned into the pillow. She lifted her hips. She couldn't have stopped herself if her life had depended on it. *Touch me, love. Just a little lower.*

Spencer moved to her lower back, her touch more massage now, fingers and palms finding all the tender places and soothing away her tension. Transferring it to the thrumming in her pussy. God, she was wet.

Spencer traced the waistband of her tuxedo pants. "You're going to get another tan line."

There were some things in life that just made your heart stop. Spencer asking but not asking her to take her pants off was one of those things. She coughed to get her heart started again like a rusty chainsaw spluttering to life, and unglued her tongue from the roof of her mouth. "Uh, that's okay."

Wait, what? *That's okay?* No, it wasn't. Tan lines were the worst. Awful. Horrible. Possibly a communicable disease. She had to take her pants off right now to save humanity.

Spencer tsked. "Your skin is so delicate, and turning just the right shade of gold. You sure you want Casper ass?"

Avery laugh-snorted into the pillow. That was her girl, the world-class smartass. "When you put it that way." Avery toed off her shoes and lifted her hips. It took Spencer a second, but then her hands slid into the inch of space Avery had created and she undid the button on her pants, then the zipper, then slid her hand inside.

"Spencer." The word was a gasp. Oh, sweet Jesus. She hadn't expected Spencer to just go for it. Hot ribbons of need curled and spread inside her, expanding, cloning themselves until everything was warm and wet and needy.

Spencer's fingers traced her clit through her underwear and Avery yelped. Oh yeah. Such a very sexy yelp it was too. God. This woman could undo her like no one ever had. "Love, I…" She pushed hard into Spencer's hand. She wanted very, very badly to come. Spencer slid her hand out and tugged on the fabric of her pants, pulling them and her socks down and off with more finesse than a virgin should've had, leaving Avery in nothing but her underwear.

Avery's unreliable heartbeat had officially moved residence to the spot between her thighs, thumping a steady beat that was driving her mad. She pushed up on an elbow again and glanced over her shoulder at Spencer. "Let me touch you, please." Finding herself spread-eagle, more or less naked while her girl was fully dressed, and she hadn't done anything more than kiss her, was not a position Avery was used to occupying.

Spencer smoothed a palm over her ass and Avery collapsed into the pillow again. Ohpleaseyesmore.

Spencer giggled. "My, my, you're easy."

So fucking easy.

Spencer moved up to look Avery in the face. "Are you okay?"

Avery nodded. She was okay. The okayest of all varieties of okay. But if she didn't touch Spencer soon she was going to implode. "I want to touch you, make you feel even half of what I'm feeling right now."

Light danced in Spencer's eyes. "What are you feeling right now? I need to know. It's for my paper."

Avery bit her lip. As much as Spencer tried to fit back into the mold of an innocent teenager, she'd grown into a woman with an insatiable, and frustratingly intellectual, curiosity about sex. "I'm feeling very aroused."

Spencer settled down next to Avery who automatically turned to face her. Spencer's gaze dropped from her eyes to her breasts faster than a meteor falling from the sky. Avery snorted. Maybe not completely intellectual, then.

Spencer reached out and cupped Avery's breast in her palm, her mouth slightly open and her eyes unfocused. Avery let her. She remembered her first time touching boobs and wasn't about to interrupt the sanctity of the moment.

"Wow," Spencer breathed, brushing Avery's nipple with her thumb and making everything south of her belly button tense in anticipation.

"They're pretty average."

Spencer shook her head. "They're perfect." She traced the curve of Avery's breast with a touch worthy of worship to the gods. Then, as if remembering herself, she looked up again. "Why did you get aroused? How? Can you explain it?"

Sure. No problem. Easy as two plus two. Avery closed her eyes and put her thoughts together, not an easy task with Spencer's hand still on her breast. "When you touch me, or kiss me, or tell me you like something I'm doing, I start to feel hot all over."

Spencer frowned, a tiny wrinkle between her brows. "Like actual sunburn?"

"No, it's on the inside, like my blood is heating."

"Does it feel good?" Spencer brushed a thumb over her nipple again, and Avery caught the whimper and held it back right before it escaped her lips.

"Yes. When you touch me, it feels like my skin is coming to life after a long hibernation. Tingly. I feel…"

"What?" Spencer asked, her voice nothing more than a whisper.

"A little weak," Avery murmured. "You turn my knees to jelly and all the blood rushes from my head, making it hard to think." Great. Could she be a little less honest next time? Weak? She was painting herself as a right little submissive. No wonder Spencer had her flat on her stomach. "I'm blushing, aren't I?"

Spencer grinned. "According to you, seventy-two percent of women blush."

"It's sexier on you."

"I could argue that point, but I'd be willing to let it go if you told me how your pussy feels right now."

"Jesus, fuck, Spencer." Avery pulled air into her lungs like she'd just run a marathon.

"No? Is that the wrong word? I only used it because it's what you used, before, when we were talking about me, and the textbooks say it's good to match vocabulary where you can, creates connection and empathy."

"It's not wrong. But the textbooks didn't tell you that it makes me wet to hear you say *pussy*."

Spencer's smile was shy. "Yeah? I'll send an email to the publisher. Demand a revision."

"Really wet. I've been wet all night."

"Since the kiss on the balcony?"

Avery brushed a strand of Spencer's hair from her face and tucked it behind her ear. "Since the moment you said hello."

"I—"

"What?" Avery asked, tracing a fingertip over the perfect shell of Spencer's ear.

"It's so scandalous. That word. *Pussy*."

"Do you think so?" Avery whispered and kissed her again because she'd never been able to resist Spencer's mind-blowing innocent sex goddess combo.

She ran her palms through Spencer's long straight hair, wrapping it around her hands over and over again, using her hold to angle Spencer's head for more, for deeper. She poured all her desire into a kiss that was at once both meditative and desperate. It was like coming home to the most exciting adventure of her life. Spencer made a sound in the back of her throat and Avery kissed her harder. She couldn't breathe but she didn't care. She wanted to find every thread of good girl Spencer had left and tug until she'd unraveled the amazing, sexy woman Spencer had become. Until Spencer opened for her, panting and sweaty and helpless with need. She curved her hands around Spencer's skull and held her, fighting the urge to move over her, to push faster, to take it all. Her body responded to Spencer's on an elemental level, instinct to instinct, and the sweet sounds she made when Avery kissed her were driving her over the edge.

"Please." Spencer gasped the word. Breathless, chest heaving. "Avery, I—"

"What, love?"

"Touch me."

God. There were only two words in the English language that mattered a damn and those were it.

"Lie back." Avery gently pressed Spencer's shoulders until she was flat on her back. She gathered her dress in a bunch until she could pull it up over Spencer's head, leaving her in nothing but pale aqua silk and the warm amber glow of the bedside lamp. Spencer instinctively moved to cover her stomach, and Avery caught her hands. Girls were always anxious about their waists, but Avery knew there was nothing sexier. She pressed Spencer's hands to the quilt, pinning them with her larger, stronger ones on top. "Don't cover up."

Spencer squirmed.

"You're stunning." Avery planted a kiss just below Spencer's rib cage, another under that and then another and another, long, slow kisses that would leave marks in the morning. She dipped her tongue into the indent of Spencer's navel and sucked. Spencer moaned, her eyes closing, her body going liquid under Avery's hold. Avery stroked her from collarbone to hipbone, unfastening her bra and cupping Spencer's small breasts, running her fingers over Spencer's nipples until they hardened and her hips started to rock.

"Tell me, Dr. Sex Brain, how does *your* pussy feel?" Avery asked in a voice less than steady, running short, blunt nails across Spencer's pelvis, watching as her back arched and her ass lifted off the bed.

Avery bent and licked a path along the edge of Spencer's panties. "Hmm?"

"I have no idea," Spencer said, keeping her eyes closed and gripping the quilt like it would save her. "What was the question?"

Avery bit down on the soft flesh under her tongue.

Spencer's eyes popped open at the same instant her knees fell apart.

Avery smirked, just a little. "How does your pussy feel, love? You'll want to remember it for your paper."

She ran a knuckle down the center of Spencer's silk panties.

"Oh my God."

"That's not an answer that will earn you an acceptance to

NYU." Avery pressed a little more firmly at Spencer's pussy, the wet heat of her arousal seeping through the silk to perfume the air. She imagined how easy it would be to slide a finger into her.

Spencer's first.

Spencer's only, if she had any say in it.

"I'm getting impatient," Avery said.

"Me too." Spencer moaned, slowly grinding her hips against Avery's knuckle. "It feels…" Spencer fell silent, her ragged breath the only sound in the room. "Hollow. Like I want it to be filled up. I'm so wet. I need you to touch me."

Avery's head began to pound, her vision to haze. Fuck. Fuck. Fuck.

"Please."

Something flipped inside her. One minute she was the slow, tender lover drawing out Spencer's pleasure like a five-course meal at a fancy hotel, and the next she wanted nothing more than to fuck her blind.

She dragged Spencer's panties down her hips, groaning at the soft patch of pale hair between Spencer's thighs. Fuck. So sexy. "Bend your knees, love. That's it, as much as you can." Avery slid her hands under Spencer's deliciously round ass and positioned her for pleasure.

"Look at me," Avery commanded. She knew Spencer had kept her eyes squeezed shut because all the new sensations were too overwhelming to take in all at once. But for this next part she required all of Spencer's senses. All she had to give, and then a little extra.

When Spencer opened her eyes, their gazes clashed, leaving Avery open and vulnerable. "Look at yourself. Look at what I'm about to do to you."

Spencer glanced down and the sound that fell from her lips was guttural. Avery lowered her head and pulled Spencer's ass toward her to fit her mouth over her pussy. Spencer watched her, thighs shaking as she licked every inch of Spencer's folds and pushed her tongue inside her. "Oh yes, yes." Spencer fell back. "Please, that's what I need. That."

"That's not what you need." Avery pushed up on an elbow and looked up at her. She'd flung an arm across her eyes and the quilt was bunched up around her. She was a mermaid shipwrecked on the sea of her passion. "Tell me you're ready, love. I need to hear you say it again."

Spencer groaned and sat back up, wriggling her hips for just a little more pressure. "I'm ready. Please. Go inside me."

Avery carefully slid two fingers slowly in. First to the knuckle, then to the next, then all the way inside. Spencer went ramrod stiff and still, so quiet Avery was worried she'd pass out. "Breathe, love, try to relax."

"I can't. I—Oh God." When Spencer opened her eyes, they were shiny with tears. Avery started to pull out, her heart dropping like an anchor. She'd pushed too hard, made Spencer cry. God, why did she always fuck it up?

Spencer grabbed at her wrist and held her in place. "Don't you dare move or I'll kill you and they'll never find your body."

"Love, you need a break, you need—"

"You," Spencer finished for her. "Please. Please fuck me."

Worry was a living thing in Avery's chest. "Are you sure?"

Tears streaked down Spencer's cheeks and into her ears, but her smile was like the sunrise. "The surest."

That was all she needed. Avery slid back inside her, out again, setting a slow rhythm, allowing Spencer to adjust to the feeling of being filled. It was Spencer who increased the tempo, whose chest flushed, who watched Avery's hand thrust inside her pussy with avid attention bordering on obsession. She was driving the train of her own pleasure and she didn't even know it.

Avery had asked Spencer to keep her eyes open, to watch her as she fucked her, but as Spencer grew even wetter and tighter around her she couldn't keep her own from closing. Being inside Spencer was the sexiest fucking thing she'd ever experienced. She was all slick softness and pulsing heat and the answering need in Avery's own pussy was overwhelming. She never, ever, wanted to stop fucking Spencer.

Spencer began to writhe on the bed, her head falling back and then side to side as she lost the battle against pleasure. Her hands released their purchase on the quilt and edged down toward her pussy. "Please. God. I need…"

"Stroke your clit."

Spencer jerked. "What?"

"You heard me. Let me see how my little sex therapist in training likes to touch herself."

Spencer's eyes went from cloudy passion to carnal lust. *Oh.* Her girl liked dirty talk. Avery filed away that piece of information for next time. Because there would damn well be plenty of next times.

"Do it, love, don't be shy."

Avery watched as Spencer slid a finger on either side of her clit and circled. Her long slender fingers worked her clit, setting a slow rhythm that had heat seeping out around Avery's fingers and turned her mind to mushy peas. All the blood rushed to Avery's clit and beat there like a drum.

Spencer groaned long and low. "I'm going to come."

Avery thrust just a bit harder, curling her fingers to hit the spot she knew would make Spencer explode. "Come for me, love."

Mine. Only. Forever. Always.

Spencer was so hot she felt electric, and when she came all over Avery's fingers, crying out her passion, Avery could barely hold off her own orgasm. She was no wide-eyed innocent, but all the wild nights she'd ever had in life were blown to smithereens by the feel of Spencer convulsing around her. Her name on Spencer's lips, her fingers inside Spencer's most private and intimate place.

Making love with Spencer was as blow her mind to mush sexy as she'd always imagined it would be.

And twice as dangerous for her heart.

If only she could find it within herself to care.

CHAPTER FOURTEEN

Truth and Dare

Spencer lay stretched out on the bed, completely nude and looking as lazy as a lizard in the afternoon sun. "If only we could bottle your sexual prowess, we'd make millions selling it to lonely women in need of mega orgasms."

"Would make a unique side hustle." Avery touched a fingertip to a streak of wetness still visible on Spencer's cheek. "You okay?"

Spencer grimaced. "Sorry about that."

"Nothing to be sorry for. I just hate to make girls cry when I'm aiming for screaming orgasm."

"Your aim was dead-on. It's just, a lot. Like there's all these feelings and sensations building up inside and they have nowhere to go. It was so intense."

Avery kissed her. Spencer was her addiction and she couldn't stop touching her. "You were lovely."

Spencer rolled her eyes. "Great. I was totally going for lovely, too. That's just what a woman wants to hear when her insides are upside down with lusty goodness. She's *lovely*."

"No?" Avery considered. "Beautiful?"

She looked slightly mollified.

"Gorgeous?"

A small smile.

"Make me almost lose it in my underwear, blow my brains out sexy, I can't fucking think straight, when can we do this again, goddess of all hotness?"

Spencer laughed. "That's better. I'll take that one, please."

"Sold." Avery pulled her in for another kiss. She liked their playful banter, but naked Spencer was tempting Spencer, and the taste she'd gotten just whetted her appetite for more.

The kiss was meant to be slow and gentle, a "thank you" and a "you're amazing" and an "I want you" wrapped in gentle lips and soft strokes. But as soon as Spencer's mouth opened to her, Avery couldn't help but let her hunger show. The kiss turned desperate and Avery drank her in, all spread out and gloriously naked. She curved her hands over Spencer's hips, guiding Spencer against her in an undulating motion that had her on the edge faster than a dart to a bull's-eye. The cotton of her underwear brushed against her aching clit, and she gritted her teeth. *Don't come, don't come, don't come.*

"I want to know your dirtiest fantasy. The one you've never told anyone." Spencer's breath was hot against her lips.

"I told you my fantasy." Avery had a flash of a mysterious woman making Spencer come, and desire stroked like a thousand warm hands down her belly.

Spencer shook her head, making her lips brush back and forth against Avery's. "Uh-uh. I want the dirty one. The one that makes you the hottest and gets you off the hardest."

Avery lifted her head an inch and looked down at her. "You know, for a woman who was a virgin twenty minutes ago, you're pretty damn sure of yourself. What makes you think I have a dirty fantasy? Maybe I'm a hopeless romantic who dreams of long walks on the beach and gentle missionary position lovemaking."

Spencer tilted her head slightly, pondering this. "You are that person, I think. You're softer than you let on. But everyone has a dirty fantasy."

That caught her attention. "What's yours?"

Spencer grinned. "Not telling unless you do."

"You drive a hard bargain, love."

"Pay up."

Avery rubbed a hand over her face. Fuck. Okay, yeah, so she had a dirty fantasy, but it wasn't so much that it was dirty, more like embarrassing. It was the kind of thing she shouldn't want, and that just made it ten times hotter. "I'm not sure this is the right moment. We should do this a few more times before I'll consider freaking you out."

Or freaking herself out.

"I'm not saying we're going to do it, but I'm not a china doll. You're not going to break me with the thoughts in your head. I want to know." Spencer kissed her with the lightest butterfly touch. "I want to know you. The real you. Not the mask you put on for everyone else."

Well, hell.

Avery lay back and stared at the ceiling. It was covered in glow in the dark sticker stars that a younger Spencer must have stuck up there to look at at night. It made her smile to see such a frivolous thing in a house that prided itself on its pretentiousness. "My fantasy is, well, it's kind of submissive. But not in a tie me up and flog me till I cry like a baby kind of way," Avery said in a rush.

"Nothing wrong with being tied up and flogged if that's your thing," said Spencer.

"I know. But it's not."

"Okay."

"My fantasy is more of a specific position, a specific thing. I think about being on my hands and knees and..." God, she couldn't say the rest.

Spencer slid a thigh over hers and snuggled in close. "And what?"

Avery closed her eyes and concentrated on the feel of Spencer against her. "And you're behind me. Touching me. Touching my behind." The words were barely a whisper.

Spencer's breath was fast and sharp beside her. The hand she'd rested on Avery's chest clenched. "God, Avery."

"I know, hardly studly of me."

"I think it's the hottest thing I've ever had in my head, and trust me, I've thought about you a lot, so getting to the top of that pile isn't easy."

Avery finally tore her gaze from the stars. "Really? You're not just being nice?"

Spencer snorted. "Nice isn't what I'm feeling right now."

"What are you feeling then?" Avery asked.

"Like I want to give you your dirtiest fantasy so you come hotter and harder than you have with any other woman, ever."

Was Spencer jealous? Possessive? Damn, if that didn't make happiness light up inside her like twinkle lights on a Christmas tree. Avery suspected all Spencer would need to do was brush a fingertip over her clit to achieve her aim, but kept the thought to herself. No need to let on just how easy she was.

"It's a bit like throwing a baby elephant into the ocean, though. Maybe we should start slower. Simpler. There are so many shades of in between." And she wanted to show Spencer each and every one of them.

"Did you just call me an elephant?"

Avery paused, thought through her last comment, and winced. "A very sexy, very slender, little elephant."

Spencer's lip wobbled, and then she burst out laughing. "You're an idiot. But seriously, I want to try this. I can't promise I'll be fantastic at it, but I'd really like to give it a go. Please, please, please?"

Spencer begging to give her her most taboo fantasy? Avery had entered an alternate universe where chocolate was free and dreams came true. "If you're sure. And if you promise me you'll say something if you're uncomfortable."

"Yes. Totally. Definitely."

How could she possibly resist?

"Come here." Avery pulled Spencer on top of her. "I love you" was on the tip of her tongue, but she didn't say it. Spencer knew how she felt, and Avery wasn't going to pressure her, even if everything inside her ached for those three little words.

Spencer opened her mouth like she was going to say something, but then wriggled away. "You're not distracting me with sexy kisses or the feel of your amazing body against mine."

"Are you distractible?" Avery kissed her, brushed her breasts against Spencer's. Everything inside her churned in anticipation.

"Completely. But I'm on a mission. Roll over."

Avery hesitated. God, it was ridiculous. She wanted this. Spencer knew she wanted this, and somehow, she still couldn't bring herself to go for it.

Spencer pushed hard against her shoulder until she flipped over. "Don't think you can just dangle the sexiest thing I've ever heard in my life in front of me and then just take it away."

The sexiest thing I've ever heard in my life. Avery looked over her shoulder and for the first time saw past the blinders of her own embarrassment. Spencer was breathing fast, her eyes sparkling, her posture determined. Was it possible she wanted this as much as Avery? She tucked her thumbs into the waistband of her underwear and tugged them down and off, exposing herself to Spencer's gaze. Before she could talk herself out of it, she rose to her hands and knees. Her heart was beating so loudly she was surprised she didn't burst an eardrum.

Spencer's soft small hands curved around her hips and then swept over her ass. *Fuuuuck.*

"You have a rather elegant behind, did you know that? Such sensual curves." Spencer's hands glided down her ass and all the way to her inner thighs, bypassing her pussy that was so wet it was basically rolling out a red carpet.

"Glad you think so." She hoped Spencer didn't expect her to talk the whole time because she was pretty sure words were going to be beyond her in another minute or two.

"But," Spencer said mildly, "there's just one thing I need."

"Hmm?" Avery had her eyes closed, every cell in her body focused on the way Spencer was running her palms up and down. Up and down.

When Spencer moved to her shoulders, she was momentarily confused, but as Spencer guided her head and shoulders down so her back sloped toward the bed, need hit her like a punch to the solar plexus. If Spencer didn't touch her very, very soon, she was going to come all over herself like a teenage boy at the all night sexiplex.

Spencer dipped a hand between her thighs and swiped fingers over her folds. "Spencer," Avery said on a gasp.

"Patience, patience," Spencer said.

With fingers wet with Avery's juices, Spencer found her back entrance and stroked lightly. She clenched and ached at the same time. "Oh God."

"Relax," Spencer murmured, "let's see how good this can feel."

She couldn't possibly relax, not with Spencer's fingers tracing those maddening circles and her pussy dripping need down her thighs.

"Touch yourself," Spencer said.

Avery followed her instruction, sliding a hand down and pressing her fingers to her clit. *Oh God, oh God, oh God.* She fought to ignore Spencer's ministrations and put all her focus on relaxing her body and the pleasure fanning out in waves from her clit. She breathed deeply in and out. She'd imagined Spencer touching her here countless times, but fantasy was a pale imitation of the mind-blowingly sexy and forbidden reality. Sensation whipped through her, weakening every muscle. If Avery hadn't already been on her knees she'd have dropped as all her insides liquefied.

"Does it feel good?" Spencer asked, pressing more firmly against her.

"Yes." Avery's voice didn't sound like her own, higher pitched and laced with longing. "You can go inside if you want to." God, she hoped Spencer wanted to.

When Spencer slipped past the last of her resistance and slid a finger in, the slight discomfort was quickly obliterated by the singularly erotic sensation of being filled. Her back arched and she was falling, falling, falling. It was all too much. Too good. "My love."

"You're driving me out of my mind," Spencer said softly. "I could come just from looking at you like this."

Avery pressed the flat of her palm against her pussy, afraid she'd go over too soon.

"Look how gorgeous you are, your fingers working your pussy while mine are in your ass. Can I move inside you?"

"Yes." Later, she'd be embarrassed that Spencer was so naturally good at dirty talk and all she'd managed was two yeses between clenched teeth. But later could wait. Right now, Spencer was moving inside her and it was all she could do to breathe.

Spencer slid out to the fingertip and added a second finger. "You feel so good. Warm and slick."

Avery's toes curled and she went completely boneless. There was no way she'd be able to stop the freight train of her orgasm now. "Please, love. Please."

"Mmm." Spencer kissed around her fingers, swirling her tongue along Avery's cleft in a way that had her on the brink of toppling over into oblivion from which she never wanted to return. "I'm definitely going to need to try this, if it feels half as hot as it looks."

"God." Avery's voice was sandpaper. Images of Spencer's delicious little ass in the air and Avery pumping inside her danced in her head. "You're killing me."

She'd never expected Spencer to use her tongue, couldn't fathom ever asking, but it was exactly what she'd fantasized about. How Spencer saw beneath all her social graces and emotional reserves was a puzzle she'd never solve.

"Well, we'd better make you come nice so at least you'll go out in style." Spencer buried the fingers of her other hand in Avery's pussy in a long, deep thrust.

It was at once too much and everything. Avery came in a rush, breaking apart and coming together, pleasure shooting through her like fireworks on the Fourth of July and stealing all the breath from her lungs, leaving her gasping.

"You're not done." Spencer kept riding the wave with her, not stilling the thrust of her fingers. "Come for me again."

She fought for air, didn't think she had anything left, but the feel of Spencer inside her was so good she just held on. In a matter of minutes, she could feel the pressure rising again, like a current pulling against the waves and washing the tide to shore. Then Spencer blew her mind to pieces by pressing her very wet pussy against the back of her thigh and sliding against her.

"Oh. Jesus. Fuck. Yes." Avery was deaf and blind, focused only on the waves rising within her and the heat of Spencer's pussy.

"I want to come," Spencer panted. "Come with me."

Spencer was all over Avery, fingers losing their purchase as she was overcome with her own desire, but it didn't matter. Their skin collided and Avery's control snapped clean in two. She came with a ferocity that made her ears ring, screaming into her hand in a way she'd never screamed before as Spencer moaned and shuddered her own release behind her. It was guttural and primal and her jaw ached from trying to keep quiet.

Everything about the next moments was perfection. The way she collapsed like a house of cards against the quilt, and Spencer collapsed on top of her, the sweat on her skin, the soft words Spencer murmured into her hair. It was all exactly everything she'd ever hoped for and so much more than she'd ever imagined.

"Well, I think I can safely say I no longer feel quite so guilty about kissing you," Avery said sleepily.

Spencer rolled off her and glanced around. "How did we end up diagonal across the bed with the quilt almost on the floor?"

Avery lifted her head for a second before letting it thunk back down again, too exhausted in the happily sated way of amazing sex to move. "Guess we were a bit rowdy. We might have broken the bed."

Spencer snorted. "It would have been worth it if we did."

Avery rolled over, feeling as graceful as a hippo in mud. And there was Spencer, looking thoroughly ravished and more beautiful than Avery had ever seen her. "I love you."

Damn.

She hadn't meant to say that. Not again. But the moment was ripe for the truth. She'd never stopped loving Spencer, and she was sure she never would. Even if, after tonight, Spencer decided she didn't want to see her again, she'd take Avery's heart with her. It belonged to her whether she wanted it or not. Avery had handed it to her with a no refund policy that day in the pool house. She braced herself for Spencer to tell her she wasn't ready yet, hoping only that Spencer was willing to see where this thing lead them.

Spencer rolled against her with enough force to send Avery onto her back with Spencer on top of her. Spencer's long hair fell around them like a sensual curtain. "I know," Spencer said against her lips. "I love you too."

"It's okay, I understand—wait, what?" Avery shoved up, taking Spencer with her and almost toppling them in an ungraceful heap. *Smooth.* "You what?"

Spencer laughed, her eyes bright. "I love you."

Avery shook her head slowly. "You can't. I mean, you never did. You don't."

"But I do." Spencer kissed her, vibrating a little, almost giddy. "Avery, I love you. I think I knew I loved you the minute I saw you with stupid Daniella and wanted to shoot her. But tonight, the way you touched me. The way you trusted me. I knew. I love you." Spencer rained a thousand tiny kisses all over her face.

"You love me." Even as she said them, the words didn't seem real.

"I." She kissed the space between her brows.

"Love." She kissed the tip of her nose.

"You." Spencer kissed her mouth.

It was that kiss that did it. Spencer had kissed her countless times that night. Shyly. Eagerly. Passionately. Kisses fraught with need and soaked in desire. But this kiss was altogether different. It wrapped around Avery like the warmest hug. Sure and steady, confident and tender, the kiss was a promise of all the kisses to come.

A forever kiss.

"God. I fucking love you." Avery cupped her face and kissed her again.

"I know. You were always soft on me, you big sap." Spencer smiled in a way that made her feel like a million bucks. "Don't ever stop, okay?"

"Forever, love." Avery wrapped her arms around Spencer and drew her back down between the sheets.

Forever wouldn't be long enough for either of them.

KAITLYN

Chapter Fifteen

Anyone But You

Forget the zombie apocalypse. She'd be better off gathering doomsday provisions and heading for the hills. Either way, disaster was imminent.

If she was going to die, Kaitlyn Forrester guessed she wouldn't end up zombie breakfast, or even the victim of a global warming induced natural disaster. No, nothing like that. Nothing that would go viral on YouTube, or get her friends on *Ellen* reminiscing about how brave she was. Her heart would simply take off its battle armor, shake its head, and give up the good fight. "Sorry, hun," it would say, in a drawling Midwestern accent that somehow wouldn't surprise her at all. "I did everything I could. Better luck in the next life and all that." And before Kaitlyn took her last breath, she'd nod solemnly and thank her heart for doing its best by her, because there were only so many battles you could fight, weren't there?

Kaitlyn smiled her I'm-at-a-social-function-and-can't-run-away-from-you smile. She'd noticed Chelsey Thomas within minutes of entering the ballroom, and it had taken her almost two hours, two glasses of top-notch pinot grigio, and some sneaky reconnaissance to make sure Chelsey was attracted to the fairer sex before she'd gathered the courage to talk to her.

A minute and a half later, ninety-seven seconds to be exact, she'd realized her mistake. In that time, her white picket fence fantasy woman had turned into the perfect candidate for cognitive behavioral therapy.

"I just don't know what happened," Chelsey was saying, her voice shrill as she spoke to be heard over the people milling too close around them. "One minute we're talking about adopting a puppy together and the next she's kissing someone else like she doesn't even know me."

Kaitlyn squeezed Chelsey's hand. "I'm really sorry. You seem like a good person who didn't deserve that." Not that Kaitlyn really knew if she was a good person or not. If rich brown eyes and shoulders broad enough to fill out the man's shirt she had on made a person *good*, then Chelsey was a candidate for sainthood. Aside from that, Kaitlyn really had no clue, and it looked like she wasn't going to find out any time soon.

"I know, right? She doesn't deserve me." Chelsey sniffed, tears welling. "Sorry for just dumping all of this on you. You're so easy to talk to."

Oh God, don't cry. Kaitlyn hated herself for being one of those people who went panicky when a woman cried, but honestly, they'd only just met. What was she supposed to do? She hoped her smile hadn't reached grimace territory. Talking to sexy, dark-haired, gym-buff women was on the admittedly fairly lengthy list of things that freaked her out, but she'd tried to put herself out there, hadn't she? She'd talked to someone new, someone not connected to work, someone she wouldn't necessarily object to seeing naked. And how did the universe repay her? With a sob story and a *you're so easy to talk to*. Nothing said friend-zoned like a good ol' gal pal heart-to-heart. All they needed now was ice cream and a chick flick.

"I'm sure you'll find the right one soon." Kaitlyn patted her hand before letting it go. *But not me.* Even if Chelsey had been looking for love tonight, Kaitlyn wasn't going to be anyone's rebound, thank you very much. She'd wait for the real deal. Manhattan was full of sidepieces and good-timers. She'd seen how that ended up and wanted nothing to do with it.

Chelsey's phone buzzed in her pocket and she pulled it out. "Sorry, I'm not on call, but…" She read the text message and sighed. "I'll be right back."

As Chelsey headed toward the doors, Kaitlyn felt her fake

smile droop. Having all her carefully nurtured hopes dashed faster than you could say *not over her ex* sucked, but standing alone in the corner watching happy drunk people get happier and drunker was worse. She started for the bar. Screw it. If you can't beat 'em, join 'em.

Midway between her spot in the corner and the sanctuary of the place where the alcohol lived, Kaitlyn spotted a familiar face. Tara, the treasurer of her charity, Forrester Fund, was standing just outside a group of businessmen and looked about as bored as Kaitlyn felt. She beelined for her. "Hey, you. Charming all the bizillionaires, hoping to strike it rich?"

Tara gave her a quick hug and rolled her eyes. "As if. I mean, if Zuckerberg wanted to sweep me off my feet, maybe I'd give him half an hour. But these guys?" She gestured subtly to the suits. "They're my dad's age and not nearly as interesting."

Wasn't that the truth.

Kaitlyn had hired Tara for her accounting superpowers, but they'd become friends because Tara was one of the few people in Manhattan who said it like it was. She was thirty-two and wasn't about to give it up to some pushing-sixty, silver fox wannabe just for the chance at an all you can shop Chanel buffet.

"Oh!" Tara said, as if the cure for cancer had just popped fully formed into her head. "I almost forgot to tell you. I've found you the perfect woman."

Kaitlyn held back the *dear God no*. It was her own fault. She was the one who, in a moment of extreme weakness, too many Hershey's Kisses on a Friday afternoon, sugar-induced semi-coma, had told Tara she wanted to find someone. Someone for something serious. She'd presented this as if she was making that choice from the mature and honorable standpoint of an adult looking to settle down, and not because dating was about as scary as seeing *Texas Chainsaw Massacre* for the first time. All that small talk and feigning interest in corporate finance, or mountain biking, or Vishnu yoga. No. If she had to do it, she'd find the right one and stick to them like glue. "Oh? Who is it?" Kaitlyn asked, nodding to the business card Tara was holding.

Tara craned her neck to look over Kaitlyn's head. "I can't see where she went off to, but Mark Henderson has just hired her as an associate at Henderson, Cooper, and Goff. I was talking to her about some pro bono work for the Fund. She seemed interested."

So was Kaitlyn. She could afford to pay for legal counsel, and often did, but she'd prefer every cent of the money her mother had routed to Forrester Fund go to those who really needed it, and not overhead. Mark was no sucker. If he'd hired this woman, she must be exceptional. "Yeah? What kind of law?"

"Tax mostly, but she has experience with nonprofits."

Kaitlyn laughed. "That must've made your night. You sure she's not perfect for *you*?"

Tara gave up craning. "If I played for your team, I'd definitely want an all night primer on 501(c) regulations."

"That hot, huh?"

"Oh yeah. Like, did we just teleport to a sauna, because I'm flushed and sweaty level sexy, but nice too."

"Nice, how?" Kaitlyn asked. Nice was good. Nice was safe, comforting, reliable. Nice sounded pretty damn amazing actually, and the hot part didn't hurt either.

"Well, she listened to me when I talked, asked interesting questions, and only glanced at my rack once," Tara said.

"Only once?" Kaitlyn sighed in mock disappointment. "Maybe she's not interested in women then."

"A possibility, but she has that Rachel Maddow vibe, only blonder. She's really smart, in a totally sexy way. I hate to stereotype, but I'm calling lesbian on this one. You should definitely meet her."

"Hmm. I don't know." The last thing she needed was to embarrass herself by coming on to someone who could help them as legal counsel.

"Kaitlyn," Tara said in a tone that reeked of this is for your own good, "you need to put yourself out there. Have some fun. Maybe even get laid." She shoved the business card at Kaitlyn and, not expecting it, Kaitlyn watched it flutter to the floor.

She scoffed and bent down to pick it up. "What do I need to

get laid for when I have a perfectly good vibrator in my top drawer? Better and faster than any woman I've ever been with, if I'm honest."

She expected a witty retort. Maybe a "but slow is so much better" or even a "why not both?" but the silence had her pausing, bent at the knees.

"Hello again. Hope I'm not interrupting," said a warm voice above her.

Oh.

Hell.

No.

She rose on jelly legs to see Tara biting her lip, her eyes sparkling in a way that promised she was three seconds from bursting out laughing. Kaitlyn felt her face flush. Tara's sauna analogy wasn't far off the mark. That voice definitely had her sweaty, but what Tara didn't know was that she'd heard it before. By now it was more of a memory wrapped in nostalgia, but there was no mistaking it.

She took a deep breath and swung to face the newcomer.

"Hi, Kait, it's good to see you."

It would be petty to just walk away, right? To leave Becca standing in her dust while she stormed out. Or maybe it would be *empowering*. She'd be an example to all the women everywhere who'd had their hopes and dreams crushed, and yet were forced to make ridiculous small talk with their archenemies because it was polite.

"You too." Since she was a bigger person, hell, a *better person* than Becca, she wouldn't make a scene, but that didn't mean she couldn't use as few words as possible.

"I go by Beck now," she said. "You haven't changed, still as beautiful as ever."

Kaitlyn glared. Where did Becca get off calling her beautiful? And for that matter, where did she get off changing her name?

"You two know each other?" Tara asked tentatively, a natural cheerleader in the unfortunate position of refereeing a boxing match.

"We dated a bit in high school." Beck's smile was easy, as if the hostility currently setting Kaitlyn's hair on end completely bypassed her.

"We didn't *date a bit.*" Kaitlyn hated people who said things in air quotes, but found herself doing just that. She knew she sounded like a stuck-up librarian correcting someone's grammar, but couldn't help it. Date a bit? Seriously? Way to make her seem small and insignificant. Why was Becca, sorry, *Beck*, even here? Was she back, or just in town to see family, and why had she come over to talk to her? To rub it in? To make her feel insecure? To stir up old resentments for her own amusement? "We had a relationship. We loved each other."

Like any of that mattered now. Loved was a word saddened by past tense.

Beck inclined her head. "We did."

"Oh." Tara looked back and forth between them like a spectator at a tennis match. "Um, wow."

They stared at each other. The awkwardness like a fourth person in the conversation. Beck hadn't changed much either. Same sandy hair that looked like the wind had picked it up and tossed it around, same buttery brown eyes that reminded Kaitlyn of toasted croissants and lazy Sunday mornings. Her mouth curved when she smiled, just the way Kaitlyn remembered. Beck had grown up of course, a suit now instead of jeans, a Rolex where her Timex had been. Some muscle to even out a frame that used to look lanky. Smart. Successful. Hot.

No. Not hot. Not even in the same...oh who was she kidding? Beck Delmar was hotter than Utah in July, damn her. She'd been forget-your-own-name sexy when they'd started dating at sixteen, and the not quite a decade between then and now had only honed her appeal. Kaitlyn firmly pushed aside the urge to strip naked in front of her. She wasn't as successful in ignoring the flood of warmth that settled between her legs, and she cursed her stupid, traitorous body. Thank God they were in a public place and she couldn't get away with it, because she was pretty sure the stripping urge would win and the last thing she wanted was to humiliate herself in front of Beck. Again.

What *was* it about Beck anyway? Kaitlyn was a grown woman, and she didn't go around weak at the knees and damp in the panties for every attractive female. For *any* attractive woman. Except this one. The one that got away. The one she'd thought would be her only. The one that dumped her ass and left town without looking back. Kaitlyn hated her. She really, really wanted to be fantasizing about ripping Beck's eyes out of their sockets and feeding her intestines through a meat grinder. But was Kaitlyn allowed a perfectly acceptable under the circumstances homicidal fantasy? Oh no. Her body had to go all soft and melty, and her heart was beating too damn fast for her to think straight anyway. It wasn't fair.

"So," Tara said, a little too brightly. "Beck's the attorney I was just telling you about. I'd love to set something up, Beck, to tell you a little more about how Forrester Fund operates, see if we can work together."

No. No. No. No. The last thing Kaitlyn needed was her high school heartbreak showing up at the office looking all *GQ* magazine gorgeous and offering her services for free out of the goodness of her heart. Beck's heart wasn't good. She'd sold it in advance for the opportunity to clerk at the Supreme Court a year out of law school. She'd had it all planned out. Step one, top of her class at Harvard Law. Step two, clerkship at the Supreme Court. Step three, fast track to partner at the best law firm in DC. Step four, political career. Beck was hard-nosed, uncompromising, ambitious to a fault, and only in it for the win. Those might be good traits in a lawyer, but she didn't want this woman anywhere near her charity or the vulnerable people they served. Someone like Beck would squish them like bugs. Just as she'd squished Kaitlyn. She wasn't about to let some ridiculous biological reaction get in the way of her common sense. Beck might have rocked her world once upon a time, but she'd walked away and left Kaitlyn behind.

"Sounds like a plan. I'd be happy to help out Forrester Fund, and I know Mark has been looking to increase his profile with some good press. We could—"

"Of course," Kaitlyn interrupted. "The good press you'll get from being a savior to the downtrodden. You wouldn't want to practice law to actually help people, not when all those non-billable hours can earn you a few worthy sound bites. Think of all the brownie points you'll score with your boss, because we both know that's all that really matters to you."

Tara's mouth dropped open while Beck's pressed together in a firm line. Kaitlyn knew she shouldn't have said that, and she was making an ass of herself, but she didn't care. They weren't going to be working together. She'd pay for a lawyer from her personal bank account before she hired Beck to so much as clean the office floor.

Beck wasn't coming near her charity, her life, her heart. No way.

"We won't be needing your services," Kaitlyn said as crisply as she could manage. "Thanks anyway." But she desperately needed the services of a good psychiatrist. Someone who could tell her exactly how she could loathe Beck and want her, all in the same confusing breath. Someone who could explain to her why Beck had to look so good in her sky-blue button-down and navy pants. Even her silver edged wingtips were sexy. Kaitlyn needed to pull herself together. Stop thinking about Beck's clothes. Thinking about her clothes was a slippery slope away from thinking about her naked, and if she did that, she might actually start begging.

"Kait," Beck said, "if this is about what happened between us, don't let the past keep us from a mutually beneficial arrangement."

"Of course it's not about that," Kaitlyn said. "That was just a few dates, remember?"

"I was hoping to downplay our prior relationship status to save my dignity, considering your vibrator appears to be more talented than I was." Beck smiled, but it didn't reach her eyes. Her eyes were all you've-got-to-be-kidding-me-with-this-shit.

She was pissed and that made Kaitlyn smile. "Well, you were young. I'm sure you've improved."

Tara's cough sounded a lot like a snort, and she studied the champagne glass in her hand with intense concentration. "You know, this one's warm. I'm going to go to the bar for a refill. I plan to get very lost on the way back." She kissed Kaitlyn on the cheek and whispered, "Told you she was your type," then sped away in a swirl of blush colored chiffon.

"Was that really necessary?"

Beck's words were so clipped Kaitlyn was surprised they resembled English. Yup. Definitely pissed. Suddenly a lot more cheerful, Kaitlyn shrugged and sipped from her glass. "I'm sorry, did I say something wrong?"

"Your vibrator is not better than me."

"How do you know?" Kaitlyn kept her tone light and easy.

Beck opened her mouth, then closed it again. The faintest hint of red crept up her neck. "I seem to remember you were pretty satisfied."

"Hmm." Kaitlyn drained her glass and twirled the flute around her fingers like a baton. "I was pretty satisfied. But it doesn't take much when you're seventeen, does it? These days *pretty satisfied* doesn't really do it for me." If Beck thought she could just waltz back into her life, just show up like nothing had ever happened, she had another think coming. Kaitlyn considered herself a nice person. On a good day she'd even go so far as to say she was a kind person. But a woman scorned was a woman you didn't want to mess with, and boy, had she been scorned. Beck never should've come back, and if she had to, she should've stayed the hell away from her. Luckily, she knew Beck's weakness as well as the back of her own hand. It was one they shared. The one thing that busted promises and broken hearts didn't appear to have diminished.

Kaitlyn stepped so close that if she breathed deeply her breasts would brush Beck's shirt. She could smell the citrus of her shampoo, and for a second, she almost lost her nerve. She loved that scent. The desire that had been simmering in her belly since the moment she'd heard Beck's voice sparked again, and her inner thermostat kicked up a notch. Her nerve endings hummed in anticipation. She told herself to forget about it. She couldn't let Beck see how turned on she was. But that didn't mean she couldn't make Beck want her just as much. She'd learned a thing or two since the last time they'd seen each other, and the situation was ripe for a little revenge.

"My vibrator is called the Reducer. As in, reduce you to a wet mess of need." She lowered her voice and spoke so her breath washed against Beck's neck. "It feels so good to have it against my clit. Working me just the way I need it. Did you know I think about my new neighbor in the apartment downstairs? She's a mechanic. In a relationship with some tech guru someone or other, but that hardly matters. She comes into the building with grease on her hands every afternoon, and it turns me on so bad I have to race up to my apartment and start up the Reducer. I fantasize about how talented she must be with those fingers. There's something about manual labor that's just sexy as hell, don't you think?"

Kaitlyn spoke until she could all but see Beck's pulse race against her throat, barely an inch from Kaitlyn's lips. She wasn't going to look at Beck's face. If she met her eyes she was afraid she'd kiss her. Just grab Beck's face and plant one on her right there, and not stop until they were both hauled out for too much PDA. That would never do. Her own racing heart and trembling knees were as inconsequential as they were inconvenient.

She watched Beck swallow. "She could satisfy me, I bet. The Reducer sure does." Kaitlyn stepped back, and without looking at Beck, turned away and started walking. She took three steps in the opposite direction, enough for a little breathing room, before she stopped and tossed over her shoulder, "But you?" Kaitlyn made a show of looking her up and down slowly. Assessing her like a piece of livestock presented at auction. "You were pretty satisfying at seventeen, but I've had better."

She walked away. Away from a past that hurt too much to remember. Away from the game she'd just played, the gauntlet she'd just thrown, and the lies she'd made herself believe. Beck had been her everything once. Her first kiss. Her first orgasm. Her first broken heart. Kaitlyn slammed the door shut on all of it. It wasn't relevant, and she'd gotten over it a long time ago.

The bright lights and bustling streets of Manhattan were where some dreams came true, and others were shattered. Kaitlyn Forrester's dreams had been made to be broken, and Beck Delmar had done the breaking.

CHAPTER SIXTEEN

Faking It

The only downside of verbally seducing your ex-girlfriend, getting in the last word, then storming off, was that Kaitlyn wasn't sure where to actually storm. She couldn't leave, at least not without Sarah and Avery, and both had mysteriously disappeared after they'd come inside from the balcony. The way Sarah had looked at that chef Ryan, Kaitlyn would lay odds they were tucked up in a corner somewhere making out. And speaking of making out, Avery had kissed Spencer again. They'd headed inside arm in arm and were now incommunicado. It didn't take a genius to figure out where they'd gone and what they were doing.

Kaitlyn wanted to find the nearest wall and slide down it until the cleaning crew scraped her up sometime after two a.m. She was glad for her friends, and if this had been a regular party on an ordinary night, she'd have toasted their success and not given her own lackluster love life more than a passing thought. But this wasn't an ordinary party. Beck had hijacked her good time, and now all she wanted to do was go home and worry over why Beck was here, and why Beck had made a point to talk to her, and why Beck had said they'd only had a few dates. She'd happily spin those questions around and around in her mind, the answers growing more and more ludicrous until finally, exhausted by it all, she'd collapse on her bed in her dressing gown and fuzzy slippers and not get up again for three days. She wanted to obsess and bitch and wallow, and none of those things were half as much fun without her friends.

"Oh, thank God." Eleanor came rushing up to her, risking a broken neck in her high heels. "You have to save me."

Not the blonde she was looking for, but an Eleanor shaped distraction would do just fine in a pinch. Kaitlyn rested her hands lightly on Eleanor's bare shoulders to slow her down so she didn't end up on the floor. "Whoa. What's wrong?"

"It's Sarah. She's insane. She wants me to kiss her girlfriend." Eleanor's eyes were just a little wild, and her hair was fast falling out of its chignon. It was a good look on her.

"She *what?*" Of the three of them, Sarah had always been the go-getter, the overachiever, the one who had big plans and bigger dreams. She made stuff happen. But asking Eleanor to kiss her girlfriend was crazy. Why? The Sarah/Eleanor hate-fest was entrenched. Did Sarah even have a girlfriend now? Had her relationship status changed in a couple of hours? That didn't seem like her either. Whatever was going on tonight, Kaitlyn had missed it all.

Eleanor shook her head. "Please. You have to come with me. Talk some sense into her."

"Well, okay." Kaitlyn had no idea what was going on, but at least Eleanor knew where Sarah was, and with Sarah, she'd be halfway to her goal of getting the hell home.

Eleanor led her through the crowd. They were forced to stop every ten feet to make small talk and thank guests for birthday wishes. Kaitlyn had done just this dance so many times she could compliment a woman's shoes, shake hands with her husband, and rave over how tasty the menu had been without engaging more than three or four brain cells. Ten minutes later, they'd escaped out the ballroom doors and Eleanor led the way to a tiny parlor tucked into the side of the entrance hall. Inside, Kaitlyn found Sarah, Ryan, and seventy million wraps, sweaters, and scarves all hanging from rolling clothing racks like a tasteful fabric army.

Sarah rolled her eyes. "You didn't have to bring in reinforcements. Kaitlyn's not going to save you. She's on my side."

Eleanor turned to Kaitlyn. "See? She's insane. I told you."

Kaitlyn looked from Sarah, who was standing in the middle of the room with her hands on her hips, to Ryan, who was grinning from ear to ear while resting a hip on a table that held a handful of beautifully wrapped presents, and back to Eleanor, who was now wringing her hands like someone's maiden aunt Martha. Kaitlyn let out the breath she'd been holding. There was no blood and no fire, so the crisis level could be considered medium at best.

"Anyone care to fill me in?" she asked.

"Sarah wants to get her rocks off watching me make out with Ryan," Eleanor said.

"Oh, I do not," said Sarah. "Why do you always have to be so dramatic?"

Eleanor folded her arms across her chest.

Apparently, Sarah and Eleanor seemed to think this explained the situation, but Kaitlyn's head was spinning. She looked to Ryan as the only other sane force in the room. "Huh?"

Ryan's smile got even wider. "Sarah's had a brainwave on how to get back at Peter. The plan, more or less, is to orchestrate Peter walking in on Eleanor and me kissing, and then have Eleanor break up with him."

"Seriously?" Kaitlyn couldn't help the incredulity. She turned back to Sarah. "Don't you think that's a bit juvenile?"

Sarah grinned too. "Of course it is. But more juvenile than fucking some loser in a bar?"

She had a point.

"Why can't Eleanor just break it off? What does the fake kissing accomplish?" Kaitlyn asked.

"Aside from floating Sarah's boat?" Eleanor said. "I have no idea."

Sarah sighed. "For the last time, Eleanor, I'm not doing this to watch. You're really not my type."

Eleanor raised her eyebrows. "You said I was sexy."

"I said you could *do* sexy, and that's me giving you the benefit of the doubt frankly, because the stick up your ass must make it difficult to keep your legs open long enough."

"Sarah!" Kaitlyn and Ryan said in unison.

Eleanor narrowed her eyes and got up in Sarah's face. "You don't think I can do it, do you?"

Sarah shrugged. "I think you're an uptight little princess if that's what you're asking."

"Screw you."

"I'd rather watch Ryan do that and get my boat all floaty." Sarah smirked.

Kaitlyn could feel a headache coming on and pinched the bridge of her nose. This whole idea was ridiculous. Someone had to inject some rationality, and it looked like she was the only one for the job. "It's not going to work," she said. "Kissing isn't the same thing as having sex. As revenge goes, it's weak."

Sarah frowned and turned to Ryan. "You think you should fuck her instead? I'm not sure how I feel about that."

Eleanor gasped.

"I think that might be above and beyond, baby. Plus, well, Eleanor is as pretty as they come, but I've known her since I was five years old, and it would just be weird," Ryan said.

"*Thank you*," Eleanor said.

"You know," Kaitlyn said, not quite believing she was actually getting caught up in this silliness, "kissing isn't enough. But the three of you..." She let the thought hang as she used all her willpower not to picture what she was suggesting. Too weird. Just too, too weird.

Ryan nodded slowly. "That's an idea. Not sex. But if Peter walked in on the three of us together, and we made it look like we were seconds from an impromptu raunchy lesbian sex party, I'd say that's about on par with public bar shenanigans."

Eleanor's mouth dropped open. "You can't be serious."

"It's not all that different from the kissing idea, we'll just need to loosen some clothes and up our acting. You can't deny it would throw Peter for a loop," Ryan said.

"It would," Eleanor said. "He hates Sarah almost as much as I do. *Did*," she amended quickly. "Almost as much as I did."

"Why?" Ryan asked.

"Sarah called him a spineless little fucker," Eleanor said. "I think he must've been hitting on her. Wouldn't surprise me. He has a thing for blondes."

Kaitlyn and Ryan looked over at Sarah, who'd been suspiciously quiet on this new idea. Ryan jumped up and joined her so the three of them were standing in a tight circle with Kaitlyn on the outside. "Hey, what's wrong?"

"I can't do it," Sarah said. "I'm sorry."

They had a plan that might actually work, one that Sarah herself had instigated, and now she couldn't do it? Kaitlyn groaned.

"Do you hate me that much?" Eleanor asked, doing a decent job of covering the tremble in her voice.

Sarah leaned against Ryan and dropped her head on Ryan's shoulder. "I only hate you about fifteen percent of my usual amount. I just can't be caught in an almost sex party compromising position because Reginald owns my ass. If he gets wind of this and is pissed I fake-kissed his very real daughter, it would cause a lot of trouble for me. I could lose Cakewalk, and hell if I'm going to let you stomp on my dream a second time."

"I didn't think of that," Kaitlyn said. Sarah was right. This little scenario might put Eleanor on even ground when it came to confronting Peter, but not at the cost of Sarah's career.

"Your job too," Sarah said, squeezing Ryan's hand. "Most of your clients come via the McGregors, right? I'm sorry I didn't think of that before."

"Yeah." Ryan didn't look at all happy now. "Damn."

"For someone who's allegedly so smart, you should really work on getting over yourself," Eleanor said.

Sarah blinked. "What?"

"You heard me. Do you really think Dad would break up a business deal because you helped me out? That he'd stop sending Ryan clients because you did his daughter a favor?"

"It's hardly going to look like we're doing you a solid when he hears about us in a tangle. He'll think less of me," Sarah said.

The indignation drained from Eleanor faster than water from a bathtub, and underneath it she was pale. "He'll think less of you if he believes you kissed me?"

Sarah closed her eyes briefly. "God, Eleanor. No. He'll think less of me for treating you like the star of a do-it-yourself porno. When he hears about his business partner having an almost-threesome, in the freaking coat closet, with his daughter, do you really think that will go over well?"

Eleanor's phone pinged in the clutch she'd left on the table by the door, but they all ignored it.

"Oh, I see." Eleanor took a step back. "You think I wouldn't explain the situation. That I wouldn't tell him the truth."

"Come on," Ryan said. "You're really going to tell your father the four of us concocted a plan to get revenge on Peter by setting him up to walk in on us faking it?"

Eleanor shrugged. "Why wouldn't I?"

Sarah glared. "Because you'd have to tell him what Peter did. Because you'd have to admit to him that you didn't have the guts to break it off without evening the score. Because being honest has never really been your strong suit, has it?"

Eleanor looked like Sarah had just slapped her, and Kaitlyn felt a tug of sympathy. Eleanor might have deserved the insult, but Sarah would never understand the constant pressure of living up to your parents' impossible standards. That from birth you were behind the mark and had to struggle to catch up to an ever-moving finish line.

"I'm sorry for what I did to you back then," Eleanor said. "It was wrong, and more than that, it was spiteful." She smiled sadly. "I understand if you don't want to go through with this. We can all just go back to the party, and I'll see what I can do about finding the guts to break things off. Come on."

Eleanor brushed past Kaitlyn on her way to the door and fished silently in her purse for her phone.

Sarah bit her lip. She looked at Ryan, and then Kaitlyn, and then at the door. "Wait," she said in a tone a death row inmate might have used for deciding between the electric chair or the gas chamber.

Eleanor turned with her hand on the doorknob.

"If Reginald hears about this, you'll tell him the truth?" Sarah stared holes into Eleanor.

"I'll tell him it was all my idea, and both of you were just being friends. Even if both of those things are still technically lying," Eleanor said. "But I don't think Peter will tell him. Our families are close and he'll want to keep his own indiscretions private."

Sarah walked to the door and took Eleanor's hand from the knob. "Friends might be pushing it. But I'd be fine with not being enemies anymore. Apology accepted. I'm going to trust you, Eleanor. We both are."

Eleanor's eyes went shiny. "Really?"

"Yeah, well. Don't think it has anything to do with you. I just want to see Ryan kiss a sexy girl. Bet you're a moaner." Sarah squeezed Eleanor's hand tightly, and then dropped it and flicked her on the shoulder.

"I *knew* it," Eleanor said. "And it's fake kissing, remember? I'm so not a moaner."

"You say that now, but trust me, Ryan can fucking kiss. I may have moaned a little the first time."

Ryan snorted. "Sure, baby, let's go with a little. I won't tell."

Kaitlyn coughed. Too much information. Way too much information.

They all ignored her.

"Are you in?" Sarah looked at Ryan and Eleanor.

They nodded.

"Great. Well, glad that's sorted then. See you all later." Kaitlyn turned for the door. She was getting the hell out of this coat closet before she saw something she'd never be able to unsee.

"Wait," Eleanor said. "We need a lookout."

Sarah clapped her hands together. "Yes. Kaitlyn, stand outside, and when he's coming, bang on the door."

Was there a patron saint of patience? Kaitlyn would have to look it up for future reference. "Because that wouldn't look obvious."

"You can make it look natural," Sarah said. "Act as if you're trying to block the door so Peter doesn't open it, and just make a lot of noise."

"Acting isn't really my thing." Kaitlyn was starting to regret ever following Eleanor. Helping plan a little revenge plot between her friends was one thing. Participating, even as a lookout, was another. "I just want to go home." And didn't that sound pathetic.

Sarah frowned. "You okay?"

Kaitlyn rubbed at her nose again. Was she okay? Sure. In a had-the-will-to-get-out-of-bed-every-morning kind of way. But the longer this party dragged on, the more being okay felt like surviving. "Course I am. But even if I'm the lookout, who's to say Peter's just going to waltz by the coatroom looking for you?"

Eleanor waved her phone. "Because he just messaged me asking where I was. Said he has a surprise."

On the word *surprise*, Eleanor's voice wobbled a little, and Ryan tugged her in for a hug. "We have a surprise for him too, remember?"

Eleanor looked up at Ryan. "You really think this will work?"

"No idea." Ryan grinned. "But I never turn down an opportunity to kiss a pretty woman, and now I have two, so it's a win for me either way."

Eleanor laughed. "I forgot how much of a player you are."

Ryan leaned down and Kaitlyn could just catch her whisper into Eleanor's ear, "I'm just hoping for this one particular girl right now. Care to do me a solid too?"

Kaitlyn wasn't going to think about the fact that Ryan was essentially asking Eleanor to play along because Sarah would find it hot. She wasn't going to think about the fact that Sarah likely found it hot because she didn't really like Eleanor. God. She was going to explode from keeping out all the things she knew and didn't want to know.

What happened to the good ol' days where you met, fell in love, and never looked at another girl twice? Where you spent your days building a life together, a family together, and love was the ignition for passion? That's what her parents had had, and Kaitlyn refused to believe it didn't exist anymore. In the meantime, however, it looked as if she'd be the stupid lookout for her sexed-up friends.

"I'm texting him back to tell him I need some air and I'm grabbing my trench for a quick walk in the gardens," Eleanor said.

Kaitlyn sighed. Really? They were all so terrible at this it would be comical if it wasn't real. "Tell him you're exhausted talking to so many people and need a few minutes alone in the gardens. If you imply you *want* him to come and find you, it'll look too much like a setup."

"Oh, that's good," Sarah said.

No, it wasn't. If Eleanor was really about to indulge her Sapphic side, the last thing she'd do was text Peter, but why inject rational thought now?

When Eleanor's phone pinged again, Kaitlyn took it from her and read the screen. "Okay, he's coming to look for you, but don't open the text. You're supposed to be busy."

"Right." Eleanor turned to Ryan and Sarah. "So how do we do this?"

Kaitlyn had no desire to find out. The only good part of being the lookout was that she could stay on the other side of the very solid, not at all see-through, door and hopefully have the opportunity to skulk off as soon as Peter arrived. If she hadn't seen for herself the way he'd mauled that girl in the bar she'd almost feel sorry for him.

As Sarah, Ryan, and Eleanor began a hasty discussion on the best angle and the most compromising position that didn't involve serious loss of dignity, Kaitlyn made her escape. She'd never been happier to leave a room in her life. She'd use the next few minutes to give herself the mental pep talk she'd need to get through the last dregs of this night. She could do this. One more hour. Tops.

Kaitlyn squared her shoulders and opened the door. All thoughts, the good, the bad, and the TMI, flew from her head, because standing on the other side was Beck Delmar.

Chapter Seventeen

Caught Kissing

"What are you *doing here*?" Kaitlyn stepped out and shut the door behind her, lest Beck get a glimpse of whatever configuration Sarah, Ryan, and Eleanor had chosen. Taunting Beck with tales of her vibrator was one thing, but if Beck thought she'd been involved in what was going on behind that door…Beck wouldn't know it was all fake, and even if she did, she'd never understand why it seemed necessary. It didn't bear thinking about.

"I was looking for you, and someone said you and Eleanor had come this way." Beck looked at Kaitlyn curiously. "What are you up to?"

"Nothing. None of your business," Kaitlyn said too fast and with too much squeak in her voice for any semblance of sincerity.

"Right," Beck said. "Can we go somewhere private? Talk for a bit?"

Kaitlyn shook her head. She couldn't move from this door, and even if she could, she wouldn't go anywhere with Beck.

Except to bed.

Her inner thoughts needed to shut up. She just had sex on her mind right now after talking with the others, that was all. It had nothing to do with the way Beck was biting her luscious bottom lip. Why was it that the ones who got all the natural beauty—sexy lips, long lashes, thick golden-brown hair—were also the ones who didn't even notice they had them, let alone appreciate them? God wasn't fair.

"Come on," Beck said. "I just want to talk, and you owe me."

"I *owe* you? Oh, this is going to be good." Kaitlyn could hear the resentment in her voice and consciously worked on toning it down. She was over Beck. All she felt now was pity that Beck felt the need to chase her down for a conversation they weren't going to have.

"The Reducer was mean." Beck's eyes locked on Kaitlyn until she was pinned in place by the stare.

She gulped. "I was merely correcting your frankly arrogant assumption that you were better than my vibrator. It wasn't mean. It was factual."

"I don't remember you being quite so merciless. You made up that stuff to make me sweat. Mean."

"And did you?" As soon as the question left her mouth Kaitlyn wanted to scoop it back inside. Way to show her cards. It shouldn't matter if Beck was affected by her words or not, because Beck didn't matter. Not anymore.

"I have a heartbeat." Beck gave her a small smile. "So yeah, thinking of you turned on and getting yourself off…"

"Floats your boat?" Kaitlyn asked.

"What?"

"Never mind." Kaitlyn waved it away. "I'm just shocked you still have your heart. I thought it belonged to Washington. And yet here you are, in the city, again. Talking to me. Again." Tiny little butterfly wings of hope launched in her chest. Beck had come back for her, after all this time. Not that Kaitlyn wanted her back. She had more pride than that. She visualized herself as the butterfly hunter, slashing all those hope-wings with her shiny feminist sword.

Sorrow clouded Becks eyes. "You don't know?"

Kaitlyn frowned. "Know what?"

"Dad. Cancer."

Dad. Cancer. Two words that changed everything, and Beck said them like they held the weight of the world.

"Oh God." Kaitlyn flung herself at Beck and wrapped her arms around Beck's shoulders. "I'm so sorry." Whatever had happened in the past, whatever was going on between them now, none of it mattered. Kaitlyn knew what it was like to lose a parent, and she didn't wish it on her worst enemy. As much as she tried to remind herself that she hated her, Beck wasn't even close to worst enemy status. Kaitlyn clung to her as memories of her mother flashed through her mind: laughing as Kaitlyn blew out ten birthday candles, looking like a fairy princess as she danced alone in the kitchen with the radio playing, as broken and pale as the snow around her on the day she died.

Kaitlyn buried her head in Beck's shoulder, cocooning herself in citrus and comfort. "I'm so sorry. I'm so sorry."

"Hey." Beck eased back half an inch and cupped Kaitlyn's cheek. "He's going to be okay. It's in his kidneys, but the prognosis is good. They caught it early."

"What do you need? How's your mother? I'm so sorry, Beck. You'll survive. I know it doesn't seem like it, but—"

"Kait." Beck cradled Kaitlyn's face in her palms. "Listen to me. He's going to be okay. He's sick and that sucks. But the outcome looks good."

"He's not going to die?"

Beck shook her head. "No, honey. He's strong as an ox."

"God. I'm sorry. Wow. Overreaction much." Kaitlyn didn't even know she'd been crying until Beck used a thumb to brush at the tears on her cheeks.

"Don't you dare apologize. I'm the one who's sorry. I should've led with that. I wasn't thinking."

Kaitlyn stared at her, not sure what to say next, and worried her knees would give way if Beck let her go. All she could think to say was, "You're back because your dad's sick, but he's going to get better." Fantastic. Bonus points for summarizing the conversation like an idiot, as if Beck didn't know this. It was Kaitlyn who hadn't known, who'd seen Beck and hoped against hope that she'd come back for her. She hadn't. She'd left before, and as soon as her dad was on stable ground, she'd leave again. It was what she did best. Why couldn't Kaitlyn remember that?

"That, and other things. I really need to talk to you."

Just as Beck finished speaking, Peter came their way, and

Kaitlyn's heart thudded. Crap. She'd totally forgotten she was supposed to be the stupid lookout. What was she going to say? How was she supposed to convince Peter to open the door, while acting as if she didn't want him to? And what in God's name was she going to do with Beck? The whole thing was lunacy and panic clogged her throat, clouding her thoughts.

With her chin still resting in Beck's fingers she did the only thing she could think of to distract everyone for a few precious seconds while she figured out how to warn the others. She hardly had to move at all, it was so easy, something they'd done a thousand times before.

Kaitlyn closed her eyes, leaned in, and kissed Beck.

❖

If she was honest, and Kaitlyn always tried to be, she'd imagined kissing Beck more than once in the years that had passed. Imagined it in the way of remembering what had been, sweet, desperate, awkward, funny. Two teenagers exploring their bodies. But she'd also thought about what it would be like to kiss her now, as an adult with some experience under her belt. Would Beck's kiss still make her head swim, or would it pale in comparison to the others she'd had in between? Would Beck match her passion for passion? Was Kaitlyn remembering Beck's hold on her heart through rose-colored glasses, because you never forgot your first?

Of all the scenarios she'd played out in her mind, what happened was something she'd never expected. Beck's fingers on her face gentled, stroking her cheeks as their lips met in perfect alignment. Good kisses were all alike, but perfect kisses were all perfect in their own way. It wasn't the thunderclap of desire she'd expected, and okay, maybe had secretly hoped for. It didn't overwhelm her, or drown her, or make her want to pass out. Beck kissed her with a tenderness she'd never thought possible. Gentle and sincere. The kiss was slow, like every minute they'd ever spent apart had been building up to this moment. This kiss. Her mouth on Beck's, Beck's hands on her face, Kaitlyn's arms wrapped around her neck. Joined together in defiance of reason and logic.

Her heart ached. Opened. Wanted.

No. God, she couldn't go there. She wouldn't survive it a second time.

Kaitlyn threaded her fingers in Beck's hair and opened her mouth, tugging on the bottom lip she'd just been admiring, making Beck groan. Seizing the opportunity to move them past the danger zone, she parted Beck's lips and deepened the kiss. Trying not to lose it, trying to remember they had an audience, Kaitlyn couldn't stop her body from growing heavy, like the desire was actually weighing her down, making it hard to move, hard to stop. She couldn't hold on to a thought for more than a second, and she was pulsing everywhere. Wasn't kissing the best thing in the entire world?

"Kait," Beck gasped her name.

But Kaitlyn wasn't ready to quit. She didn't want to talk, she didn't want to feel, at least not what Beck had just stirred in her. Feeling with only her body was so much better. Easier. More satisfying. "Shut up." She fit her torso against Beck's, pulling her in until they fell against the door with a thump loud enough to alert the others.

Okay, job done. Time to stop now.

Just as she was about to pull away, Beck sighed and melted against her like butter warming in a pan. Kaitlyn's mind started to shut down, wanton desperation taking over. When Beck planted a hand on the door for leverage and trailed a string of wet kisses down her neck, Kaitlyn could finally focus on why she'd kissed her in the first place. Why she was standing in the entrance hall on the other side of a door where…Oh no.

Kaitlyn eased back, rested her head against the solid wood for a second, and caught her breath. Whatever happened next, it wasn't going to be pretty for anyone. When Beck cupped a palm around her hip and tried to pull her in again, she put a hand on her chest to stop her. Beck's heart hammered under her palm. One kiss and they were both on the edge like they hadn't touched anyone in years.

"Peter's behind you." Kaitlyn hoped Beck didn't know exactly when Peter had appeared.

Beck's eyes widened. She turned and tugged at the collar of her shirt in the sweetest self-conscious gesture. "Oh, hey, man. Did you need something?"

The adorable I'm-embarrassed-to-be-caught-kissing thing was making Kaitlyn feel bad for using Beck as a distraction long enough to alert the others. Not bad enough to regret having done it, but…

Peter smirked. "I'm looking for Eleanor. She was coming this way to find her coat."

Kaitlyn made a scene of looking worriedly at the door and back to Peter. She was going to kill her friends when this was all over. "She, um, well, I think you should just go back into the ballroom. She'll find you when she's ready." She was talking too loudly, hoping the others could hear her, since the sound of her and Beck falling against the door might not have been enough. Was it enough? She hated being the lookout. So much pressure.

"Do you know where she is?" Peter looked confused.

Kaitlyn looked to the door again and gave guilty and clueless her best shot. Honestly, if Peter was too thick to join the dots, she couldn't help him.

"Is she in there?" Peter asked, like it wasn't crazy obvious.

"Well, I, um…" *Come on, just push past me and open the door so I can go home.* She couldn't look at Beck. The truth had to be plastered all over her face.

"Peter, I—"

"Move," Peter said.

Kaitlyn let out a silent breath. Thank God. She scooted out of the way, and Peter swung the door open.

Kaitlyn didn't want to see. She really didn't. She was the kind of girl others loved to bring home to their parents. Family oriented. Traditional. She didn't do threesomes, not even the fake kind. Her idea of a wild Saturday night was a glass of wine and a Sandra Bullock movie. But when Beck moved to follow Peter inside, her heart seized and she rushed to stop her. Oh God, if Beck saw. But she was too late. From behind her, Kaitlyn saw the way Beck's spine stiffened in shock, heard all the air whoosh from her lungs. Uneasiness churned in her belly, and against her better judgment, Kaitlyn looked over Beck's shoulder.

If she hadn't known what to expect Kaitlyn would've lost her breath too. They were positioned against the wall opposite the door, Ryan behind Eleanor, her black shirt unbuttoned and her hair a rumpled mess. Eleanor was curved into her body like a spoon, and they were kissing with their arms around each other in a display worthy of a love scene in a movie. Maybe it was fake kissing, maybe it wasn't. She didn't want to know, she didn't want to know, she didn't…God. Sarah stood in front of Eleanor with Eleanor's bra-covered breasts in her hands, watching them while shielding most of Eleanor from the doorway.

Once you got past the shock factor, it was a pretty good setup. Plainly obvious what they were doing, but Ryan was covered by Eleanor, who was covered by Sarah, who was still fully dressed. You couldn't really *see* anything except the kiss and Eleanor's bra. And it was quite a kiss.

Kaitlyn touched her lips remembering her own quite a kiss.

"What the fuck, Eleanor," Peter yelled, and they all made a commendable attempt at shock and scrambling. It was maybe a tad too seamless. Sarah whipping up the front of Eleanor's dress, and Ryan zipping the back in less than three seconds. They separated, Ryan casually fastening the buttons on her shirt, her white chef pants still buttoned.

"What…" Peter was turning puce. "Are you *doing?*"

None of them spoke. A picture was worth a thousand words. That'd been the point, after all.

Sarah touched Eleanor's hand and she jumped. "Just having a little fun on my birthday, Pete. Surely you're not going to hold it against me." Her voice wobbled.

"Not going to…" Peter couldn't seem to finish a sentence on the first try. "You're cheating on me, you little bitch."

Ryan took a step forward, but before she could defend Eleanor, Sarah spoke up. "Just like you were cheating on her."

She winked cheerfully and traced a fingertip lazily down

Eleanor's bare arm. "Can't blame you for being put out though. Damn. She's a firecracker, isn't she? Got a body like Jennifer Lopez. Too bad you walked in. I was really looking forward to fucking her."

Peter's fists clenched at his sides. "I was coming to find you to *propose*, Eleanor. I..." He faltered, looked completely baffled. "I was going to ask you to be my wife."

With Ryan and Sarah flanking her, Eleanor found her voice again. "Sorry. I've decided I'm done with you. Maybe there's still time to ask the girl you met at a bar this afternoon, though? I hear she's as stupid as she is ugly."

Kaitlyn tugged on Beck's hand. "Come on," she whispered. "We need to leave."

In all the drama, no one had noticed Beck standing two feet behind Peter in the doorway, and Kaitlyn wanted to spare her any further awkwardness. Okay, and spare herself too. *Just what were you doing with your ex-girlfriend, Kaitlyn?* She winced. Yeah, she'd put that conversation off for as long as possible.

They left without a word, leaving the door open behind them, now that everyone was decent.

Once again, Kaitlyn had no idea what to say. There wasn't anything she could say. Nothing that didn't make her sound like an ass. How exactly did you explain that you had to make a bunch of noise so your friends could fake a threesome? That you just had to kiss the one woman you'd vowed never to kiss again? That you never expected the kiss to actually mean something? That it'd seemed like a good idea at the time, wasn't going to cut it.

"What was that?" Beck asked once they were standing just outside the doors to the ballroom. "I mean, were they really...you know. With you standing outside the whole time?"

Why had Beck shown up at just the wrong moment? Why had Kaitlyn panicked and kissed her instead of sending her away? Now it looked as if Kaitlyn had been in on the whole thing, and the worst part was that she *had* been in on it, fake or not.

"It's complicated," she said, hedging.

"Are they all..." Beck paused, searching for the right word. "Having an affair together?"

Kaitlyn flushed. "No." God. This was so much worse than she'd expected. "It was staged. We caught Peter cheating, even though he didn't see us see it, so they decided it would be a good idea to get a little revenge, before Eleanor broke up with him. Even the playing field a bit. I was just looking for Sarah, and then Eleanor wanted my help because Sarah was suggesting she kiss Ryan, and honestly, I happened to walk in on them devising the plan. I wasn't a part of it at all, well, expect for the fact that it was kind of my idea. The threesome, I mean. They were just going to kiss at first, but it wasn't enough, and I suggested they make it look like more." Kaitlyn sucked in air and hoped she'd shut up soon. Did her motormouth have an off switch? She was so completed screwed.

Beck frowned. "That was *staged*?"

Kaitlyn wanted the floor to open up and swallow her. "Yeah. I know it was dumb, but Eleanor didn't think she could just break it off without dinging Peter's ego a bit."

"Girls are vicious," Beck said with more than a hint of admiration.

"Well, he did have sex with another woman, at a bar downtown, in public," Kaitlyn said.

"And you saw it?" Beck wrinkled her nose.

"We saw enough. We had to tell Eleanor, and thus a plan was hatched. A dumb plan. But effective, it seems."

Beck fell silent. She didn't speak for so long the silence started to ring in Kaitlyn's ears. "And kissing me, was that part of the plan too?"

Kaitlyn closed her eyes. Maybe, if she couldn't see Beck, then she wasn't really there, and she wouldn't have to answer.

"Kait?" Beck asked.

Kaitlyn opened them again, and there she was. All sexy lips, and long lashes, and thick, wavy hair that was two weeks overdue for a trim. Dammit. "Yes and no. I was the lookout, obviously. I was supposed to alert the others when he arrived, but then you showed up, and I panicked. I didn't know what to do, so I kissed you as a distraction, and so I could bang on the door without being too suspect."

"Wow," Beck said. "Just wow."

Kaitlyn risked a glance at her face, and the barest hint of a smile was playing on Beck's mouth.

"I stand by my earlier statement, girls are vicious."

"You're not mad?" Kaitlyn asked.

"That you kissed me as a distraction because I was a handy hunk of beefcake?"

Kaitlyn groaned. "I didn't! You're not! I mean…what is a beefcake, exactly?"

Beck made a sad puppy face. "I feel so used."

"You're not mad, are you?"

"I'm irate. I'm going to call my senator and complain. Loose women, of looser morals, hatching plans to take down the patriarchy by appearing scantily clad in intriguing sexual positions. It has to be stopped." Beck grinned.

"Beck." Kaitlyn couldn't help smiling back.

"Sarah fondling Eleanor has been the highlight of my night so far. Who knew they were a thing? Didn't they hate each other, or am I misremembering?"

Kaitlyn swatted her on the arm. "No one was fondling, you pervert. It was staged."

"Yeah. It looked terribly staged. All that kissing and stroking."

"You're enjoying this far too much," Kaitlyn said. "Maybe I should be jealous you seem more interested in Sarah and Eleanor than in our kiss."

"Well…" Beck made a show of considering her options. "You were pretty satisfying, but I've had better."

Kaitlyn winced. She'd set herself up for that one. "Then I guess we'd better head back in so you can find better."

Kaitlyn turned to walk away, but Beck grabbed her hand. "I need to talk to you."

"What could we possibly have to say to each other?" She couldn't blame Beck for flinging her own words back in her face. Kaitlyn had said them first. But, well, maybe it stung just a little that Beck had gotten more of a rush out of Sarah and Eleanor's faked rendezvous than the actual kiss she'd shared with her. Ugh. This night sucked.

"I came back to support Dad, but I wanted to see you as well."

The butterfly wings started to reincarnate in Kaitlyn's stomach. "You did?"

"Yeah, I—"

Mrs. Davenport, a widow of seventeen years, and, as legend had it, the one who wielded the knife that killed her husband, bustled out of the ballroom laughing merrily with a man half her age on each arm. They looked like all their Christmases had come, and Kaitlyn guessed it had a lot more to do with the zeros at the end of Mrs. Davenport's bank balance than her fading beauty. She didn't believe the rumors for a second, but had always steered clear nonetheless.

Beck and Kaitlyn had to step to the side or risk being run over.

"Can we go somewhere more private?" Beck asked.

Did Kaitlyn want to? Before tonight, she'd have said no way and not even blinked. Beck had left her, her heart dead by crush injury and her dignity in tatters. But damn if that kiss hadn't brought it pumping back to life. Not to mention other parts of her anatomy.

"I have no idea where. If you think I'm going upstairs with you, Delmar, you have another thing coming. The kiss wasn't *that* good." She was such a liar. It was totally that good.

Beck grinned. "Sweet talker. I know just the place. Follow me." Beck grabbed her hand and headed toward the front doors.

Kaitlyn bit her lip. She'd followed Beck with stars in her eyes and dreams in her head when she was just sixteen. She was older now, but was she really any smarter?

CHAPTER EIGHTEEN

For the Love of Kait

Kaitlyn stopped so abruptly Beck almost pulled her shoulder out of its socket as she forged ahead, Kaitlyn's hand still in hers.

"What's wrong?" Beck asked.

"We're in the parking lot." Well, what served as a parking lot anyway. It was more an orderly assembly of town cars and sports cars, and many other kinds of cars Kaitlyn didn't know the names of. All of them expensive.

"Yup. Mine's here somewhere. Damn valet, where did he put it?" Beck tugged Kaitlyn along, and too perplexed to put up a fight, Kaitlyn followed.

"We're going to your car? Why?"

"Because spring is playing peekaboo and it's getting too cold to stand around outside. The car's warm, and best of all, private." Beck stopped at a red SUV with black accents and a barely discernible Range Rover logo. She opened the back passenger door for Kaitlyn. "It's this or a bedroom upstairs at the McGregor place, and something tells me if we get in a room with a bed, you won't be able to resist my charms."

Kaitlyn scoffed. "Don't count on it. I only kissed you to facilitate a threesome between my friends, remember? You were collateral damage."

Beck grinned. "Oh, honey, I remember. Where are they, and kiss me again."

Why did she keep doing this to herself? Kaitlyn was being ridiculous, she knew she was, but it wasn't fair. She wanted Beck to think she'd kissed her as a means to an end, because there was no way Kaitlyn was going to admit she'd *wanted* it, but when Beck was on board with that, and completely unaffected by their kiss, Kaitlyn wanted to stamp her feet.

Why couldn't Beck be weak-kneed and desperate for more? Begging her for a second chance? That way Kaitlyn could be the one who shrugged it off and pretended like it was nothing special. Like Beck was nothing special. She wanted Beck to want her, just so she could be the one who did the dumping this time. She was a terrible person.

It hit a little too close to the "let's fake a threesome to get back at your cheating ex" scenario for her comfort zone. She might not do something as crazy as a threesome, but she wasn't above her own need for revenge, and that was small and shallow. What Beck did to her had broken her heart, but they were adults now, and setting someone up to fall wasn't her style. She was better than that. Or she hoped she was.

"Two questions before I consent to getting into a strange car with an untrustworthy woman." She'd meant it as a joke, but the flash of pain in Beck's eyes stalled anything else she might've said. "I didn't—"

Beck smiled and winked at her, the emotion masked almost as quickly as it had appeared. "I promise, if you hop inside, pretty girl, I'll give you candy."

Kaitlyn swallowed. Candy was the last thing on her mind, but the deliciously devious tone Beck was using had her thinking of some very specific things that, if memory served her, tasted even better. "I wasn't born yesterday." Kaitlyn prayed Beck couldn't tell where her mind had just been.

"Damn. That usually works too." Beck sighed dramatically. "Okay, what are your questions?"

"Why is your car unlocked, and since when do you drive a Range Rover?"

Beck pulled a key fob smaller than a matchbox out of her pocket. "The car senses the key and unlocks itself."

"Huh." Kaitlyn could fit what she knew about cars on the back of that key. "So, the car is telepathic? That's cool."

Beck looked at her like she'd just said the sky was green. "It's not telepathic. It's a smart key. There's a sensor inside the car that picks up on the sensor inside the key, and——" She stopped herself. "Do you actually care?"

Kaitlyn shrugged. "Not really."

Beck rolled her eyes. "To answer your other question, it's Dad's car. I gave mine up when I moved to DC. He's letting me borrow it."

"Ah," Kaitlyn said. "Midlife crisis red didn't seem like your style. You're more of a low-slung sports car in muted gray type."

"Oh, I am, huh?"

"Yup. Expensive, but too classy to flaunt it," Kaitlyn said before she could think better of it.

"If I promise to be classy, will you get in?" Beck asked.

Kaitlyn got in. Beck walked around front to start the engine, ran the heat, and turned on the overhead light, before hopping in the other side.

"So here we are," Kaitlyn said in an ominous horror movie voice. "What's so secretive you had to whisk me away?"

Beck had turned to face her, but she stared somewhere past Kaitlyn's right ear. She was a little pale in the glow of the overhead light, and Kaitlyn couldn't help but reach out and touch her cheek. "Hey. I'm sorry. Is it your dad? Is something else going on you didn't tell me?"

"No," Beck assured her. "It's not that. I wanted to say I'm sorry. I was a real shit to you in high school. I loved you like crazy, but getting into Harvard, and Mom and Dad's expectations. It blew my mind."

Kaitlyn rubbed at her nose. Okay, so apparently, they were going to go there, even though it helped no one and solved nothing now. Pain stabbed her chest, turning an emotional ache into a physical one. Why did it still have to hurt so much? "I appreciate that. But if you really are sorry, then admit that you left because it's what *you* wanted. Your parents might have pressured you the way anyone would with an acceptance to an Ivy. But if you'd really wanted to stay, New York has some pretty great colleges, too."

Beck shifted on the seat. "I wanted to stay. But I wanted to go too. I was seventeen. I wanted to prove myself. I had to find out who I was outside my family's shadow. Can you understand that?"

Kaitlyn wasn't sure if Beck had phrased the question that way to suggest Kaitlyn couldn't understand because her family was dead, or if Beck was simply pleading for forgiveness for a decision that had cost Kaitlyn everything she'd ever truly cared about. Either way, Kaitlyn wasn't handing out redemption.

"What I understand is that you wanted to go more than you wanted to stay," Kaitlyn said, fighting to keep her voice from wavering. "I couldn't have followed you, not with Forrester Fund on my shoulders. You knew that. You had no such obligation at that age, and you chose to leave. It's not like we're from Podunk Nebraska. We live in one of the best cities in the world. You could've been a lawyer here too."

"I am," Beck said. "I took the bar again a few months ago. I'm licensed to practice in New York now."

"You're moving back?"

Beck's mouth tilted up at the corner in a half smile. "Yeah."

"Because of your dad?" Kaitlyn asked, hearing her own words without realizing she'd said them.

"Partly." Beck flopped backward and stared at the back of the driver's seat. "Have you ever made a decision, which at the time you genuinely thought was the right one, only to discover it didn't make you as happy as you'd hoped?"

Kaitlyn's heart did a tap dance in her chest. "Does too much eggnog on Christmas Eve count? Every year, Uncle Henry convinces me to have that second glass, and every year, it's a mistake. Alcoholic beverages made with dairy should be generally outlawed."

"Kait," Beck said.

Maybe Beck wasn't getting at what she hoped she was getting at, but the implication had her nerves on end. Kaitlyn shook her head slowly. "Honestly, no. I've always been pretty sure of what I wanted." *You, and us, and maybe even a baby or two.*

Beck laughed. "Yeah. That's why it's taken me so long to explain. You've always been sure, so put together, so rational. It's intimidating to the rest of us mere mortals who occasionally fuck up."

"I got a head start," Kaitlyn said. "I didn't just lose my mom. I stopped being a kid and started being an heiress. People were counting on me."

"I'm sorry, I didn't mean—"

Kaitlyn waved away the apology. "No need. It's not your fault." She paused, and with her heart in her throat, asked, "Did you fuck up, Beck?"

When Beck looked at her, her eyes filled with sorrow. "In so many ways. I wanted politics because I wanted to change the world. I wanted to be the person others looked to to make decisions. In some ways, I wanted what you have."

"What?" Of all the things Beck could've said, that was the last Kaitlyn would've expected. What did she have that Beck could possibly want?

"You were stepping up to run Forrester Fund. Back then I had no real concept of how big it was or how many people were counting on you. I just knew it was important, and it was yours."

"God," Kaitlyn said. "My mom died. I *had* to step up. I was the only one. Do you know how much pressure I was under?"

Beck nodded. "I know that. Knew it then too. But it didn't stop me from feeling as if I didn't measure up, that I wasn't good enough."

Ice settled on Kaitlyn's skin so fast she was sure she'd crack. "You left because you didn't think you were good enough?"

"I think so. I wanted to make something of myself. Be someone who deserved a woman like you," Beck said.

Kaitlyn was master of the stoic stiff upper lip. But she wasn't a masochist, and she couldn't take this anymore. She flung the passenger door open. She had a foot on the ground before Beck grabbed her hand to stop her.

"Whoa. Where are you going?"

"I'm leaving. Screw you."

"What? Why?" Beck looked adorably confused, but Kaitlyn didn't have it in herself to care.

She wished Beck had never come back, that they hadn't kissed, and that it hadn't made her want things she'd promised herself she'd never want with Beck again. But especially that they hadn't sneaked out of the party and ended up right here, right now, having this conversation. Kaitlyn had built her life in spite of Beck's leaving. She'd had no choice. Falling apart wasn't an option. But she'd pushed her broken heart down and built the woman she'd become on top of it. Her pain was her foundation, and Beck had just pulled it up. Kaitlyn was starting to crumble. She couldn't let that happen. Beck shouldn't be allowed to have that kind of power.

Love completely sucked.

She got back in the car and slammed the door with more force than necessary. "You left because you didn't think you were good enough for me? How about my feelings? How about asking me what I wanted?"

Beck shook her head. "No, honey. I wasn't good enough for *me*."

Kaitlyn wanted to scream. "What does that even mean?"

Beck sighed. "My parents are successful by anyone's standards. My brother was a Rhodes Scholar, and my girlfriend was not only an heiress, but about to run a company that balances a checkbook worth more than my whole family put together. I felt as if I had some catching up to do. Like everyone around me was five steps ahead. I wanted to forge my own path."

"You do realize I was only *successful* because my mother died, right? That I'd give it all back and then some to have her back? I inherited both my money and my company. I didn't earn it. Not then."

"I know," Beck said. "And I'm so sorry. But surely you can see it from my perspective too? I wasn't anyone special, I was a loner in school, I wasn't quite as smart, or as good looking, or as wealthy, as anyone else. I had to make it on my own terms."

So the hell what? How did that make it okay? Kaitlyn refused to accept Beck's choice. It had been the wrong choice. "We were kids. We could've learned to be adults together. Why did you have to leave?"

If Beck had still wanted her, why did she go? She could've had everything in New York, and Kaitlyn as well. They could've made it together.

"At the time I felt like it was the only way to distinguish myself. To figure out who *I* really was, the same way that Forrester Fund has defined life for you," Beck said.

The anger drained away until Kaitlyn felt like a wrapper someone had tossed out a car window to be blown around by the wind. How could the person you loved so much be so completely wrong about you? Did you ever really know someone, or did people just bump up against each other as they went about their lives, forging their own solitary existence? "Forrester Fund isn't what defines me. I enjoy it. I'm proud to carry on the legacy, but what defined me was *you*. It was us. That's what I really wanted. A nice quiet life in a quaint brownstone with a couple of kids running around and you by my side. I lost my family so young. All I've ever wanted was to make one of our own." Kaitlyn sagged back in her seat, weary of it all. "Did you become the person you wanted to be? Is that why you came back?"

She caught Beck shaking her head in her peripheral vision. "I came back for you. I love you."

I love you. Kaitlyn supposed she should be shocked it was still true, but part of her had always known their love was forever. That's why Beck's leaving had hurt so badly. High school sweethearts rarely lasted, everyone knew that. But they'd been soul mates, not sweethearts. Their love meant for a lifetime.

Beck started to speak again, but Kaitlyn held up a hand. If she hadn't been clear when they were kids, she was certainly going to be crystal now. Beck was about to get a taste of just how sure she could be. "I'm sorry, but you've wasted your time. I can see how you must've felt insecure. It's not easy growing up here. The expectations are high, and mine more than most. But you put us in opposition when we should've been a team. My career, whatever it was, shouldn't have been something you had to compete with to feel worthy. I never wanted that. *You*," she poked Beck in the chest, "are worthy by virtue of my loving you. You are my everything, and you screwed it up because your brother is scary smart and I have a little more money?" Kaitlyn rolled her eyes. "That was really dumb, and I don't forgive you."

Beck was staring at her in a way Kaitlyn had never seen before. She wasn't sure what the look meant, but it made her squirm. "What?"

"You said you love me."

"No, I didn't," Kaitlyn said. Had she? Oh, dear God.

"You did. You said I was worthy because you loved me." Beck touched Kaitlyn's cheek. "You still love me."

Panic rose in Kaitlyn's throat until she was sure the salmon she'd had for dinner would end up all over their laps. "I didn't. I meant back then. I loved you back then."

Beck traced her finger down Kaitlyn's cheek and along the line of her jaw, mapping her face. "I don't think so. You said I'm your everything. You meant now."

Kaitlyn's heart was beating so fast she felt light-headed. She didn't. She hadn't. She couldn't. Not again. "No, I can't…"

Beck moved in close, tilting Kaitlyn's face toward her. "You can," she murmured right before she crushed Kaitlyn's mouth in a kiss.

This was the kiss Kaitlyn had thought about endlessly. Gone was perfection, gone was gentle and considerate. Beck pressed her back against the seat and took what she wanted. Her breath went all shuddery, and intelligent thought emptied from her brain. Beck threaded a hand into her hair, cupping the back of her neck and pushing her lips apart. She reacted instinctively, wrapping her arms around Beck's neck, as sensation raced down her belly to pool between her legs. Her head went all *guhhh* as Beck's kiss walked the line between pleasurable and unbearable, reminding Kaitlyn with every brush of her tongue and nip of her teeth what they'd once had, and what had been denied her. As much as she wanted to hold on to her anger, Beck's mouth was making her a hot rush of promises. *This is how I'll touch you. This is how I'll savor you. Remember how good it was.*

Kaitlyn groaned, feeling Beck's hip press into her stomach as they moved closer in the tight space. Beck palmed her breast through her dress and Kaitlyn whimpered, darts of electricity shooting from her nipple down to her clit like they were connected by a live wire. She was losing her mind. It wasn't fair. There was something unbearably arousing about Beck's power over her, the way she couldn't help but want her even after all this time. But wanting Beck was one thing, loving her was a whole different story, and love wasn't an emotion to be trusted.

As if sensing her whirling thoughts Beck pulled back, breathing hard. "Relax, honey."

Kaitlyn looked away. She was panting like a dog in heat. God, she had to pull herself together. She was so turned on she was surprised she hadn't come already. But underneath the desire her chest hurt. Her entire life hurt. Kaitlyn wanted Beck inside her more than she wanted to breathe, but she hated herself for wanting it. Why was she throwing herself at Beck after everything she'd done to her? She didn't forgive her, but she wanted her anyway. What did that say about her? About her values, and what was truly important?

Beck stroked Kaitlyn's hair, her eyes as open and trusting as a Labrador retriever, though currently clouded with concern. "What can I do? Tell me what you need and I'll do it. Anything. I'll take you back to the party and round up your friends so you can go home if that's what you want. You'll never have to see me again."

Kaitlyn knew that if she told Beck to leave, she'd be gone for good. But that thought had the ache in her chest transforming into knife sharp pain. Never seeing her again might be what she wanted, but it wasn't what she needed.

Kaitlyn took a deep breath. All she'd ever wanted in her life was to love Beck and make a family. But that was then. Now, even if only for tonight, she could be a different version of herself. The version who took what she wanted and damned the consequences. A braver, sexier woman, less tied to unreliable dreams. She wanted

Beck, and Beck wanted her. That part was simple, always had been. Sex. This was about sex and nothing else. She'd never done casual. Never had *just sex* before. But there was no time like the present to try, and God, did it sound appealing.

"I'm so sorry," Beck said gently. "I ruined us, didn't I?"

Had she? Kaitlyn didn't know. But at least one thing between them had only gotten stronger. Kaitlyn made her decision and, as advertised, she was sure. "No more apologies," Kaitlyn said. "Just for tonight, we don't have a past, okay? We just have right now."

"Right now," Beck echoed, staring at her so intently Kaitlyn felt as if Beck was reaching inside her head to read her thoughts.

"Yes," was all Kaitlyn could manage over the pounding of her heart. She wanted this. It made no sense. It wasn't like her at all, but her engine was revving as if this was the start of a race, and she wanted desperately to win.

"And what are we going to do right now?" Technically, it was a question, but Beck said it in a way that implied she had a million unique answers and wanted to try each and every one of them. Slowly, and with excruciating attention to detail.

Kaitlyn bit her lip and squared her shoulders. "I'm going to show you exactly what you gave up when you walked away, Delmar."

Chapter Nineteen

The Best Revenge

"Put your back against the window," Kaitlyn said, mirroring Beck on the other side. They were face-to-face with only the middle seat between them. Beck looked at her curiously. Taking the lead had never been Kaitlyn's strong suit. She'd been raised to believe ladies never made the first move, and socialization was part of it. But honestly, she just plain liked it when her lovers took control.

Beck had been right; running Forrester Fund was a prestigious and demanding occupation. She made decisions all day. The last thing she wanted was to make them in bed too. Yet tonight she'd taunted Beck with the story of her vibrator. She'd kissed her to provide a warning for her friends, and now here she was, alone in the back seat of a car with her. Tonight was no ordinary night, she wasn't her ordinary self, and she was going to do something she'd never had the guts to do before.

She slipped off her sling-back heels and placed them on the mat. Then she brought one leg up, bent her knee, and rested it in the crease in the seat where the back support met the bench. She faced Beck with her legs splayed open as much as she could manage in the cramped space.

"Fuck," Beck breathed. "What are you doing?"

Kaitlyn's floor-length dress covered most of her legs, but Beck's gaze was glued to the spot where, underneath the layers of satin, Kaitlyn had her legs spread like an invitation from a broke hooker.

"I'm going to give you a show," Kaitlyn said. "After-dinner entertainment, if you like."

"A show," Beck said, as if not quite believing her.

"Or perhaps we should call it a demonstration." Kaitlyn edged the layers of pale material up her legs until it started to bunch in her hands. "It's been a long time. You'll need a primer before getting back in the game."

Beck groaned. "If you had any idea how primed I am right now…"

Kaitlyn shook her head. "Not you, Delmar. You need a primer on me. On what I want, how I like to be touched."

Heat flared in Beck's eyes. "I already know how you like it."

God, did she ever. But Kaitlyn wasn't ready to give her the upper hand just yet. She wanted to see Beck squirm a little. She needed Beck to need her and not be able to have her. Not real revenge, but sexy, drive Beck out of her mind revenge. Then, just maybe, she'd be able to face her mirror in the morning. "Maybe what I like has changed."

She inched her dress up past her knees.

When she'd pulled it up far enough to reveal rose pink panties, Beck grasped Kaitlyn's ankle, like touching her *anywhere* was imperative.

"People don't change that much." Beck's voice sounded as if someone had scoured her vocal cords with a Scotch-Brite pad. "I know you like me on top."

Kaitlyn released a shaky breath, her heartbeat a bass drum, and her clit pulsing in tune. The overhead light was harsh. Beck would be able to see she'd soaked through her panties.

"I know there's a spot right behind your ear, and when I kiss you there you get wet instantly." Beck's fingers tightened on her ankle. "Look me in the eye and tell me another lover has found that spot, that they know what it does to you to be touched there."

Beck's words flayed her open. Of course no one else had ever found that spot. No one had ever hung around long enough, or taken the time, to discover her most obscure turn-ons. Beck knew them all. Knew *her*.

Kaitlyn shrugged. "There's plenty of ways to make me hot. Maybe some other lover has found a few you haven't."

"Trying to make me jealous?" Beck traced the bones in her ankle one by one.

Kaitlyn tilted her head to the side. "Are you?"

"Maybe a little. I'm glad you haven't been lonely, but I'd be lying if I said I didn't wish it'd been me every time."

Sex without love had scratched an itch, but it hadn't made Kaitlyn less lonely. Another woman's hands felt nice, but it was the touch to her heart that really mattered. "What about you? Been lonely?" There she went again, asking questions she didn't want to know the answer to, and setting herself up for disappointment. She really had to stop doing that.

"Yes."

"Yes, what?" Kaitlyn asked.

"Yes, I've been lonely."

Kaitlyn didn't know what to say to that.

"My life didn't exactly work out the way I thought it would." Beck's fingers moved to the arch of her foot, massaging in a way that made Kaitlyn's eyes roll back in her head. Standing for hours in heels was hell on your feet, and Beck knew right where to apply pressure so her toes curled in pleasure. "At first, a new city was fun, but after a while the drinking and partying got old, and I was working more and more. I thought the work would make me happy. Make up for what I'd left behind."

"But it didn't?"

"Nothing could ever make up for losing you."

Kaitlyn's breath caught. The words sounded so heartfelt. So big and open. They terrified her. How could she possibly trust that they were true?

"Oh, I don't know." Kaitlyn reached between her legs and stroked over her panties. Nerves she'd forgotten she had lit up like fairy lights, making her shiver. "This might rank as a decent consolation prize." Because that's all it was. A bit of fun. A tying up of loose ends and rowdy libidos.

It was nothing more than a long good-bye.

Beck watched her stroke herself with such focus Kaitlyn felt her stare like a flame on her skin. Heating. Burning. Branding. *You're mine* Beck's eyes seemed to say to her. Kaitlyn's throat was so dry it was difficult to swallow. She hadn't even done anything yet and already she was in over her head. She didn't want to think about that.

Kaitlyn let her head rest against the chilly window and brought her fingers to her clit. She was so wet she slid easily against the silk of her panties, a sensation that both excited and frustrated. So good, yet so much less than what it would be if there was no barrier. She traced the line of her panties down the crease where her thigh met her center. Stroking there, dipping the tips of her fingers under the edge of silk. Teasing herself. Teasing Beck.

"Take them off." Beck's voice was full of gravel. It made Kaitlyn burn hotter. This was what she'd wanted, to make her suffer, make her want. She hadn't considered how much it would make her want in return, though. Beck's breathing was unsteady, her pale blue shirt wrinkled from where she'd leaned into Kaitlyn to kiss her. She looked about as undone as Kaitlyn could remember seeing her, and it made her want to keep applying pressure to Beck's composure until it snapped in two.

"You're not in charge right now." Kaitlyn pressed her thumb to her opening. It felt amazingly good and she couldn't stop the sigh. She pressed deeper, stretching the material of her panties as far as they'd allow.

Beck's expression was caught between that of a voyeur who never wanted her to stop and a predator about to seize control. Kaitlyn didn't know which she liked more. She smiled to herself. She'd tempted Beck. She could read it on her face clear as a book. Beck wanted to rip her panties clean down the middle and shove inside her, but she was reeling herself in, allowing Kaitlyn the pretense of control. Because they both knew that's what it was. A pretense. An act. Make-believe. Beck had always been the one to call the shots. The control had always been hers. Even when Beck had used it to hurt her beyond reason, and Kaitlyn had let her.

"Take. Them. Off." Beck enunciated each word carefully, like a drunk trying to act sober.

Kaitlyn opened her mouth to toss back some cutting reply, but Beck yanked on her ankle just hard enough to jolt her. Her head slid down the window just a little and she gasped, heat flooding her pussy. God. They both knew that if Beck wanted to, she could have Kaitlyn's panties on the floor and her body halfway to orgasm in less than thirty seconds. She wasn't asking.

Kaitlyn brought her foot up from the floor and worked her panties down her thighs; the smell of her arousal filled the confined space.

Beck took the ball of pink silk from her before she could toss it. She brought the panties to her face, breathed them in. "Look at these, they're ruined. You've soaked clean through them."

The words weren't even particularly dirty, but Kaitlyn went molten. She was slick and needy, on the verge of not caring if she had to beg Beck to touch her. Revenge was fast becoming the last thing on her mind.

"You've teased me all night." Beck tucked the scrap of silk into the pocket of her pants like it was a slutty souvenir. "Making up stories about your vibrator, using me to distract Peter, displaying yourself, touching yourself. You're a vicious tease, do you know that?"

Kaitlyn whimpered. God. She was so into this. "I've been called worse."

Beck frowned at that. She put a hand on Kaitlyn's knee and used it to pry open her legs. Not that Kaitlyn needed encouragement. She was debating whether or not to sit on her own hands to stop herself from rubbing her clit to orgasm. "Look how sexy and wet you are already." Beck's hand was still maddeningly on Kaitlyn's knee. "You're such a good girl, ever the lady, always in control, always rational, but you can't hide that your pussy is begging to be fucked."

The words landed like a hot caress on her skin, igniting her. "Speak for yourself. Don't try to convince me you go around using words like *pussy* on a daily basis. You're a politician in training."

Kaitlyn had no idea what she was saying. Complete sentences were impossible right now, and why hadn't Beck touched her yet? Why was her hand still on Kaitlyn's knee, for God's sake?

Beck's smile was devious. "Oh, you're right. I don't. Not at all. I'm using them now because every time I do, you get wetter. You like it, don't you, when I explain to you how brazen you really are underneath all the polish?"

If Beck was expecting an answer to that question, she wasn't going to get it. But Kaitlyn's center was wet, swollen and pulsing with need. That was answer enough.

"I think," Beck started to slide a hand down the inside of her thigh, and Kaitlyn thought briefly that she might pass out, "it's sexier when it's not one's natural style, and you know underneath all those social niceties lies an audaciousness that's just for you." Her fingers reached the crease in Kaitlyn's thigh and stopped. "Are you audacious?"

What was with all the questions? She shouldn't be required to think right now. Not with Beck's hand so close and every fiber of her being zeroed in on what was about to happen next. "Yes."

"Only for me?" Beck pressed fingers firmly into the softness of her thigh, a reminder. A mark.

"Only you." *Please. Please. Please.*

Beck leaned in closer, almost directly between her legs now, and slid a finger on either side of Kaitlyn's lips, spreading her open. Kaitlyn's head dropped against the window again and her eyes closed. She was so ready for Beck's fingers on her clit she could feel them there already. Except they never came. Beck hadn't moved since spreading her open. Kaitlyn opened her eyes.

Beck raised her eyebrows. "Did you really think it would be that easy?"

Kaitlyn groaned. "I'd hoped."

Beck laughed at that, her sexy as hell dominant role cracking for a second. "I suppose it was worth a shot." They grinned at each other. Kaitlyn wanted to hug her. She wanted Beck to screw her senseless too, but there was something comforting about knowing the sweet, always ready for a laugh Becca was still there, waiting for her on the other side of her orgasm.

"Maybe I should have you call me mistress," Beck mused, using her other hand to circle lazy patterns on Kaitlyn's thigh.

"Over my dead body," Kaitlyn said automatically.

Beck tilted her head as if trying out the title in her head. "I suppose you ought to be grateful it's not to my taste then." Beck perused her slowly, from the top of her head all the way down to where Kaitlyn was displayed between her fingers like diamonds in a showcase. "Show me what I've been missing."

Kaitlyn blinked. "What? You're not going to touch me?"

"That's not what you said you wanted."

Kaitlyn bit her lip. Okay, maybe five minutes ago, before Beck had demanded she strip off her panties, before she'd said *pussy*, Kaitlyn had wanted to draw things out and tease her. But now? Her own hands were a pale imitation of what Beck could do to her, and they both knew it. Kaitlyn just couldn't admit how desperate she was, even when the centerpiece of her desperation was currently snuggled between Beck's fingers. Ugh. Sometimes she was her own worst enemy.

Kaitlyn reached between her thighs, access easy with Beck holding her open. God, she was wet, slippery with it. She caught Beck's gaze and, holding it, stroked her clit once. She made a choked sound halfway between a groan and a whimper as pleasure spiraled. If she wasn't careful she was going to come in three seconds, the fastest tease in the history of the world. Her libido on steroids. Avoiding her clit for now, she dipped fingers into her opening and her sex clenched around them. She wanted to climb into Beck's lap, wrap her legs around Beck's waist, come with her lips against Beck's throat. But Beck wasn't letting her change her mind.

Kaitlyn took a long, slow breath. She could do this. It took the average woman ten to twenty minutes to come, for God's sake. She could make it at least two. She pulled her fingers out, slid them back in, fucking herself slowly and watching Beck's eyes darken. The fingers holding her open tensed, the hand on her thigh stilled. It was like everything inside Beck froze, like all her insides had gone on strike and gone home to put their feet up. Oh yeah, Beck liked this. Kaitlyn smiled. Maybe she'd last three minutes.

She pulled her fingers out and offered them. "Taste me. Let's see if you remember."

Beck's eyes fluttered shut when the pads of Kaitlyn's fingers hit her tongue. She didn't just lick them clean, she worshiped them. Rolling her tongue up and down Kaitlyn's fingers and sucking thoroughly before letting her go. Kaitlyn's stomach quivered. If Beck's tongue on her fingers felt this oh-my-God-amazing, what would it feel like when Beck finally touched her? The question was moot. She knew exactly how Beck's hands, and mouth, and skin felt on hers. The knowing made her want it even more.

"Even better than I remember." Beck placed Kaitlyn's fingers back at the apex of her thighs. "Keep going. Show me how you pleasure yourself."

"I don't know if…I've never actually…not in front of anyone." God, she was pathetic. She was the one who'd initiated this little game of show-and-tell, but she'd never expected Beck to actually keep her hands to herself long enough for Kaitlyn to follow through.

Beck leaned forward and rubbed at the spot between her brows where Kaitlyn knew she had a premature worry line. "Trust me?"

She nodded. She had a million and a half reasons not to trust Beck, but inexplicably, none of those mattered right now.

"Then touch yourself, honey. Show me how it's done. Close your eyes if it helps."

Kaitlyn nodded. Closed her eyes. Focused on her body. She traced fingers up and down her entrance, casting a wide circle around her clit, making it ache. A flood of arousal hit her. She slid the fingers of her other hand inside herself as she made the circles around her clit smaller and smaller, closer and closer, until she was stroking herself exactly where, exactly how, she needed. Every muscle in her body tightened, every sense sending out an alert, her whole body readying for the orgasm she wasn't sure she could hold back for much longer. She took it all in, the scent of her passion, the spark and swirl of pleasure coming from her clit, Beck's ragged breathing so close she could feel it against her skin. It was all at once too much, and not enough. She pumped her fingers faster inside herself and the sound they made was wet, crude, obscene in the near silence. Kaitlyn gasped and her eyes flew open. "I want—"

"Come," Beck said instantly, her body tense and leaning toward Kaitlyn like a runner at the start of a race. "Come for me."

Every cell in Kaitlyn's body exploded at once. *Bam!* Her moans ricocheted around the tight space as she rocked her hips and rode the wave of her orgasm from a trillion straight down to zero.

CHAPTER TWENTY

The Long Way Home

It was a good thirty seconds before she had the energy to open her eyes. Okay, so maybe ten of those thirty were because looking at Beck after doing *that* was a feat of self-confidence she wasn't sure she possessed. "That was—"

"Amazing," Beck supplied for her. "I take back everything I ever said about knowing what you like. I have amnesia. You'll have to remind me of every one. Next time, with props."

Next time. Beck seemed to take for granted that there would be a next time. That this strange night in this cramped car was the start of something, or rather, the continuation of something. Beck had taken her for granted once. Had considered her replaceable, even disposable. She'd thought ambition, and work, and women would somehow replace Kaitlyn's love. If this night *was* something, and she wasn't saying it was, how was she ever supposed to believe she mattered at all, let alone that she mattered the most?

She sat up and pulled her dress down to cover herself. Without the rush of desire to distract her from reality, her cheeks burned. "I can't believe I did that."

Beck laughed. "*Now* you're embarrassed? After you just gave me the performance of my life?"

"Was it the performance of your life?" Surely there'd been other women much bolder than her.

"I couldn't have looked away if a Krispy Kreme truck had pulled up alongside the car," Beck said.

Kaitlyn made a shocked face. "Wow, better even than a raspberry filled? Now I know it must've been good."

Beck scooted closer until she'd maneuvered Kaitlyn around so they were shoulder to shoulder, Beck's arm tucked around her. "It was perfect. You're perfect."

Perfect. Such a bland little word. Cardboard cutouts were perfect. Sex wasn't supposed to be."Does perfect mean sexier than all the other women you've been with?"

Beck gave her a don't-be-such-a-girl look. "Come on. You know I wasn't thinking about anyone but you."

"But you've been with other women."

"As have you," Beck said in an oh-so-reasonable tone.

It was true. She couldn't be mad at Beck for getting laid. But that wasn't the point.

"Okay, yes, but I didn't leave you for them." Kaitlyn winced. Her anxiety had just showed up out of nowhere and sucker punched the sexy revenge girl that she tried so hard to cultivate. She'd told Beck to leave the past in the past, and here she was bringing it up again. A sore tooth she couldn't help niggling, rotting just beneath the surface.

"Is that what you think? That I left you for some girl I hadn't even met yet?"

Kaitlyn shrugged. "A girl, a job, a chance to prove yourself. It's all the same thing, isn't it? You wanted different. You wanted someone, something, that wasn't me."

Beck huffed out a breath and tugged at the collar of her shirt like it was choking her. "I've always wanted you. I went to DC *for* something. Something that turned out to suck in comparison with what I left behind. I'm sorry. Sorrier than you'll ever know. But I never left to *leave* you, to get away from you. Leaving was the hardest thing I ever did, and the worst mistake I've ever made. I've never stopped loving you."

It was the second time Beck had told her she loved her, but Kaitlyn shoved aside the flutter of *she likes me best* that was making her heart pitter-patter. *I love you* used to fill her to the brim with mushy goodness, but love wasn't ever forever.

"You don't leave the people you love. You don't choose your career, your dreams, *yourself*, over the people you love. I believe *you* believe you love me. But if you love me now, and you loved me then, what's stopping you from walking away again, when some other opportunity comes calling?"

Beck's eyes were a fierce swirl of brown, like autumn leaves in a hurricane. She shifted her weight and none too gently grabbed Kaitlyn under the arms and hauled her into her lap so they were nose to nose. The warmth of Beck's skin bled though the material of her clothes, and the heat of her made Kaitlyn's mouth water. Shivers traced over her skin everywhere they touched. Twin surges of need and adrenaline skated up and down her body, wrapping themselves around her brain, poking into her belly, pooling between her legs, making her ultra-aware Beck hadn't bothered to give her back her panties. *OhdearGod.*

Kaitlyn went to speak, but Beck shook her head. "No. You're not hearing me. The difference is that I came back for you. I recognized my mistake and I came back. I was seventeen and I screwed up. I was selfish. I didn't know what I had. But I'm here now. I'm yours, and I want the whole shebang. All the stuff we talked about once upon a time. Marriage, family, the clomp of little toddler feet. But most of all, I want you. I'm moving back to New York, and I'm staying. I'll wine you, dine you, and beg for forgiveness as much as you need. But these are my cards. I'm laying them all out, Kait. This is what I want. You are who I love, and I'm not going anywhere ever again. Believe it."

When Beck said things like that, things she so badly wanted to be true, Kaitlyn could feel herself start to waver. But love wasn't a four-letter word bandied about on Pepto-Bismol pink Valentine's Day cards. Love was a verb. It was a day-by-day set of commitments. It was that kind of love, that side of Beck, that she didn't know if she could trust again.

"For now." Kaitlyn didn't even realize she'd spoken until the words were already out of her mouth, Beck's passionate declaration no match for her inner cynic.

"I don't remember you being this persnickety." Beck frowned at her.

"Well, I don't remember you manhandling me into sharing

personal space either, but here we are," Kaitlyn shot back. She was *not* persnickety. Persnickety was a stupid word, anyway.

"No? You've forgotten the homecoming game when I cornered you behind the bleachers and slid my hand up your skirt?" Beck raised her eyebrows. "That's a shame. That memory has a prime spot in my lonely nights fantasy bank. Okay, well, maybe you remember the time you got ridiculously mad because some forgettable brunette flirted with me at a party? You sulked the entire way home. Do you remember that I threw you on your bed? How I tore your panties? Do you remember how wet it made you? How prettily you begged? How hard you came?"

Kaitlyn couldn't speak. She just didn't have access to the part of her brain that handled words. Her body, however, was screaming. *Get over it. Hurry up. Give in.* Her skin felt too tight and her center throbbed.

"Tell me you forgive me." Beck clamped a hand to the nape of Kaitlyn's neck and held her as if she owned her. "Tell me you trust me."

When Kaitlyn didn't respond, the silence stretched. Beck's eyes went bleak like the last dead leaf falling from a tree. Her hand fell. It was the utter defeat that flicked across her face that forced Kaitlyn to conjure words, any words, anything to change that look.

"It's not that." Her heart constricted. But of course, it was exactly that. And why should Kaitlyn trust her? Beck hadn't given her any reason to. Well, except coming back, seeking her out, explaining her side of things, telling her she loved her, kissing her with blow-her-to-smithereens intensity, with melt-her-bones tenderness. Except for making her feel special, and beautiful, and one of a kind. Except for those little things.

Except that Beck was her everything, dammit.

"Sure, it isn't. Maybe it's exactly what I deserve. You get to do to me what I did to you. Walk away. Go back to the party and find your friends. But this time it's you who's leaving. You're the one who won't let me in." Beck let her head fall back against the headrest, not looking at Kaitlyn any longer.

No. The word expanded in her throat, caught there like a square plug in a round hole. It was exactly what she'd thought she'd wanted. Revenge. To make Beck hurt. To pay her back. But now that she had it, it was coal in the bottom of her stocking.

"No," Kaitlyn said, out loud this time.

"No, what?"

"I'm not walking away." *Not when I love you so much I can't breathe.*

"Then tell me you want this. Tell me you love me too."

"I'm scared."

"Why?" Beck kissed her slow and soft. Tasting. Inviting. Showing her how it could be between them. All the things she'd be turning down if she couldn't let go of the past.

Kaitlyn sagged. She rested her forehead against Beck's. The tight space of the car, the way she was crammed up against Beck's chest, it should've been uncomfortable, but rather than making her claustrophobic, she felt safe. Like this moment was wrapped in time. Just theirs. The world outside didn't exist, and there was only her and Beck, and this connection that never seemed to break no matter what they did to stretch it.

Kaitlyn wanted to believe her, wanted to forgive her. She wanted everything that Beck wanted. She should be jumping for joy right now. They should be having fantastic makeup sex. Picking out baby names. Snort-laughing over all the dumb things they thought were so cool in high school. But she couldn't get past herself, and for the first time, she understood that it wasn't Beck, it wasn't just the past that was keeping them apart. It was her and all the walls she'd built. All the bubble wrap and sticky tape she'd wound around herself from the age of ten to survive in a world where you lost the people you counted on the most. Where nothing and no one was a guarantee. Where you had to find a way to live in the aftermath of loss. To live with the absence of love. To be the one who was left behind.

"Everyone leaves." Two words that defined her life. Her motto. Her oh-so-cheery catchphrase. Print it on a bumper sticker and never leave home without it because it was the truest statement she'd ever known.

"Sometimes people come back," Beck said.

Kaitlyn shrugged. "You'd be the first. Nothing can bring Mom back. Nothing can change how I felt when you left. How I feel now that Sarah and Avery seem to be paired up and happy. They'll leave too, eventually. They'll all move on. But I'll still be here. After everyone has left, I'll still need to survive. If I forgive you, if I let you back in, I won't survive if you leave again. I won't be able to bear it."

"I'm here. I'm never leaving again. I'm yours." Beck's lips brushed her hair, trailed down her cheek, nipped at her earlobe. "Trust me, honey. I promise I won't let you down again." Beck brushed back a loose curl of hair and kissed the special spot right behind her ear, the one that only she knew, the one they'd discovered together. *Hers.*

Kaitlyn's walls crumbled.

The bubble wrap popped.

The hurt healed.

"God," Kaitlyn whispered.

Beck's fingers were on the zipper of her dress, her lips all over Kaitlyn's neck. Kaitlyn's bones melted together like Popsicles in the sun. Beck eased her dress down and kissed the tops of her breasts that were spilling over her bra. "Tell me you forgive me." Beck's voice was full and throaty.

"Or you'll what, Delmar?" Kaitlyn was breathless.

"Or I won't let you come for hours."

Kaitlyn laughed. "I'm not sure who that would be worse punishment for, you or me."

"Oh, definitely me. But I'd do it to convince you I'm yours. I'm here. I love you."

Kaitlyn sucked in a ragged breath. She let everything go and sank into the moment. "I forgive you. I love you back. Forever."

"Thank God. I promise you won't regret it."

Kaitlyn's skin went goosebumpy. Happiness flowed in her veins, washing out the last seeds of doubt. Beck was hers. Beck loved her. Like, really, really loved her. They'd make this work. For forever.

But first, they had work to do.

Kaitlyn gathered Beck's shirt in her fists and yanked until she'd pulled it free. Making quick work of the buttons, she tore it open and palmed Beck's warm skin. Beck's mouth went to her neck, her shoulder, her breasts, and Kaitlyn moaned. It felt so good to be touched again. She released the button on Beck's pants. She needed skin on skin. They kissed and fumbled, hands and mouths everywhere.

"Do you remember the last time we did this?" Beck asked.

The sound of Kaitlyn tugging down Beck's zipper cut the air. "The last time we had sex?"

Kaitlyn knew every detail. She could fill out a police report with the specificity to which the slide of Beck's skin on hers was ingrained in her head.

Beck shook her head. "The last time we were all over each other in the back seat of a car."

Kaitlyn paused. Then it came to her. "The Lexus your dad bought you when you first got your license." She laughed. "I'm pretty sure we used it half the time for driving and the other half as a convenient place to make out."

"Mm, those were some prime makeout sessions." Beck wrapped her arms around Kaitlyn and pressed flush against her.

Kaitlyn's eyes clicked shut, all her senses sinking into lusty quicksand. This was what she wanted. What she'd always needed. Beck's skin on hers, Beck's hands stroking her, Beck's touch making her melt. But she had no time to process it with Beck kissing her again. Fucking with her mouth, that's what she was doing. Long, deep strokes and hot, quick nips and thrusts. Kaitlyn rocked against her, the soft skin of her belly meeting the open fly of Beck's pants. Kaitlyn wanted to meld with her, freaking climb inside her until they were one and the same. As close as close could be.

"Take off your pants," Kaitlyn said.

"Giving me orders now?" Beck whispered in her ear.

"I can't stand anything between us. Please." She was desperate for Beck. Desperate to fill the places inside herself that'd been reserved for Beck the moment they'd fallen in love. Places that'd been empty for too long.

They fumbled, slid, yanked, and tugged their clothes into a scattered jumble. "Tell me what you want," Beck said.

Everything was running together in her mind. She and Beck were *together* again. Together-together. They were going to do it like horny teenagers in the back seat of her dad's car. She was so turned on she couldn't stand it. So much had happened that the night had an air of unreality. She needed something to ground her.

Something real.

Something hers.

Something theirs.

Kaitlyn levered up onto her knees and pressed her center to Beck's stomach. Her groan slid out through clenched teeth. *Sososo good.* "You know what I want, Delmar?"

"What?" Beck cupped her ass, pulling her tighter, making her head fall back.

"I want you on top."

Beck's fingers tightened on her ass. "That's a request I'm happy to grant."

She flipped their positions so smoothly Kaitlyn made a mental note to marvel later. She was pinned under her, her wrists clamped together in Beck's bigger, stronger hand. She whimpered into Beck's mouth. Please. Please. Please. She was so close to flying off into a million pieces that Beck's slow and patient approach made her want to scream.

"Always in such a hurry." Beck circled Kaitlyn's nipple with her tongue. Bit down.

"It's been a while." Kaitlyn's teeth were gritted so hard she was afraid her jaw would lock.

"Long fucking years. Now stop squirming and enjoy it, or I'm going to have to make you."

Kaitlyn snorted. Ignored the hot rush of *ohmygodyes* that incited. Tied up. Unable to move. Helpless. Beck would be able to do anything she wanted. Kaitlyn would have to take it. Who cared why exactly that pushed every button she had. "There's nothing to tie me up with in here, and no room."

Beck shifted her weight, forcing Kaitlyn's breath out of her for a quick, delicious second. "You think I need ropes and room to make you submit? You've forgotten who you're dealing with."

Kaitlyn literally couldn't move an inch. Her heart was going to put a dent in her chest it was beating so hard. She struggled, luxuriating in the way their skin slid together. "You think you can just do whatever you want because you're bigger and stronger, Delmar? Do you know who I am? I could buy you and everyone you know a thousand times, and still have money left over."

Beck wedged a hand between them and found her clit. "Nice try, honey. We both know your money means shit right now. This," Beck ran a deft finger round her clit, "is all that matters."

A tiny part of Kaitlyn's brain, a very small part right in the back, cheered. Her money, her job, her status, it really didn't matter. Not anymore. The thought splintered as Beck began to stroke her with maddeningly gentle fingers. Kaitlyn moaned. Her body lit up like a birthday candle. Beck's gaze, pure lustful hunger, ate her up. Beck looked like she wanted to fuck her into oblivion and Kaitlyn couldn't think of anything she wanted more. "Please."

"Please, what?" Beck dipped a finger inside her, and everything clenched and tightened.

"Please," Kaitlyn said again, her hips pinned beneath Beck but struggling to rise all the same.

"So shy." Beck slid her finger out, then back in. In and out, torturously slow, maddeningly precise. "I love that you can't say the words. You can't tell me you want me to fuck you, can you? You can't tell me how wet this is making you, how you love my weight on top of you, how you like to struggle under me even though we both know you'd never win. That you'd never want to."

Pleasure climbed up Kaitlyn's spine, made her toes curl. The dirty words a soundtrack to her desire, edging her higher. Blood rushed to her head. Her ears buzzed. Her mind blurred at the edges.

Those patient, clever fingers never let up. Stroking her clit, sliding in and out. "Please."

Beck laughed. "So shy."

She added a finger, curled them in just the perfect way, and thrust back into her, harder this time. Not stopping. Not letting up. Fucking her. Overwhelming her. The thrust of Beck's fingers, her palm pressing against her clit, her weight all but crushing her, it all wound tighter and tighter inside her. Around, and around, and around. All she knew was Beck. Coming back for her. Loving her. Giving her just exactly what she needed.

The orgasm slammed into her, hard and unrelenting. So much. Too much. She was coming. She was flying. She was falling.

Beck hugged her. "Shh. I've got you, honey. I've got you. Ride it out."

Beck stroked her hair, the curve of her back, down the length of her arm. Soothing, caressing. Her heartbeat finally slowed from Ironman marathon to gentle stroll in the park. She was more than naked. Coming in Beck's arms, beneath her, held in place by her, she was exposed in a way that went deeper than skin. Beck knew everything there was to know about her, had seen the best and the worst of her, and she wasn't afraid. Tonight was the first time all over again. Their fresh start.

"Get off me, you brute," Kaitlyn mumbled, almost too swirly, and floaty, and postorgasmic to speak.

"You're so beautiful," Beck said.

"Mm." Kaitlyn shoved her. "Off."

Beck rolled off her, and Kaitlyn struggled to pull her noodle bones into a sitting position. "Pretty good, Delmar."

Beck swatted her on the arm. "Smartass. I was phenomenal. You went off like a rocket and you know it."

Kaitlyn snorted. "Pretty sure of yourself."

Beck kissed Kaitlyn gently on the forehead. "Pretty sure of us."

Us. Two letters that felt so good she wanted them tattooed on her skin. *Us. Them. Hers. Forever.*

CHAPTER TWENTY-ONE

Woman On Top

"Can I touch you?" Kaitlyn asked, snuggled half in Beck's lap, their legs entwined under the space blanket Beck had found in the emergency kit stashed in the side door pocket.

"You don't have to ask." Beck brushed her lips against Kaitlyn's hair, an unconscious gesture that spoke of companionship, of togetherness and obstacles overcome. They might've spent the last half dozen years apart, but they'd come back together like no time had passed. Like love had been waiting with outstretched arms and an all-access pass for them to pick it back up again.

Kaitlyn pressed her lips to Beck's ear. "I want you on top."

Beck ginned. "Didn't we just do that?"

"You're a smart woman, you'll figure it out." Kaitlyn smiled up into toasty brown eyes that for the first time tonight seemed content. Light, and sure, and sparkling.

She loved that she could make Beck happy in this simple way. Sex was awesome. The necessity of all necessities, as far as she was concerned. Nothing said *I love you* quite like a heart pounding, can't breathe, don't ever want to stop, turn your brain to soup, orgasm. But happiness, the kind of quiet uncluttered contentment that came after, was even better. Nothing could be more satisfying than being the one who mattered, and Kaitlyn felt it from the top of her head all the way to her toes. This time, they'd make it.

Beck's mouth quirked. "You know what, you're right."

She whipped the blanket off them so fast Kaitlyn squealed. "Cold!"

"You can throw it over yourself again in a minute. Lie down on the seat."

"Don't you need room?" Kaitlyn asked. "We really should've found a more comfortable place to do this."

Beck poked a finger at her. "Are you going to trust me to figure it out or not? Lie down. Plus, I like it here. Reminds me of the time I fast-talked you to second base in the back seat of the Lexus."

"You did too," Kaitlyn said, the memory surfacing. "I seem to remember I wanted to wait for…Why did I want to wait, again?"

"No idea." Beck grinned at her.

"If I'd known then how good sex was, I'd have given everything up on the first date."

"And deny me the thrill of the chase? That's half the fun."

"Going to get bored now that you've caught me?" Kaitlyn asked.

"Hell, if things get stale, I'll just have Eleanor kiss you. Spice it up a bit. Seems to work for Sarah."

Kaitlyn exaggerated a frown. "Don't even think about it, Delmar."

Beck touched her cheek. "Oh, I'm definitely thinking about it. But that one's for the lonely nights fantasy bank, not real life. I hate to share what's mine."

Mine. The word was archaic. Anti-feminist. Possessive. Domineering. Over the top. It lit her up like sunrise after endless night. *Hers.*

"No lonely nights for either of us anymore." Kaitlyn lay down on the seat as Beck instructed.

When Beck threw a leg over her and settled directly above her mouth, Kaitlyn's stomach dropped as if she were barreling down a death-defying incline on the world's fastest roller coaster. God. Okay, yeah. This was Beck on top, all right. An endless expanse of smooth skin. Beck's small, perfectly shaped breasts were mouthwatering at this angle. Her stomach tapering to hips that flared just a little. Strong thighs holding Beck up, and her center an inch from Kaitlyn's lips. So close and so delicious looking that she couldn't help but swipe her tongue over Beck's folds.

Beck jerked. "Fuck."

"Mm. What's that you said about going off like a rocket?" Kaitlyn licked her again. "I think you like making me come, Delmar. You're all wet."

"You have no idea." Beck slid a hand under her neck, stroked her nape. "Ever done it like this?"

Kaitlyn winced. The sexy answer would be no. The last thing she wanted was to bring up past sexual encounters, but she couldn't lie. "This would be my first time with you."

Beck laughed. "How diplomatic. You must be a socialite."

Kaitlyn pinched her on the thigh. "I'll have you know I'm the CEO of one of the biggest nonprofits on the East Coast."

"And the difference is?" Beck grinned at her.

Kaitlyn rolled her eyes. "You're an ass."

"Right now, I'm a bit preoccupied with another part of my anatomy." Beck tilted Kaitlyn's neck to position her exactly how she wanted. Kaitlyn might be the one about to wrap her lips around Beck's clit, but Beck was completely in control of the pace. It was oddly reassuring.

"I love you, you know," Kaitlyn said right before she used her tongue to trace every inch of Beck's center.

Oh God. She had more than a few unforgettable memories of Beck in her own fantasy bank, but memory didn't do justice to the real deal. Beck was wet, and soft, and tasted heavenly. Kaitlyn couldn't imagine needing anything in life as much as she needed Beck to explode all wet and messy over her face. The need went bone-deep, more a part of her than any career ambition or bank account would ever be. *This* is what mattered. *This* is what she needed.

She was going to show her woman where home and happiness really was.

She raised her hands to Beck's hips and pulled her down firmly, unwilling to be separated from her by even an inch. Beck groaned, and even though Kaitlyn could no longer see her, Beck's thighs tensed and her breath came in harsh pants. Kaitlyn thrust her tongue inside, grasping Beck's hips to encourage her to ride her face. She thrust her tongue in and out as Beck writhed on top of her, painting her face from nose to chin.

The faster Beck panted, the faster Kaitlyn's pulse raced, like they were equally matched in a race and determined to outdo each other. She slid her hands to Beck's ass and squeezed, the muscles there firm and tight, her skin baby smooth. Kaitlyn whimpered. A UFO could've landed on the roof of the car, aliens invading earth to use up what was left of its natural resources, human life a negligible sacrifice. She could be whisked away to Saturn to live out her days in servitude to a green-skinned alien prince, and she wouldn't have cared as long as she could make Beck come first. The world outside this car, outside the sphere of Beck's body against hers, failed to matter.

"Fuck," Beck said, the word sounding more like a prayer than a curse. "That's so good. I love that you love this."

Something else that hadn't changed. Of all the many, varied, and somewhat improbable ways Kaitlyn knew to make a woman come, oral sex was by far her favorite. Simple, maybe. Not really kinky, or even particularly adventurous or inventive. But there was something deeply intimate about using her mouth on a woman. Tasting her passion, exploring every corner of her most private and vulnerable place. The feel of slick skin on her tongue, the scent of her arousal, the way her body responded to Kaitlyn's touch. It did it for her like nothing else.

Going down on a woman was *satisfying*. Going down on Beck was a seven-course meal. Beck groaned above her, rubbing herself all over Kaitlyn's face. The muscles in her thighs and ass tensed as she climbed toward release.

She'd been content with others, but not like this. Not full to overflowing, so connected she could drown in her. As if some terminally thirsty part of her was finally being quenched. It made her feel alive. Complete.

"Honey," Beck said, her voice guitar-string taut. "I'm going to come."

Kaitlyn stopped just long enough to say, "You'd better wait

until I'm done, Delmar," before she got back to work, redoubling her efforts, the leisurely tourist-on-a-Sunday-morning pace of her licks and thrusts replaced by focused intention. Kaitlyn circled Beck's clit, now swollen and standing proud. Just how ready Beck was made Kaitlyn throb with an interest that should've been biologically impossible after two orgasms. She wrapped her lips around Beck's clit and sucked it like a lollipop.

Beck made a grinding sound and her fingers flexed on Kaitlyn's neck like she was trying not to shove Kaitlyn's face tight against her and use her like a human sex toy. A big part of Kaitlyn, the part she'd rather not analyze, wished Beck would. But what was sacrificed in power play was made up for in the opportunity to savor. It'd been so long since she'd tasted Beck. The salt of her skin, the unique not-quite-sweet flavor of her arousal. Beck tasted like sex, like strength wrapped in softness, so very, very female. Kaitlyn inhaled, her nose all but crushed against Beck, giving her the most intimate sensory overload. She took another long, slow suck. Flicking her tongue back and forth over Beck's clit in a firefly wing caress.

"The sounds you're making are driving me nuts...*Fuck*."

Kaitlyn hadn't realized she'd been making any sounds, but her response to having her mouth on Beck was impossible to contain. Every swipe of her tongue earned her a tensed muscle or a hitched breath, a gush of wetness against her lips. It was making her crazy in the best possible way. Kaitlyn groaned.

"Do you know what it does to me knowing you get off on this?" Beck asked.

Kaitlyn just barely registered the words, the rumble of Beck's voice floating over her. She hummed her response against Beck's clit and felt it swell.

"Can't hold it much longer." Beck ground against Kaitlyn's mouth, her movements jerky and unfocused.

Kaitlyn whimpered. She didn't want her to hold it; she wanted Beck to come screaming all over her face.

"Oh God. Oh Fuck. Fuck."

Beck's words sparked across her skin. Kaitlyn flicked her tongue across the tip of Beck's clit one last time and she exploded, pumping roughly against her mouth, her hand a vise grip on the back of Kaitlyn's neck. All manner of sweet, dirty things fell from her lips. Kaitlyn rode it out with her, licking and sucking and savoring every moment until Beck insisted she stop.

All too soon, Beck was easing herself away and rubbing soothing fingers against her neck. "Jesus. I'm sorry. I think I've left fingerprints."

Kaitlyn blinked. A soft fuzziness enveloped her, making it hard to think. "I don't care. You know that."

Beck tossed the space blanket back over them and sat with Kaitlyn's head in her lap, stroking her hair, her nape, across her forehead. "You're incredible."

"I'm glad you think so because I'm yours," Kaitlyn said. The truth that used to scare her, now made her all glowy.

"Nothing means more to me. You're my heart." Beck brushed a thumb across her lips and Kaitlyn kissed it. All she'd ever wanted was the love of this woman. Being her love, being the one, was a gift she'd never tire of.

"We belong together like jelly and donuts," Kaitlyn said.

Beck laughed. "Hungry? I think all the birthday cake is gone."

"It's your fault. You and your Krispy Kreme truck." Kaitlyn poked her in the belly.

Beck smiled. "I'm so sorry. I vow never to bring up sugary fat again."

"Alternatively, you could just buy me a donut shop. That'd solve the problem nicely."

"Done. Anything for you."

Kaitlyn rolled her eyes. "You're just saying that because I'm naked and you're all postcoital."

"True. But it's the thought that counts, right? I'd give you a million dollars right now."

"How about a million years?" Kaitlyn held her breath. Thoughts did count, but actions spoke louder.

Beck cradled her face and stared directly into her eyes. "Make it two million and you've got yourself a deal."

"You drive a hard bargain, but I think I can make that work."

Kaitlyn's smile felt so big she was sure her face would crack open at any second.

"I'll spend the rest of my life making you happy," Beck promised her, sealing their deal with another of her brain melting kisses.

Kaitlyn rested her forehead against Beck's. "As much as I hate to say it, we should probably drag ourselves back to the party. It's got to be well and truly over by now."

Beck checked her watch. "No kidding."

Kaitlyn found her dress at the far end of the seat and wriggled into it. She glanced around. "Do you know where my panties went?"

"I do know," Beck said sagely.

"Where are they? The last thing I want is for your dad to find my underwear when he gets the car back." Kaitlyn ducked to check the floor. Nothing.

Beck patted the pocket of the pants she was pulling on. "They're safe. Don't worry."

It was only then that Kaitlyn remembered Beck had taken them from her. She made a grab for them, but Beck fended her off. "No way, pretty lady. These are a priceless memento."

Kaitlyn laughed. "A memento of what?"

"Of the night we pledged two million years together," Beck said.

Kaitlyn's throat closed. Tears stung her eyes. Sometimes, with the right person, love really was forever. "Used and ruined panties will forevermore signify our love. You're such a sentimental fool."

Beck pulled on her shoes and hopped out of the car, holding out a hand to Kaitlyn. "See? This is why I love you. You get me."

The next two million years were going to be amazing.

EPILOGUE

Endings Are Beginnings

Sarah yawned so wide the corners of her mouth hurt. God, she was happy to be heading home. The seductive call of her rickety old bed; her mattress that dipped in the middle; her fluffy pillow; Bob, the three-legged wonder cat, curled up purring like a locomotive made her ache with longing. If heaven were a theater, her bed and Bob would be center stage. She was used to putting in sixteen-hour days and had no excuse for being this sleepy, but amazing sex and executing the world's raunchiest breakup would put anyone down for the count.

She pulled on her duck egg blue peacoat on her way from the coatroom into the entrance hall. Her phone vibrated against her hip, and she slid it from the pocket.

Miss you already, Aphrodite.

She smiled. Ryan was probably loading her van and hauling her own tired ass home by now. That she'd thought to text made leaving without her just a little easier.

Ryan.

Who would've thought she'd find her perfect stranger at Eleanor McGregor's party? For that matter, who would've thought she'd find Eleanor so alluring? Once you got past the hefty dose of bitch, she was pretty decent. With emphasis on the pretty. Plus, she had amazing breasts. Sarah hadn't ever been particularly attracted to breasts, but damn if Eleanor's hadn't made her mouth water.

Avery held Sarah's purse and tugged on a tan Burberry trench coat. "Stellar night, huh?"

Sarah raised her eyebrows in a way she hoped exuded fervent judgment and disapproval. "Did you sneak away with that poor girl and deflower her, Avery Anders?"

Avery blanched for half a second, then flicked her scarf at Sarah before wrapping it loosely around her neck. "I did. It was very, very dirty."

Sarah laughed. "Was it now. Details, please."

The humor slowly ebbed from Avery's face, but the sparkle in her eyes seemed to be permanently ingrained. "I told Spencer I love her."

Sarah gasped and launched herself into Avery's arms. "It's about time, you broody, mopey mush-bucket."

"Aw. You give the best compliments."

Avery spun her around in circles until Sarah was giddy. She landed on her feet and they smiled hugely at each other until Avery resembled the scary clowns at the circus.

"I take it Spencer was happy to hear this?" Sarah said.

Avery lifted a shoulder in an aw-shucks gesture. "She loves me too."

"No way." When Avery choked on a laugh, Sarah added, "I mean, that was unexpected, right? You didn't think she was into you like that."

"Apparently, I was wrong, thank God."

"Why are you two standing there grinning at each other?" Kaitlyn asked as she walked inside with…

Wait. With *Becca Delmar*? Holy shit.

"You're not trying to convince Avery to kiss Ryan too, are you?" Kaitlyn said.

The grin fell off Avery's face like she'd dropped it on the floor. "What the fuck is she doing here?"

If looks could kill, Becca would be on a slab in the morgue.

Kaitlyn held up her hand as if her palm alone could stop the fistfight about to break out. "It's okay, Avery."

Avery glowered, and Sarah wasn't too far behind her on that. But the longer they stood there, the clearer she saw things. Becca's clothes were rumpled, and Kaitlyn's cheeks were flushed, her hair mussed. She was practically glowing. They both were.

"Looks like love's in the air tonight." Sarah turned to Becca. "If you hurt her again, I'll murder you. I know how, and I don't care if I go to prison."

Kaitlyn made a protesting sound, but Becca nodded. "If I hurt her again, I'd deserve it."

Well, that was okay then.

Sarah walked over and slung her arm around Becca's waist, giving her a quick side hug. "Always knew you'd come back. You're not as stupid as you look."

Becca hugged her back. "You're just as charming as I remember."

"It's a gift." Sarah grinned.

Kaitlyn started toward the coatroom. "We should get going. Looks like we're the last ones left." She disappeared and came out with her ankle length white woolen coat. A coat only Kaitlyn could pull off without looking like Cruella de Vil. She draped the strap of her purse over her shoulder and looked hopefully at Beck. "Can I give you a lift?"

Beck's smile was so sensual Sarah shivered. Wow. "Got the Range Rover, remember?"

Kaitlyn pouted, but there was heat in her eyes. "I remember."

"I'll call you tomorrow." Becca grasped Kaitlyn by the shoulders and kissed her so thoroughly Sarah had to look away. Double wow.

"Kaitlyn and Becca sitting in a tree," she sang as they headed toward the front doors and out into the cold. "K-I-S-S—"

"Sarah," Kaitlyn interrupted her, "if you don't shut up, I'll gloss over all the best details and leave you hanging."

Sarah shut up.

❖

Avery buttoned her coat and wished for the eleventy-billionth time that Spencer wasn't a McGregor. Tonight particularly because Spencer was spending the rest of the weekend right here with her family, and Avery had to go back to Manhattan without her. She'd just gotten Spencer to love her, and leaving now felt like parting with a limb. The most gorgeous limb ever. She'd kissed Spencer good-bye only fifteen minutes ago, but she was already deprived of her beautiful voice, her sweet smile, her sexy body. Deprivation made her cranky.

"So, you two are back together?" Avery asked Kaitlyn as they waited for the valet.

Kaitlyn nodded. "For approximately the next two million years. After that we'll need to renegotiate."

Sarah squealed, but Avery wasn't so keen to join the celebration. "She kicked you to the curb."

Sarah frowned at her, but Kaitlyn looked thoughtful. "That's how it felt at the time. But it wasn't about me. She needed to leave. Then she needed to come back."

"And you, what? Just spread your legs like nothing happened?"

"Avery," Kaitlyn said in a voice edged with steel. "Who I spread my legs for isn't a decision I make by committee."

Avery struggled against the smile that wanted to break through her missing-Spencer-asshole-ness. Only Kaitlyn could tell her to mind her own fucking business in such a prim and proper, CEO of a major corporation way. She was awesome like that.

"Okay, okay. I just don't want to see you hurt again. How do you know she's back for good?"

"Because I trust her," Kaitlyn said simply.

Huh. How could you argue with that?

"It's so romantic," Sarah said as the town car stopped at the curb and they all piled in. "You're torn apart as innocent teenagers, but a decade later she comes swooping back to town and sweeps you off your feet to live happily ever after in a castle far, far away."

Kaitlyn grimaced. "Don't quit your day job, okay? Fairy tales aren't your calling."

"It *is* kind of romantic." Avery smiled at Kaitlyn in a way she hoped said sorry for being an ass.

The car pulled slowly out of the McGregor estate, and Avery stared at the warm glow of light illuminating Spencer's bedroom window as it grew smaller and smaller. The bedroom Spencer would be sleeping in tonight. The bedroom they'd made love in. Said I love you in. Committed to forever in. Avery'd rather Spencer be with her, but tucked up under the quilt they'd all but sent to the floor wasn't a bad consolation prize.

"It is. And she has my very compromised panties in her pocket to prove it." Kaitlyn winked at Avery. All forgiven.

"You're not wearing underwear?" Avery glanced at Kaitlyn's lap automatically like she'd be able to tell through the layers of silk and wool. She looked away hastily. Jesus. Kaitlyn without underwear. How long had she been walking around like that? So much for prim and proper.

"Good for you," Sarah said, apparently completely unfazed. "Bet she's hot in bed."

"You have no idea," Kaitlyn said.

"Well, you know, we could maybe…" Sarah trailed off, laughing as Kaitlyn shoved her.

"She's all mine, you unrepentant horndog. No sharing."

Sarah sighed dramatically. "So unfair."

"Speaking of sharing," Kaitlyn said. "Did you tell Avery about your threesome with the sexy chef and your frustratingly beautiful archenemy?"

"*What?*" All the blood rushed from Avery's head, making her dizzy. "You had *sex* with Elle?" She couldn't picture it. Well, okay, she was already picturing it, but holy mother of God. Sarah had a threesome with Elle, and Kaitlyn's underwear was in her ex-girlfriend's, now current girlfriend's, pocket. This night couldn't get any stranger.

Or hotter.

"It wasn't a real threesome," Sarah said.

She relayed what'd gone down in the coatroom, and Avery

wasn't sure whether to be impressed or horrified. "Is Elle okay? How did you leave things?"

"I didn't ask her for her number, if that's what you mean. Seemed too needy," Sarah said.

Avery rolled her eyes. Sarah had never met an uncomfortable emotion she hadn't attempted to deflect with humor. "I mean, is Elle okay? How's she feeling? Is she upset about Peter?"

Avery remembered Elle's empty expression and haunted eyes when they'd parted on the balcony. She should've made sure Elle was okay. She should've been there for her. She'd been too wrapped up in Spencer. It was difficult to feel guilty for that, but she was sorry she hadn't looked after her friend.

"She's a real mess," Sarah said. "She's going to spend the next twenty years in therapy examining how she could've possibly been such an awful meanie to the nicest, cutest, smartest girl in her senior class. A girl she was secretly attracted to. But after she's processed that, I imagine she'll be just as sane as the rest of us."

Avery stared at her. "Sometimes I don't know whether you're joking or being a dick."

Sarah laughed. "Relax. She's fine, just a bit shaky and lost. But I have a plan."

"Sarah, no." Kaitlyn had gone pale. "No more plans."

"It's brilliant." Sarah looked pleased with herself. "I'm going to introduce Eleanor to Hot Bartender."

Avery groaned.

"The bartender where Peter had sex?" Kaitlyn asked. Hot Bartender was apt all right. The woman was stunning. She'd also been sending Sarah signals. Maybe setting her up with Eleanor wasn't the best idea. "It looked like she was interested in you. It's a bit rude to shove someone else at her."

"Then I'll do my best not to *shove* Eleanor at her. I'm capable of finesse, you know," Sarah said.

Kaitlyn glanced at Avery.

"Hey." Sarah was indignant. "I am."

Kaitlyn shook her head. "We'll help you. It's one of your better plans. Eleanor could probably use a nice rebound relationship to get her confidence back."

Sarah snorted. "Pretty sure Ryan gave her that when she stuck her tongue down Eleanor's throat."

"Ryan was kissing her for *you*, and you know it. Eleanor needs someone nice and steady, not to get caught up in your..." Kaitlyn trailed off, at a loss for words to explain exactly what Eleanor would be getting caught up in.

"Horndog shenanigans?" Avery suggested.

Kaitlyn pointed at her. "Exactly."

Sarah harrumphed. "What's wrong with horndog shenanigans?"

"Nothing, if that's what you're looking for," Kaitlyn said.

"It's totally what I'm looking for," Sarah said. "All the sex. So much sex. Sexy sex."

"Glad to see you're committed to getting over your dry spell," Avery said.

"Haven't been dry since dropping off the cake." Sarah giggled at her own joke.

Kaitlyn couldn't help but smile. "You're in fine form." She looked at Sarah closely for the first time since getting in the car. "Look at you, you're all smiley."

Sarah instantly frowned. "I am not."

"You are. Why?"

Sarah fidgeted with a button on her coat. "I have a date for next Saturday."

"With a certain drop-dead gorgeous chef?" Kaitlyn said.

"She made me drop something all right," Sarah said.

Avery clapped her on the back like they were bros at a football game. "Well done. Told you some crazy hot sex would sort you out."

Crazy hot sex had sure sorted Kaitlyn out. She wanted to be scrambled just so she could be sorted out some more.

"Where are you going on your date?" She needed a distraction. She couldn't think about sex. Right now, getting turned on thinking about Beck would be a disaster. She crossed her legs surreptitiously and hoped her cheeks weren't burning. If Beck had stolen her panties to make her extremely sensitive and aware of how very bare she was under her dress, she'd achieved her goal. The sadist.

"Swingers," Sarah said.

Avery shot Kaitlyn a worried look over Sarah's head. "I know you're happy to be back in the saddle, but maybe a bar for swingers isn't the best place for a first date."

"Do you know this woman? Is she safe?" Avery asked Kaitlyn.

"I don't know her. I know someone who's hired her though. I'll ask around."

Sarah rolled her eyes. "You will not, you idiots. *Swingers* is the name of the new mini golf complex in Queens."

"Mini golf," Avery said like Sarah had just told them she'd be having her first date in the party room at McDonald's.

"Yup. It's cool. There's a bar, and food, and golf balls you attempt to hit into very small holes in the ground."

"Oh," Kaitlyn said. "I get it. It's upscale mini golf. I read about it in the culture section. Very trendy." And way better than a swinger's club or McDonald's.

"It's going to be great," Sarah said, her face all smiley again.

"Maybe you should suggest that Hot Bartender take Eleanor there," Avery said, grinning. "Think of the double date potential."

Sarah closed her eyes and moaned theatrically. "So much mini golf hotness. We should all go out sometime, me and Ryan, Kaitlyn and Becca, and you and Spencer. Even Eleanor and Hot Bartender if it works out for them. We could…" She frowned. "What's the word for four things?"

"Quadruple," Kaitlyn said.

"Yes, an epic quadruple date," Sarah said.

"Also known as hanging out with your friends?" Avery laughed.

"We should go to a strip club," Sarah said.

"I am *not* going to a strip club." Kaitlyn was firm on that. Strip clubs were for middle-aged men who couldn't get it up for their wives.

"Fine, we'll go to the *movies* or something boring." Sarah

rested her head against the window and closed her eyes. "You're missing out not going, though."

"I am?" Kaitlyn looked at Avery, who just shrugged, laughter in her eyes. "What am I missing out on?"

But she wouldn't get her answer because Sarah was fast asleep, a ghost of a smile still on her lips.

Kaitlyn tilted her head back against the seat and let the night wash over her. What a party. The angst of telling Eleanor about Peter. Avery holding hands with Spencer, both of them so goofy happy. Accidentally telling Beck her vibrator was a better lover. Being a lookout for the most ridiculous revenge ever. Finally understanding why Beck had walked away, forgiving her, trusting her. The most gut-wrenching, blood-sizzling, panty-ruining sex of her entire life, in the back seat of a car no less. And now here she was chatting with her friends, teasing them, making plans. Kaitlyn's cup of gratitude for her life was full to overflowing and just being alive had never felt so right. She couldn't think of anything she needed.

Except maybe going to a strip club? But, really, what was she missing?

About the Author

Sandy has a master's degree in publishing from the University of Sydney, Australia, and is the senior editor at Bold Strokes Books. *Party of Three* is her first novel.